A Conspiracy of Aunts

Sally Spencer

Table of Contents

PART ONE: The Deal

1

My mother was swept out to sea one moonless night, shortly after my ninth birthday. She was not washed up onto the shore again for several days, by which time she was, of course, quite dead.

But though she is gone, she is far from forgotten. I had, back then (and still have now) a most remarkable memory, and not a single word of the sage advice and honest common sense that Mother imparted to me has ever been lost. I carry this philosophy – this World According to Jennifer Bates, as I sometimes fancifully think of it – around in my head, and it has been as essential to me as a good guidebook is to a tourist who suddenly finds himself lost in a strange foreign land. In fact, I would put it even more strongly than that. It has served as a lantern to light my way along the darker paths of life – a lantern which circumstances have sometimes, most regrettably, forced me to use as the proverbial blunt instrument.

But wait! Before going any further with this narrative of mine, I have a confession to make. When I said I remember everything, I was not being entirely accurate, and that, in Mother's eyes, would have been almost the same as lying. For though I have total recall now, there was a period – nearly twenty years, in fact – when, apart from the occasional dream-like flashback, the last few days of Mother's life were almost a complete blank to me.

Yet isn't such a single lapse excusable? The person who made up most of my universe had been taken from me. What could be more natural than that I should block out the circumstances of her death? The gap, then, was not cognitive, but traumatic. And, as I said, I've got those memories back now. Oh yes, thanks to the merciless probing of Rosalyn, my late fiancée, I've got them all back.

I can pin down the period of my blackout exactly. It started the moment that I climbed excitedly into the taxi which was to whisk us away on the initial stage of our last, fateful holiday in Cornwall – and it ended with the convocation of the aunts.

2

My first impression on this side of my memory gap is of standing in the hallway of the small terraced house that Mother and I shared with Grandfather. It was raining outside, though not heavily, and only the occasional raindrop was foolish enough to go into a kamikaze dive and end up spattered against the panes of coloured glass in the front door.

'Your aunts are waiting for you,' whispered Mrs Kowalski, a neighbour who, I now remember, had been looking after me during the funeral.

My aunts? I thought in a panic.

My aunts?

Those strange women who my mother had often talked about, but who were all still completely unknown to me?

Mrs Kowalski knocked softly – almost reverently – on the door. Standing beside her, my eyes only just level with the handle, I was suddenly afraid, not only of what lay on the other side of that door, but also of what had lain beyond another door, many miles away, on the wild Cornish coast.

Mrs Kowalski knocked again, louder this time.

'Yes?' called out a voice as grating as a ragged fingernail being scraped down a blackboard.

Our neighbour opened the door and ushered me in.

'I bring the child,' she explained.

'Thank you,' said the owner of the grating voice.

I looked across the room at her. She was a tall, gaunt woman, dressed in black from her scrawny neck to her blue-veined ankles, and she had not only invaded our living room, but was even now occupying Grandfather's favourite chair. I was outraged at the usurpation – but I didn't show it, because that would have been rude.

'Other people may forget their manners, but that's no excuse for you forgetting yours,' Mother used to say.

'If there is anything else I can do …' Mrs Kowalski mumbled.

'Nothing,' Buzzard-neck said dismissively, 'nothing at all.'

'If you're sure …'

'Thank you. You may go.'

Mrs Kowalski backed out of the room. I listened to her footsteps retreating up the hall, and heard the click of the front door as she closed it behind her, leaving me alone to face my last four surviving relatives.

'I am your Aunt Catherine,' the black-clad spectre announced.

Mother had told me all about her. She was the oldest of my aunts, a widow, and she ran an evangelical mission somewhere in Wales.

'How do you do, Aunt Catherine?' I said politely.

'And that,' she said, pointing to a short, wiry woman sitting on the sofa, 'is your Aunt Jacqueline.'

'Hello, Aunt Jacqueline,' I said dutifully.

Aunt Jacqueline snorted what may have been a reply, took a heavy drag on her untipped cigarette, and blew some smoke from her nostrils. Her hair was closely cropped, and had it not been for the fact that she was wearing a skirt instead of trousers with her hound's-tooth check jacket, I might have mistaken her for a man.

I had expected to be introduced to the other woman on the sofa next, but Aunt Catherine – always a believer in pecking orders – pointed instead to the round figure almost curled up in Mother's armchair.

'That's your Aunt Peggy,' she announced.

'Oh … err … hello,' Aunt Peggy said vaguely, then turned her head away as if she were about to take a nap.

She kept cats, Mother had told me – hundreds of them. I'd always imagined that she resembled a cat herself, but it was still quite a surprise to discover how closely she conformed to my fantasy. With her fat little body and the ginger hair which cascaded over her eyes, she looked like nothing so much as a big, spoiled moggie, lying in the sunshine and watching lazily as a parade of birds and mice passed it by.

'And she,' said Aunt Catherine, pointing with some distaste at the other occupant of the sofa, 'is your Aunt Sadie.'

What can I say about Sadie – other than that before I met her, I'd thought Mother was the most beautiful woman in the world?

Sadie had long hair, the colour of ripe corn, and eyes that were as blue as the most enchanting lagoon. Her skin had an almost translucent quality, her lips invited kisses, and her delicate jaw gave her a vulnerability which was almost irresistible. Is it any wonder then, that even as a young child, I was captivated?

I felt an urge to run across the room to her and bury my face in her silky hair, but even though her eyes were kind and inviting, other eyes, far more hostile, were fixed on me too, ordering me to stay where I was – and I couldn't summon up the courage to defy them.

'Hello, Rob,' this golden goddess said to me. 'It's really lovely to meet you at last.'

I wanted to tell her it was lovely – wonderful – to meet her, too, but the only words which would come out of my mouth were, 'Where's Granddad?'

Sadie looked at each of her sisters in turn, and I think there were tears in her eyes.

'He doesn't know,' she said. 'The poor little mite doesn't know.'

Each aunt met her gaze in a different way. Peggy looked vaguely embarrassed, Jacqueline merely annoyed, and Catherine totally unmoved. Then, from somewhere in the folds of her black dress, Aunt Catherine produced a large pocket watch and made a great show of studying it.

'If the British Railways Board is following the Good Lord's injunction to run on time, then my train for Llawesuohtihs leaves in three hours and twelve minutes,' she said. 'And in those three hours and twelve minutes, there is a great deal to be settled.'

Sadie turned her attention back to me. 'Would you do something for me, Rob?' she asked.

'What, Auntie?' I replied, knowing, as she spoke, that whatever her request – be it to get her a glass of water or throw myself under a bus – I would have done it willingly, because I was already her grateful slave.

'Would you go and sit quietly in the corner, next to the standard lamp, while we have a talk?' Sadie said.

'Yes, Auntie Sadie.'

'What a good boy you are.'

What a good boy you are!

I have been awarded international Bridge trophies to thunderous applause. I have seen the adoring fans of my television programmes literally throw themselves at me. And nothing – nothing! – has ever had the same effect on me as those six words Aunt Sadie spoke on the morning of my mother's funeral.

'Is it wise to have the boy in the room?' asked fat Aunt Peggy, emerging temporarily from her lethargy. 'I mean, if we're going to talk about … talk about … well, you know … shouldn't he be sent upstairs?'

'Waste of time, sending him upstairs,' Aunt Jacqueline snapped. 'Only a child. Won't understand a word.'

'You're right for once, Jacqueline,' Aunt Catherine said.

Ah, dear Aunt Jacqueline, dear Aunt Catherine – how you both always underrated me! If only you'd credited me with just a little more intelligence then, you might still be alive today.

3

A frozen tableau: me, short-trousered and grey-wool-stockinged, sitting cross-legged under the standard lamp; my four aunts, on their various chairs, as rigid as waxworks' dummies.

Outside, the rain was becoming more confident, and began to beat out a tattoo on the bay window – *rat-a-tat-tat, rat-a-tat-tat* – but inside, there was only silence.

'Well, isn't anyone going to make a start?' Sadie asked finally.

The other aunts said nothing.

'Oh, for goodness' sake!' Sadie sighed.

It seemed to be the opening that Aunt Catherine had been waiting for. 'Goodness!' she repeated. 'There is very little goodness in this house.'

Aunt Sadie tugged nervously at her skirt, pulling the hem down over her beautiful knees. 'Please, Catherine,' she said, 'I don't really think it serves any useful purpose to—'

But Aunt Catherine was warming to her theme, and was not to be interrupted. 'God is not mocked,' she thundered, 'and neither is He cheated. As sure as Tesco stays open for late-night shopping on Thursdays, had Jennifer left home as the rest of us did – as even *you* did, Sadie – this shameful tragedy would never have occurred.'

'We shouldn't talk about it!' Sadie said, her tone a mixture of earnestness and alarm. 'For Rob's sake, we should come to an agreement, right now, that none of us will ever tell him exactly how his mother died.'

I heard the words – "exactly how his mother died" – and they came as no great shock. So though I had no memory of Mother dying, or of her being buried, part of me at least must have known that she *was* dead.

'Will you promise?' Sadie persisted. 'All of you?'

'Promise?' Aunt Catherine repeated. 'There's no need to promise. I would never soil my lips with such filth.'

Aunt Peggy shifted uncomfortably in her chair. 'Me neither,' she said. 'I mean, I just couldn't. I wouldn't know where to put myself.'

Sadie turned to Aunt Jacqueline. 'And you? Do you promise, too?'

'Yes, yes,' said my chain-smoking aunt impatiently. 'Now let's get back to what we're here for, shall we? Which of you is going to take the boy?'

'Which of *us*?' Aunt Peggy asked. 'Oh no, you don't get away with that, Jacqueline. I mean, if he's the responsibility of any of us – and I'm not saying that he is, mind you – then he's the responsibility of all of us.'

Sitting, shivering, under the standard lamp, I knew what I wanted to happen. I wanted Aunt Sadie to hug me and take care of me.

But it was not to be.

'I'd look after him,' my beautiful aunt said. 'I'd really like to. But living in France …'

'Don't see why that should stop you,' Aunt Jacqueline interrupted. 'Very educational place, France – bags of culture. Live by the sea, don't you? Fresh air would be good for him.'

Sadie shrugged her pretty shoulders. 'If I had a permanent base, it might be different,' she said. 'But I don't. In my work, I have to move around a lot.'

Aunt Jacqueline laughed – a nasty, rasping laugh which carried with it the evidence of a million cigarettes.

'Course you move around a lot,' she said. 'Clients expect it, don't they? If they wanted somebody who just lay there like a sack of potatoes, they might as well stay at home with their wives.'

I didn't understand the remark, nor could I see why it should make Sadie blush as she did, but the odd, incomprehensible comment from an adult was the least of my worries at that moment. Sadie couldn't take me, so it would have to be one of the others – roly-poly Aunt Peggy, bony Aunt Catherine or masculine Aunt Jacqueline.

None of them seemed a very attractive prospect – but what was the alternative? I'd read *Oliver Twist* – not in a simplified, sanitised version for kids, but with its full adult horror – and anything, it seemed to me, would be better than that.

'Why couldn't he live with you, Catherine, dear?' Aunt Peggy asked.

'Me?' demanded the senior aunt, as if the suggestion were both unreasonable and obscene.

'Why not?' Aunt Peggy asked, stalking her sister as cunningly as I would later see her numerous cats stalking sparrows. 'I mean, you're always saying what a good Christian you are, aren't you? Well then, here's your chance to bring another soul to Jesus.'

But Aunt Catherine was too wily a sparrow to be caught like that.

'I am engaged in the Lord's work,' she told her fat sister, 'and, like the work of the little yellow heathens at the Chinese take-away, it is almost never-ending. The boy would be to me as a window-shopper is to trade – an obstruction.'

'You take him, Peggy,' Aunt Jacqueline said. 'Got hundreds of cats already. A kid's no more trouble. Plate of meat, saucer of milk, and that's it.'

A woolly look came to Aunt Peggy's face. 'They're so helpless, cats, aren't they?' she said reflectively. 'But so demanding, too. And they will keep on having babies, won't they?'

The Angel, the Scarecrow and the Dumpling having turned me down, all eyes were suddenly fixed on Aunt Jacqueline.

'No,' she said with absolute determination. 'Don't want a child. Got my bridge tournaments to think of.'

'Well, somebody has to take the poor boy in,' Aunt Sadie protested. 'We can't just abandon him.'

Couldn't they? From where I was sitting, that looked like exactly what they were intending to do, and I felt the shadow of Dickens' beadle already hovering over me.

Aunt Catherine consulted her watch again. 'Time is passing,' she said, standing up. 'We must get about our business.'

'Get about our business!' Sadie protested. 'Isn't Rob's future our most important business?'

'Indeed it is,' Aunt Catherine agreed, 'but unlike most commercial enterprises, the boy has no closing time.' Her right hand disappeared into the vast leather handbag, and when it emerged again, it was holding two cheques. 'This is the balance owed to the caterers,' she said, passing the first to Sadie, 'and this is the amount still due to the solicitors,' giving it to Aunt Peggy. 'I will go and see the undertaker myself. The flowers drooped during the funeral. They were an insult to the glory of God, and I shall certainly demand a discount.'

'What about Jacqueline?' Aunt Peggy demanded peevishly.

'Jacqueline will be as the floorwalker is to his merchandise, and the Lord is to his flock,' Aunt Catherine told her.

'You what?'

'She will look after the child while we are away,' Aunt Catherine said. She walked over to the door, then turned to face her sisters again. 'And as you carry out your missions, examine your consciences with regard to the boy,' she told them. 'My account with the Bank of Heaven is in healthy credit, but the rest of you could use a few good works to help pay off your spiritual overdrafts.'

4

Life, I've often thought, is very much like a game of bridge …

Oh God, that sounds awful, doesn't it? It's the sort of line a satirist might use in a sketch about a vicar.

'You know,' – plummy voice, elongated face – 'as I was on my way to church this morning, it struck me forcibly that when we play the game of bridge we are, in a very real sense, playing the game of life.'

But life *is* like bridge in so many ways. For a start, the cards you receive are pre-dealt, and there's no way you can alter that. But what you do with your hand is up to you. If you are to be successful in the game of life, you must first sort out your cards until you can see a pattern. Having done that, you must decide which cards within the pattern will be important, and which are merely peripheral. It is this decision, this ordering of priorities, which will determine your play.

A word of warning: a good player will inevitably make more of his hand than a poor one with the same cards, but however brilliant he is, he can never go beyond the hand. I was dealt a quartet of aunts, but the eventual outcome was far from determined at that point. Had Fate shuffled a little less, or cut at some other point in the pack, the play would be entirely different. Or to put it another way, if – when Aunt Catherine had divided up the errands – it hadn't fallen to Aunt Jacqueline to look after me for an hour, I might indeed have ended up as one of Dr Barnardo's little sunbeams.

But Aunt Jacqueline *was* deputed to look after me, and when the other aunts had left – Sadie gliding across the carpet, Peggy wobbling through the door – she and I found ourselves alone together.

I have always had a quick, active mind, and as I sat under the standard lamp, watching my aunt steadily smoke her way through a Virginia sharecropper's annual quota, I began to feel boredom setting in. I had the solution to my ennui in my pocket – a small pack of cards – but I had not dared to take them out while Aunt Catherine was in the room.

Now, however, I plucked up my courage and said, 'Can I play cards, Auntie Jacqueline?'

My aunt snorted. 'Don't want to play cards,' she said. 'Not with a kid.'

'I don't need you,' I pointed out. 'I can play by myself.'

'By yourself?' Aunt Jacqueline scoffed. 'How? Fool yourself at Happy Families? Surprise yourself at Snap?'

Happy Families! Snap! The idea of playing either of those childish games would never have occurred to me.

'I was going to play Patience,' I said, very much on my dignity.

'Patience,' my aunt said, the surprise evident in her voice. 'How old are you, child?'

'Nine.'

Aunt Jacqueline's eyes narrowed. 'All right,' she conceded, 'you may play Patience.'

As I dealt the cards, I felt her gaze on me, but apart from the occasional sucking sound as she drew on her cigarette, she kept perfectly silent.

The game I'd chosen to play had a one-in-three chance of working out. It was fairly standard – black on red, red on black – except that the appearance of a jack necessitated a change in the order – black on black, red on red – until another jack came up and reversed the process. I became so absorbed in the game that I did not notice Aunt Jacqueline rise from her seat, cross the room and kneel down next to me. In fact, it was not until I had played the final card – a seven of clubs – that I even became aware of the cloud of smoke which was encircling my head.

'It looks like an interesting game,' my Aunt Jacqueline said. 'Tell me the rules.'

I explained them. Aunt Jacqueline took the cards from me, shuffled them with her deft, sure, nicotine-stained fingers, and dealt a new hand. It took her five minutes to play it out, and when she'd finished, she nodded her head several times, as if confirming an earlier suspicion.

'It *is* a good game,' she said. 'Who taught it to you?'

'Nobody, auntie.'

Aunt Jacqueline snorted again. 'Somebody must have taught it to you. Didn't make it up yourself, did you?'

'Yes, auntie.'

'Did you? Did you really?' Aunt Jacqueline nodded her head reflectively. 'How long have you been playing cards?'

How long?

Forever!

Playing cards, like reading, seemed to be something I'd always done.

'Well?' Aunt Jacqueline demanded. 'How long?'

'Since I was three?' I hazarded.

'Don't know how to play Bridge, do you?'

'No,' I agreed, humiliated.

'Of course you don't,' Aunt Jacqueline said airily. 'You're far too young to understand.'

My feeling of humiliation was rapidly replaced by one of injured pride.

'Teach me,' I said.

'No point,' Aunt Jacqueline replied. 'It's well beyond your comprehension, child.'

'Teach me,' I insisted.

My aunt glanced at her watch, and shrugged.

'I suppose I might as well try,' she said. 'After all, it will be another half hour before Catherine the Great comes back.' She shuffled the cards. 'Now the first thing to remember is the order the suits come in. Clubs is the lowest, then diamonds, then hearts, and spades is the most valuable suit of all. Think you can remember that?'

'Clubs, diamonds, hearts, then spades,' I repeated. 'Oh yes, I'll remember that, all right.'

5

By the time Aunt Catherine returned from the undertaker's, we were half-way through our fourth game of Honeymoon Bridge.

The senior of my aunts was not at all pleased with the way things had developed.

'Cards are the Devil's handiwork,' she stormed from the doorway. 'As surely as Fairy goes further than any ordinary washing-up liquid – as surely as that – you are gambling with your salvation by leading this child astray.'

'I'll take him,' Aunt Jacqueline said, not looking up from her game.

'You'll what?'

'I'll take him. The boy. Richard.'

'His name is Robert.

'Robert, then. I'll take him.'

'I would not let you have him now,' the senior aunt said. 'Not after I've seen, with my own eyes, the tub of evil in which you seek to immerse him.'

'All right – you take him,' Aunt Jacqueline said, trumping both my return diamond and her sister's objection.

From the corner of my eye, I could see that Aunt Catherine was torn between duty and expediency.

'If I *were* to allow it,' she said, expediency having won an easy victory, 'you would have to promise – here and now – that you would never again play cards with the child.'

'Agreed,' Aunt Jacqueline said, cashing in her ace of clubs.

PART TWO: The Queen of Clubs

1

Holding a large suitcase in my small hand, I stepped awkwardly off the train and onto the platform of Lewes station. My aunt, her feet already firmly on the ground, looked around her.

'Where the hell is Tom?' she demanded belligerently.

'Tom?' I repeated. 'Is he my uncle?'

'No, he is not,' my aunt said curtly. 'Your uncle's name was Charles, but he's long gone. And bloody good riddance. The man couldn't bid a grand slam to save his life.' She scanned the station once more. 'There he is. Late as usual.'

The object of her criticism, it appeared, was the man in a pale fawn overcoat who was making his way towards us. He was middle-aged, of average height, and had neutral brown hair and a wispy moustache which was only remarkable for its complete lack of remarkableness.

'How did it go?' Tom asked when my aunt, a cigarette stuck firmly in her mouth, had turned her head slightly so he could kiss her on the cheek.

'How did it go?' Aunt Jacqueline repeated. 'It was my sister's funeral. We buried her. That's what people do at funerals.'

If Tom noticed the sarcasm, he didn't show it. Instead, he merely nodded his head. It was his eyes I noticed now I could see him from close up. They weren't exceptionable in themselves – pale brown and revealing no particular depth of intelligence, they fitted in perfectly with the rest of his face – but what *was* exceptional was the look in them.

They burned!

With love!

I looked beyond Aunt Jacqueline to see for myself at whom he was gazing. The train had pulled out. The disembarked passengers had all gone. We were the only three people left on the platform.

I turned back to my aunt. Could she – this stringy woman in a severe suit, this aunt I had at first mistaken for an uncle, this smoking machine on knobbly knees – could she, I say again, be the object of Tom's adoration?

There was no one else there. Incredible as it might seem, it simply had to be her.

'Who's this?' Tom asked, noticing me for the first time.

'He's my nephew,' Aunt Jacqueline said. 'His name's … err …'

'Bobby,' I supplied.

'I didn't know you even had a nephew,' Tom said.

'Well, I do. And he's coming to live with me.'

Tom frowned.

'Any objections?' Aunt Jacqueline demanded.

'No, no,' Tom said hastily. 'It's just that I never thought that you … somehow you just didn't seem the type to …'

The type to do what, Tom?

To take in a poor, helpless orphan?

Spot on. It had been puzzling me, too.

But then, at that point, neither of us knew what plans Aunt Jacqueline had for me – for both of us.

I didn't talk much on the drive back from the station. Neither did Tom. Instead, we were both subjected to a bridge monologue delivered in short, sharp sentences by my Aunt Jacqueline. She began by analysing a new overcall as we pulled off the car park, continued with her views on the Texas convention while we were negotiating the traffic on the High Street, and concluded with a few disparaging remarks on Tom's play as we drew up outside her semi on the edge of town.

'I can play bridge,' I told Tom as he reached into the boot of his ancient Morris Minor for my suitcase. 'Auntie taught me yesterday afternoon.'

'Did she?' Tom asked.

'Of course not,' Aunt Jacqueline snapped angrily. 'How could I teach a child something I can't even teach my own partner?'

'But Auntie …' I protested.

Ignoring me, my aunt turned to Tom. 'It's half past three,' she said. 'Be back here at six-thirty.'

Tom looked puzzled. 'Don't you want me to come in?'

My aunt lit another cigarette. 'What for?'

'Well, I thought Bobby might want some help with his suitcase.'

'The boy's carried it this far,' my aunt said. 'No reason why he can't manage it the rest of the way.'

Tom seemed as if he were about to argue, then, with a hangdog expression on his face, he climbed back into his car.

'And remember,' Aunt Jacqueline called after him, 'six-thirty sharp.'

Struggling with my case, I followed my aunt up what would have been called the garden path if the collection of weeds growing on either side of it could ever have reasonably been called a garden.

At the front door, Aunt Jacqueline stopped and turned around. I expected her to take the keys out of her handbag, but she seemed much more interested in making sure that Tom was really leaving. She waited until his car had finally turned the corner, then crouched down in front of me, so that her eyes were level with mine. Her cheeks burned with anger, her thin lips were twisted in an ugly snarl. She could never have been an attractive woman at the best of times, but now, I recognised instinctively, I was seeing her at her worst.

'There's an orphanage just up the road,' she hissed at me.

'An … an orphanage,' I stuttered.

'It's a terrible place. The orphans are kept half-starved, and at night there are rats which climb onto your face, and eat your eyes out.'

My lower lip was beginning to tremble. 'Please, Auntie …' I begged.

'And if you *ever* talk to Tom about playing bridge again, if you even *hint* to him that you know the basic rules, that orphanage is where you're going. Do you understand me?'

'Yes, Auntie,' I said, fighting back the tears.

What else could I have replied? For the moment, she held all the cards, and I had no choice but to obey her.

3

It is almost impossible to describe the state of my aunt's living room as it appeared to me when I saw it for the first time. The abandoned site of a rock concert would have looked tidy in comparison. The epicentre of a dustbin bomb explosion could scarcely have looked worse. It was every housewife's worst nightmare, a composite of all the "before" pictures ever used in adverts for miracle cleaners.

Bridge magazines, for which at least a square mile of pine forest must have laid down its life, lay in piles all over the ash-grey carpet. Scatter cushions were scattered far further than their designers had ever intended. A layer of dust, as thick as plywood, lay smugly on top of the sideboard.

It was more of a shock to me, I suppose, because it was such a contrast to the home I had just left. Every Saturday morning, for as long as I could remember, Mother and I had cleaned the front parlour, polishing the furniture and photographs, vacuuming the carpet and picking hairs off the velveteen sofa. It had been a labour of love for Mother, and I had loved doing it with her.

'*You could eat your food off the floor in here,*' Mother used to say – and she'd been quite right. Only one thing in Aunt Jacqueline's house had ever been the object of her love – the trophy case. There it stood, to the right of the gas fire, the glass front sporting a shine which would have made any professional window cleaner green with envy. And how many cups and medals there were! For all my aunt's complaints about Tom, he couldn't be such a bad partner, I thought – though I wisely decided to keep my observation to myself.

My stomach rumbled, and I realised I had had nothing to eat since the sandwich Sadie gave me when I got on the train.

'I'm hungry, Auntie,' I said.

My aunt lit up a cigarette. 'See what there is in the kitchen.'

'The kitchen?'

'It's through there,' Aunt Jacqueline told me, pointing to the door next to the trophy case. 'But I don't expect you'll find much.'

Tom arrived, as instructed, at exactly half-past six.

'How are you, young Bobby?' he asked, tousling my hair, and favouring me with a colourless smile. 'Settling in all right?'

'Yes, thank you,' I said politely – just as Mother would have wished.

It was the truth, too, if by "settling in" you mean being assigned a room and making yourself a meal of Marmite and crispbreads.

My aunt came down from her bedroom, where she'd been changing into a severe suit of black and white check.

'I'm ready,' she announced.

'Where's the baby-sitter?' Tom asked.

'Baby-sitter?' my aunt repeated, as if the word was alien to her vocabulary. 'What baby-sitter?'

'You're surely not intending to leave young Bobby on his own, are you?' Tom said.

'Why not?' my aunt questioned. She turned to me. 'You're a big boy now, aren't you … err … Bobby. Look after yourself, can't you?'

'Yes, Auntie,' I said, acting the Brave Little Trooper – as my mother had always taught me to.

'Still and all, I don't think it's right,' Tom objected.

Aunt Jacqueline stubbed out her cigarette in an already-overflowing ashtray. 'The only thing you need to worry about is your bidding once you get to the club – that is, if you're coming to the club,' she said. 'If you're not, tell me now, while there's still the chance I can get another partner.'

Tom hesitated then shrugged his shoulders apologetically in my direction.

'We won't be late,' he promised.

'Watch some television if you want to, then get yourself off to bed,' my aunt told me as she headed for the front door.

I didn't go to bed, of course. After all the excitement of the day, I simply wasn't sleepy. Besides, a strange empty house can hold innumerable terrors for a nine-year-old, and I was afraid that if I allowed myself to fall asleep, the demons would get me. Thus it was that I was still wide awake when Tom's car pulled up in front of the house a little after eleven.

Crouching at the top of the stairs, I heard them come in.

'Whisky?' Aunt Jacqueline asked.

'Please,' Tom replied gratefully. 'Err … how do you think we did tonight, Jackie?'

'Not badly,' my aunt conceded reluctantly. 'But if you'd played for a two-two trump break on Board Twenty-Seven – as you should have – we'd have done even better.'

For the next half hour, Aunt Jacqueline talked over the evening's games, re-living her triumphs in all their glory and occasionally lavishing faint praise on her partner. Only when she finally paused for breath did Tom speak – and then, what he said had nothing to do with bridge.

'Could we … could we go upstairs?' he asked tentatively.

Silence.

'Please!'

'I suppose so,' Aunt Jacqueline said, with a sigh.

There was a pattern to this, I was to learn later. If my aunt considered her partner had played well, she'd invite him in for a drink and eventually – after making him almost beg for it – she'd take him to bed and administer some soldier's comfort. However, if she was displeased with his performance at the bridge table, she would refuse to perform too – and he wouldn't even get through the front door.

I used to ask myself why he bothered – how he could even *want* to sleep with my aunt. It must, I thought, be rather like making love to a mound of old bicycles, except that – chances were – the bicycles would be more appreciative.

Now that I've seen more of the world, I accept that however weird Tom might have appeared to me then, he wasn't even half-way up the twisted scale of weirdness. Take, for example, the petroleum engineer from Peterborough, who I met while I was on the lam in the Gulf, shortly after Aunt Sadie's unfortunate accident. His name was Brad, and he was a Hollywood dream – tall, broad and handsome. He could have had any woman he wanted, yet he was totally infatuated with a camel – and a bad-tempered, ugly one, at that.

So Tom's obsession with my aunt, whilst hard to understand, is not totally inconceivable. Even so, if I were given the choice between Jacqueline and the camel, I'd plump for the camel every time.

4

I don't wish to create the impression that I had the kind of childhood which would have made Oliver Twist's experience look like a fortnight at the Club Med. It was difficult at first, I admit, but conditions did gradually improve. Aunt Jacqueline was quite prepared to shop for food, as long as I organised it, and, thanks to Mother, I already knew how to cook a few simple meals. Nor did my aunt object when I started to clean and tidy up, and by the end of the year I had the living room so presentable that even Mother would have approved.

And whilst it is true that Aunt Jacqueline wasn't the most affectionate of relatives, nor was she really intrusive, either. She was out most of the day – pounding at the keyboard of an estate agent's PC with her nicotine-stained fingers – and her nights were usually spent at the clubs.

How many clubs there were! She and Tom put in thousands of miles every year, just travelling to different venues. They played in the Liberal Club and the Conservative Club, the British Legion Club and the Country Club. Had the National Union of Poisoners opened a branch in the area, they'd have played there, too – as long as there was a Strychnine Cup to compete for.

How ironic it is then, that for all her fanaticism, Aunt Jacqueline was not that good a player. I don't mean she was actually bad. She came consistently top of the list, and no doubt impressed all her local opponents, but as I came to really understand bridge properly over the next couple of years, I began to appreciate just how limited *her* understanding of the game was.

'I can't see how they could squeeze an extra trick out of that,' she said, one Sunday afternoon when we were analysing the 1968 World Championship.

'I can't see it either, Auntie,' I told her.

'How could he have known the king was lying there?' she asked on another Sunday, in reference to the 1971 European heats.

'I don't know, Auntie.'

Of course I saw. Of course I knew. It was all so obvious to me, but I thought it wise not to make her aware of the fact that, although I'd never sat down at a proper bridge table in my life, I was already out of her class.

So I lied, knowing that Mother would have understood and forgiven me, because Aunt Jacqueline was the only person standing between me and the orphanage where – I still believed – the rats ate your eyes out in the night.

****

Oh, that aunt of mine! How she dreamed of going on to greater things.

'One day,' she'd repeat over and over again, almost as if were a prayer, 'one day I'll be an international player.'

It was pathetic really – rather like hearing an amoeba expressing the wish to become Brain of Britain.

5

A few days after I went to live with her, Aunt Jacqueline enrolled me in the nearest primary school. It was a pleasant enough place – light and airy and filled with all those kinds of resources that middle-class parents provide from the proceeds of countless bring-and-buy sales – but on the whole, it bored me.

I don't blame the school. The teachers were all caring, well-meaning people, but I had little interest in the knowledge they attempted to impart to me. What did I care about how Eskimos lived, when sitting at home – just waiting for me – was an account of the 1934 Culbertson-Lenz clash of the bridge titans?

How could I show enthusiasm for the New Maths, when the only mathematics which concerned me was the percentage variants on a finesse?

The other kids, equally, failed to stimulate me. I tried, once or twice, to teach a few of the brighter ones how to play bridge, but they were soon floundering. I did my best to share their interests, but moronic children's television quiz shows held no appeal for me, and kicking a ball to and fro seemed so pointless as to be hardly worth contemplating.

In the end, I found I was spending most of my time alone, and it's not surprising that despite attending the school for two years – and being blessed with an exceptional memory – I'm unable to recall a single person I met there.

Actually, that's not quite accurate – I do remember Les Fliques.

But does he count? After all, he was a visiting lecturer, not a teacher or a pupil at the school, and perhaps my memory of our first meeting has been reinforced by the fact that since then we've locked horns far more regularly than I personally would have chosen to.

No! Thinking about it, I'm sure that if I'd only seen him once, the image of Les Fliques – only a humble constable back then – would still have been firmly burned into my mind. That was the kind of impact Les had – once seen and he'd be visiting your nightmares for years.

We'd had several guest lecturers that term before Fliques made his appearance. A large man, whose face contained so many broken veins it resembled a road map, had preached temperance to us. A thinner man, with a hacking cough almost as bad as Aunt Jacqueline's, had warned us of the dangers of smoking. An obese woman, weighed down with jewellery, had asked us to collect used stamps for the starving millions in Africa. So it was as veterans that we trooped into the gym/hall and sat on the floor in class lines to await the arrival of Constable Fliques.

Looking straight ahead – as we'd been taught – we watched Fliques march up to our minuscule stage. He was certainly a sight to see. His lean body seemed – like that of a jack-in-the-box – to have been constructed on a very tight spring which was held down for the moment, but would shoot forth with considerable force whenever he blew his top. His eyebrows resembled malevolent stinging caterpillars, and the eyes below were small, yet missed nothing. His nose looked as if it had been broken, then set again by a drunken doctor with poor vision. The picture was completed by a wide mouth which looked big enough to swallow a child whole, and a chin like a crudely re-shaped house brick.

He was not a tall man – I'd guess he only just made the regulation height – but he exuded a power and ferocity which, without him having to do a thing, made several of my small companions wet themselves.

'My name is Constable Fliques,' he said, fixing each and every one of us with his piercing eyes.

From the back of the hall came the sound of the door closing, as our teachers stepped outside for a quick smoke or – in the case of at least one of them – a stiff slug of McMeths' Finest Accrington Whisky from his hip flask.

Fliques wrote his name on the whiteboard.

'You don't say the "s",' he told us. 'It's pronounced "Flick".' He gave us another piercing stare. 'It's Huguenot.'

The eyes swept the room, searching out any kid willing to dispute that his forefathers had been 16th Century French weavers of a Calvinistic persuasion.

No one did.

'Road Safety,' he announced, writing it on the whiteboard in thick, intimidating capitals. 'How many of you have got bicycles?'

When it came to conditioning, our teacher would have put Pavlov to shame, and though I had no particular desire to participate in this exercise, I found my arm – surrounded by a forest of other arms – being held high in the air.

'You!' Fliques said, homing in on me. 'Do you go out after dark on your machine?'

'Yes, sir.'

'And do you have proper and adequate lighting mounted on it?'

'I think so, sir.'

'Think so isn't good enough, is it, laddie? Think so could not only have you under a lorry, your head squashed like an over-ripe tomato – think so could also cause you to contravene the Road Traffic Act, couldn't it?'

'Yes, sir,' I replied obediently, though I had absolutely no idea what "contravene" meant.

'What type of illumination is operative on your machine?'

'Pardon, sir?'

'Do you have a battery lamp or a dynamo, laddie?'

I searched desperately for some way of saying that when he'd asked us who had a bike, I hadn't realised that what he'd meant was a *bike*, and that I, personally, travelled everywhere on foot.

No good.

I looked down at the floor, and wished I was dead.

'Well?' Fliques demanded.

'It's got a battery, sir.'

'And how long, under normal conditions, would you expect the battery to last?' he asked witheringly.

'I don't know,' I confessed.

'Then find out,' he roared.

Fliques turned his back on me, and I thought, for one glorious moment, that my ordeal was over.

But it was just a policeman's trick. A second later, he swung round again, and his accusing finger was back in place.

'Have you had a look at your brake blocks recently?' he asked.

'Yes, sir. Yesterday,' I lied, feeling sure that on this occasion, Mother would have forgiven me.

'Don't believe you,' Fliques told me. 'I'll be watching you, laddie.' But he did seem, finally, to have finished with me, and his eyes swept the hall again. 'Who's used a zebra crossing?' he asked.

Apparently, no one had.

'Black and white stripes,' Fliques said helpfully. 'Can't miss 'em. Run right across the road.'

Still, nobody volunteered to step onto the firing line.

'You,' Fliques said, pointing to a girl called Jane who was so sickeningly good that she was both the library monitor *and* the flower monitor. 'You've used them, haven't you?'

'Yes, sir,' the class paragon reluctantly admitted.

'Then why didn't you say so in the first place?' Fliques asked belligerently. 'Now what do you do before you step off the kerb?'

It took less than a minute of Fliques' blistering interrogation for goody-two-shoes Jane to break down and confess that once, when she was much younger and much less responsible than she was now, she'd crossed the road without looking right, left and then right again.

We'd gone into the hall as lively and reasonably optimistic children, but when Fliques released us, forty-five minutes later, we filed out like broken men and women, weighed down by our faults and convinced we were doomed to a life of inadequacy and failure.

Never, ever, would I go within a mile of Constable Fliques again, I promised myself – which only goes to show that even with a near-genius IQ, it's still possible to get things totally, hopelessly wrong.

If only I'd known the truth back then. If only I'd realised then that Les Fliques was going to be with me for a long time, pointing the finger of guilt at me after Aunt Jacqueline's death, Aunt Peggy's untimely demise, Aunt Catherine's …

But I'm getting way ahead of myself – a fault that I've often been prone to.

'*Your brain works too quickly, Bobby,*' Mother used to say. '*Slow down and give your body a chance to catch up.*'

Quite right, Mother.

6

If I were to pick a point at which life began to change – at which *my aunt* began to change – I think I would have to select my eleventh birthday. We didn't celebrate it – birthdays, like most other aspects of existence away from the bridge table, had no relevance for Aunt Jacqueline – yet it did have an impact on her.

I noticed it in little things at first, like the way she looked at me – quizzically, appraisingly.

And then there was the question of the uniform I would need for my new school.

'Shall we go and buy it on Saturday, Auntie?' I asked her one day towards the end of July.

'Plenty of time yet,' she told me.

'We still haven't got my new uniform,' I reminded her at some point in the middle of August.

'Don't worry about it,' she snapped.

But I *did* worry, or, at least, I was puzzled. Whatever her faults – and they were legion – my aunt was not a mean woman. Indeed, having no interest in the merely material world, meanness and generosity hardly featured in her outlook at all. If she had money, and I requested it, she'd usually give it to me – so why did she baulk at the idea of a new uniform, which she knew she'd have to buy eventually.

Nor was the issue of the uniform the only mystery. With the exception of Tom, people hardly ever phoned us at home. Now, however, she began to receive a large number of calls. Not only that, but when the phone rang she would rush into the hall to make sure she reached it before I did, and, when talking to the caller, would keep her mouth close to the receiver and speak in what was almost a whisper.

I caught snatches of the conversations – 'Don't ring me at the office'; 'Thirty-five thousand pounds'; 'By the end of the month' – but never enough to explain the sudden change in my aunt's telephonic habits.

But I have yet to reveal the strangest thing of all – there were nights when Aunt Jacqueline did not play bridge!

It's true.

'I'm too tired,' she told Tom, one balmy August evening.

Too tired?

For bridge?

Even when she did play, her killer instinct seemed to have completely deserted her.

'We did well tonight, didn't we?' Tom asked enthusiastically, after a session at the Liberal Club.

And my aunt, who could normally out-crow a cockerel, simply said, 'Yes, we did,' without any suggestion of triumph in her voice.

'So could we ... err...?' Tom asked, glancing towards the stairs.

I was there at the time, I should mention – right in the living room – but they'd long since given up trying to hide from me that it was in the bedroom that Tom got his reward for his services at the bridge table.

'Could we?' Tom asked again.

'Could we what?' my bloody-minded aunt replied.

'You know ...' Tom awkwardly. 'Go upstairs ... for a lie-down.'

'No,' Aunt Jacqueline said firmly. 'I've got a headache, and besides, I don't feel like it.'

Did she notice the look which flashed briefly in his eyes – the look of a much stronger man than he normally appeared to be, a man who was tired of being treated as a doormat? I don't know, but she must have at least *suspected* that such a man existed, or she would not have executed her plans in the way that she did.

7

It was not until the beginning of September, a few days before I was due to start my new school – uniform-less – that Aunt Jacqueline finally chose to confide in me. We were engaged in our joint household tasks at the time – me polishing the sideboard, my aunt covering the sofa arm with a protective layer of cigarette ash.

'I shouldn't bother doing that,' my aunt said, from out of nowhere.

'Why not, Auntie?'

'It'll only get dirty again during the move.'

The move?

Suddenly, the spate of phone calls and her refusal to buy me a new uniform both made sense. But what about her waning interest in bridge? Even the move didn't explain that.

'Where are we going, Auntie?' I asked.

'A long way away,' Aunt Jacqueline replied. 'Better you don't know where until we actually leave, just in case you let it slip out.'

'Why is it all such a secret?' I asked, alarmed. 'We're not in any trouble, are we?'

Aunt Jacqueline laughed drily, like a snake with a bad case of laryngitis.

'Not in trouble,' she said. 'Just want to avoid a scene. Tom won't like it.'

Tom won't like it. What could that mean?

'Are you saying you're not going to tell him we're leaving?'

'That's right.'

Poor, faithful Tom! For years he had sacrificed himself to her obsession for bridge, and now she was abandoning him as if he were nothing more than a cigarette she'd smoked down to the filter.

'He loves you, you know,' I said earnestly. 'You'll break his heart if you just go away.'

'I'd never have got anywhere with him,' my aunt said dismissively, as if broken hearts didn't really come into it.

I didn't understand, although, having lived with her for two years, I certainly should have done.

'I'd have been stuck in the minor bridge leagues for ever if I'd kept playing with Tom,' my aunt continued.

'But if you're not going to play with Tom any more, then who is going to be your part—?' I began, before realisation suddenly struck. 'Me!' I said. 'You want *me* to partner you.'

'You're too young to play in the big tournaments yet,' my aunt said, 'but there's no reason why the local clubs shouldn't accept you.'

She'd waited for this moment ever since the day of my mother's funeral, when we'd played our first game of Honeymoon Bridge. No wonder she'd lost patience with playing with Tom as the time for our departure grew ever closer. He'd never been anything but her hors d'oeuvre – I was to be the main course.

'You would *like* to be my partner, wouldn't you?' Aunt Jacqueline asked.

Her voice was strained, as if the effort of forcing the question out had been monumental. In all the time I'd lived with Aunt Jacqueline, I'd never heard her sound like this before. Her impatience, I was used to. Her brusqueness, I'd learned how to handle. But this was neither of those things. What I was hearing now was pure, blind panic. She was terrified I'd refuse to partner her, because she knew that I was her one chance – her only chance – to become a big name on the bridge circuit.

'Yes, I'll partner you,' I told her.

Well, I had no choice, did I? I didn't dare defy my aunt – I was still a mere child, and the threat of Mr Bumble and his orphanage continued to hang heavily over my head. Besides, if the truth be told, I quite liked the idea. True, Aunt Jacqueline was not my ideal choice as partner, but I was sure that as long as I controlled the situation, she would prove quite adequate on the provincial circuit. And when the time came for me to move on to a better player, I'd try to drop her with a little more sympathy and understanding than she was about to show to Tom.

'We're moving on Monday,' Aunt Jacqueline said, walking over to the sideboard and taking out a new pack of cards. 'There must be a game somewhere near our new place on Monday night, so we'd better get our signals right.'

How like my aunt! I still didn't know exactly where we'd be going, but she had indicated it would be a long way from Tom, so we'd probably be travelling for most of the day. And when we finally arrived and the removers had departed, we'd be surrounded by our own personal chaos. But none of that would bother Jacqueline – she'd find the nearest bridge club, and off we'd go.

She sat down opposite me and dealt out the hands, as she'd done so often in the past. I picked up my cards and sorted them. I had a solid opener – a good spade suit, a diamond doubleton.

'What bidding system are we using?' I asked. 'Acol's always seemed a bit restrictive to me, and the Blue Club, for all its faults, is—'

'Doesn't matter,' my aunt told me. 'Just bid.'

'One spade,' I said, keeping it simple.

Aunt Jacqueline nodded with satisfaction. 'We've hit a grey area already,' she said. 'Look at my hand – only don't make it too obvious.'

Don't make it too obvious?

If she was going to lay her cards down on the table, how *could* I look at them without making it obvious? And why should I want to, anyway?

'Well, look at it!' Aunt Jacqueline said impatiently.

But how could I look while she kept her cards pressed tightly against her scrawny chest?

'Do you mean you want me to look at the backs of your cards?' I asked, wondering if her earlier fears that I'd refuse to be her partner had temporarily unhinged her.

A look of comprehension appeared on my aunt's face. She at least understood me, even if I still didn't understand her.

'Not the cards, you bloody fool,' she said. 'My hand ... the thing at the end of my arm, with fingers attached to it.'

'You mean the one you're holding your cards in?'

'No, the other one, you idiot. The one that's resting on the table.'

Not having a straitjacket readily available, I decided to humour her, and let my gaze fall on her left hand.

Four stubby fingers – two of them stained a dark nicotine-brown – all perfectly still. Then her index finger gave a barely perceptible twitch.

'See that,' my aunt asked.

'Yes,' I replied, wondering if lunatic asylums, like dispensing chemists, had a late-night rota.

'Less obvious than facial signals,' Aunt Jacqueline said with satisfaction. 'Index finger shows a void in a major suit, little finger a void in a minor.'

Now, finally, I did understand her – and I was horrified.

'Cheating!' I gasped. 'You're talking about cheating.'

'Everybody does it,' Aunt Jacqueline said, matter-of-factly. 'It's even happened in international tournaments. Gives you the edge, and you'll never get anywhere without the edge.'

'Perhaps some people *do* cheat,' I admitted. 'But I won't do it.'

Aunt Jacqueline's eyes narrowed. 'You won't, eh?' she said, with an edge of menace in her voice.

'No,' I said firmly.

'You'd prefer the orphanage, would you?'

I no longer believed in the eye-eating rats, but, even without them, I knew the orphanage would be bad enough.

'Well?' Aunt Jacqueline said harshly. 'What's it to be – partnership on my terms, or the orphanage?'

'I haven't … I can't …' I stuttered.

'Make up your mind.'

'The orphanage,' I gasped.

'You really mean it, don't you?' Aunt Jacqueline asked incredulously.

'Yes,' I said, trying not to cry. 'I really mean it.'

My aunt's mouth drooped, and her skin sagged as if it had been made for a much larger person. Tears poured from her eyes and cascaded over cheekbones which had turned chalky white.

I reached across the table and gently stroked her cropped hair. It was the first real physical contact we'd ever had.

'Why won't you do it for me?' my aunt sobbed. 'Just tell me why.'

'I won't do it because Mother would never have approved.'

Aunt Jacqueline's head whipped suddenly back. I watched – mesmerised – as burning anger dried her tears, and her ever-growing rage stained her pale face blood-red.

'Mother would never have approved,' she mimicked. 'Think your mother was perfect, don't you?'

'Yes.'

'She wasn't. My God, she wasn't! Do you want to know how she died?'

A wave of inexplicable dread swept over me, chilling me to the depth of my bones.

'*For Rob's sake, we should come to an agreement that none of us will ever tell him exactly how his mother died,*' Sadie had said just after the funeral.

And all the other aunts had agreed.

'You promised never to tell,' I told my Aunt Jacqueline, in a frightened whisper.

'So what?' she asked bitterly. 'Why should I see all my hopes turn to ashes just because you've got some cock-eyed idea about your mother? I'll tell you everything – then maybe you won't think cheating's so bad after all.'

Memories which my brain had long since buried began to claw their way out of the graveyard of my mind.

I could hear the sea roaring.

I could smell the salt in the air.

And when I closed my eyes, I could see a woman walking along the beach – Mother, beautiful Mother, her golden hair gleaming in the sunshine, the hem of her green silk dress swirling in the breeze.

She was not alone! Another presence walked by her side, but whereas my vision of her was as clear as if she'd been in the room with me, this other figure – this spectre – was nothing more than a sinister black outline.

My fear was increasing by the second. I knew – don't ask me how – that though I didn't recognise the apparition at that moment, it was no stranger to me. I knew, too, that if I gazed on the scene much longer, the layers of darkness would be stripped away, and I'd be forced to acknowledge the figure for what it was.

And I didn't want that. I couldn't … take that.

I searched desperately for something else on which to focus my mind.

The 1968 Gold Cup! Harrison-Grey had been playing West and held the King of Spades and the Ace and King of Hearts …

The phantom of my nightmare vision was becoming less obscure by the second and was moving closer and closer towards being recognisable.

North had five hearts, and so did South. East had a void and …

38

Now, where there had only been a black emptiness, I could make out the beginnings of eyes and a nose.

'Think,' I urged myself. 'Concentrate on the game.'

North bid Six Hearts, and Harrison-Grey immediately doubled, but at the next table … yes … yes …. that's it … that's better … at the next table they were playing the "unpenalty double" and Jonathan Cansino was forced to pass, even though he had the top two honours in trumps.

I had succeeded in my exorcism. The evil black figure had disappeared, and I was back in my aunt's living room.

How long had I been gone?

I didn't know for sure, but it couldn't have been more than a few seconds, because my aunt hadn't moved or even begun to tell her terrible tale.

'What your mother was doing …' Aunt Jacqueline began.

I clamped my hands over my ears.

'Don't want to listen,' I chanted loudly. 'Don't want to listen … Don't want to listen … Don't want to listen …'

I could see my aunt mouthing at me, but I couldn't hear the words. Then she reached across, grabbed my arms and slammed them down on the table.

'You will listen,' she screamed. 'I'll *make* you listen.'

'Can't make me,' I shouted. 'Can't make me. No, you can't.'

'All had the same temptation …' my aunt screeched.

'Jack and Jill went up the hill to fetch a pail of water—'

'… even that self-righteous prig Catherine—'

'… and Jill came tumbling after, sing a song of sixpence a pocket full of rye. Four-and twenty blackbirds—'

'… but only your mother, *your precious bloody mother*, gave in to it …'

My aunt's fingers were gripping me tightly – digging into my flesh. I couldn't hold out much longer, and we both knew it.

I prayed to God, then to the Devil, then to whatever passing deity might listen – for the strength to break away, and heaved with all my might.

I felt Aunt Jacqueline's fingers start to slip, and suddenly my thin, bruised arms were free.

'Mary had a little lamb, its fleece was white as snow ...' I shouted as I jumped up from my chair.

'Ride a cock horse to Banbury Cross ...' I bellowed as I rushed down the hallway.

'Mirror mirror on the wall, who is the fairest of them all ...?' I roared as I flung open the front door.

The air outside tasted fresh and pure. I rushed down the path, leaving the Wicked Queen alone in her dark castle.

8

I have retained a few vague images of the following two hours – a dog cocking its leg against a lamppost, an old man leaning heavily on his stick, a group of normal, average, *lucky*, children playing tag – but for most of the time I neither knew where I was going nor where I had been.

My mind was in turmoil. To return home – to present myself to my aunt and stand there passively while she stabbed me through the heart with the true facts of my mother's death – was clearly unthinkable.

Yet where else could I go *but* home? I was only eleven years old. If I ran away, Constable Fliques would be sure to find me, and bring me back in chains.

Finally admitting to myself that I had no choice but to return to my aunt's house, I started to walk back towards our estate, my head bent in defeat.

It was then that I noticed the phone box! It was not remarkable in itself – its red paint was exactly like the red paint on every other phone box in the country, its floor was carpeted with the sweet papers, cigarette ends and lolly sticks you will find in boxes from Land's End to John O'Groats – but it was about to have a remarkable effect on my life and the lives of many other people. The destinies of my four aunts, of Sir Llewellyn Cypher, Pastor Ives, the residents of the Old Almshouse in Shelton Bourne, even of Ernest Fellstead (Mr) and the rest of the dirty mackintosh brigade, were, at that moment, about to be altered.

I didn't know that at the time.

All I thought then was, 'I've had an idea, Mother.'

I looked up into the darkening sky, half-expecting to see Mother looking down at me. Her face wasn't there, of course, yet I could still feel her presence.

'But is it a *good* idea, Mother?' I asked. 'Is it one you'd approve of?'

And I swear I heard her voice, as soft and clear as if she was standing right next to me and whispering in my ear.

And what did that voice say?

It said, '*Look at the change in your pocket, Bobby. If there's a 5p piece amongst it, it means you were meant to make the call.*'

I reached into the pocket and pulled out some coins. There was not one 5p among them, but two! A double endorsement!

I no longer had a sense of Mother's presence, but it didn't seem to matter. Whistling tunelessly to myself, I pulled open the phone box door and stepped inside.

9

Aunt Jacqueline died soon after that, and so I went to live with Aunt Peggy.

PART THREE: The Queen of Diamonds

1

Aunt Jacqueline's final journey to the great bridge tournament in the sky should have been a sombre affair – but her sisters, Catherine and Peggy, quickly turned it into something of a circus.

They started arguing in hushed, furious tones the moment they met over the closed coffin. The debate continued with increasing ferocity on the route to the church, and attained even greater intensity during the service.

The other mourners, mainly representatives of the various bridge clubs at which my aunt had played, showed outrage on their faces, but didn't dare put it into words. Even the vicar, an unflappable cleric of the old school, was well and truly flapped, and I'm sure it was Catherine and Peggy's presence – rather than a personal knowledge of Aunt Jacqueline's nicotine habit – which caused him to pronounce on the human condition in terms of "ashtrays to ashtrays."

And what were my dear, loving aunts fighting about?

Me, of course!

'Why didn't Sadie come?' I heard Aunt Peggy hiss, when we had finally turned our backs on the last resting place of the Olympic Class Smoker and Bridge Cheat, and were heading for the lych gate. 'Why isn't she here to take her share of the responsibility?'

'Jacqueline wished *you* to take care of the boy if anything happened to her,' Aunt Catherine replied. 'She told me so herself.'

'Then it's strange she didn't bother to tell me as well,' Aunt Peggy countered. 'Anyway, I've got enough on my hands with all my cats.'

'Your heart is as hard as the tap water in Pontypridd,' Aunt Catherine told her fat little sister, 'but a little of the Lord's miracle detergent may soften it yet.'

****

It was over the funeral tea that Aunt Catherine gave up on persuasion and turned instead to pressure.

'The man in charge of the Cheshire police is called Chief Constable Douglas Hampton,' she told her sister.

'Is he?' Aunt Peggy asked, though she seemed to be more interested in stuffing a whole chocolate éclair into her mouth than in receiving any information about her local police force.

'Yes, he's a good man – a deeply religious man,' Aunt Catherine continued. 'He's very active in the Law and Order Tabernacle.'

'So?' Aunt Peggy said, masticating furiously on the éclair, and reaching across for a buttered scone.

'He writes to me often,' Aunt Catherine told her. 'Or rather, he writes to my special post box.'

The hand which had been about to feed the scone into Aunt Peggy's pastry disposal system froze in mid-air.

'To your special post box,' she repeated worriedly.

'So far, he has only assisted my mission through financial contributions,' Catherine said, 'but I'm sure if I asked him to do something more practical, he wouldn't refuse.'

'You mean …?' Peggy said tremulously.

'I mean that if I told him there was something not quite right at your smallholding, he'd agree to investigate it. After all …' and here Catherine's voice hardened, '… he wouldn't really have much bloody choice, would he?'

'That's not fair,' Aunt Peggy choked. 'What I told you was confidential – a secret shared between sisters – and I never thought for a minute that you'd … that you'd … This is nothing but blackmail.'

'In looking after the boy, you would be carrying out our dear departed sister's wishes, and at the same time paying a fair and just penance for your life of sin,' Aunt Catherine said firmly.

'I won't do it!' Aunt Peggy protested.

'How does the song go?' Aunt Catherine asked.

'What song?'

'You know the one I mean. It's something about a kiss on the lips being quite continental, but diamonds being a girl's best friend.'

If I was amazed that Aunt Catherine should know the words of such a secular song, I was even more astounded by Peggy's reaction. The greed for food, which had blazed in my roly-poly aunt's eyes seconds earlier, was now entirely absent.

'Very well, Catherine,' she said heavily. 'I still don't think it's right, but I'll agree to take the boy for a trial period.'

'A trial period,' Aunt Catherine mused, 'an introductory offer. Yes, that should do for a start.'

2

'You have a few drinks with your sister, get a little bit tipsy, and let slip how you earn your living,' Aunt Peggy said bitterly, as she plopped down into one of the over-stuffed armchairs which dominated her living room. 'And what does she do?'

'I don't know, Auntie,' I said.

My suitcase, which I'd been carrying all day, weighed heavy in my hand, but I didn't have the nerve to put it on the floor and sit down, like my aunt had done. I considered myself very much on trial, you see, and however little the prospect of living with Aunt Peggy appealed to me, it was still better than being cast into the middle of my Dickensian nightmare.

'I'll tell you what she does,' Aunt Peggy said. 'She uses it to stab me in the back. Well, I've half a mind to use what *she* told *me* to stab *her* in the back. The only problem is I'm not sure that what she does is illegal.'

I said nothing. I couldn't think of anything *to* say.

'This arrangement will never work out, you know,' my aunt said. She reached into her handbag, took out a packet of marshmallows, and popped one into her gargantuan mouth. 'I shouldn't have let your Aunt Catherine bully me,' she continued. 'I should have called her bluff. I might *still* call her bluff.'

'I'll be no trouble,' I promised, as I tasted the panic welling up in my throat. 'And I could make myself quite useful around the place.'

"The place" was a smallholding at the end of a dirt track, some twenty miles from Manchester. It was quite a modest establishment, as I would soon discover, consisting of the house, a little land, and some outbuildings. The farmhouse itself was Victorian red brick. It was an ugly, square building and had a crooked chimney – appropriately enough! – that blew back smoke when the wind was coming from the wrong direction. Next to the house was the kitchen garden. It may once have produced cabbages and sprouts, lettuces and tomatoes, but now it was home to a flourishing crop of weeds which put even Aunt Jacqueline's urban jungle to shame. At the other side of the house lay

Aunt Peggy's only field, which had lain fallow since she took over the farm, and beyond that were the outbuildings – a tumble-down barn, a disused double-seater privy, and an ancient sty which even a pig would have turned up its snout at.

Not that there were any pigs there to express such fastidiousness. Neither was there bleating sheep nibbling the grass down to its roots, nor cows gazing vacantly as they amused themselves by passing their disgusting cud from one stomach to another.

No, my aunt raised none of the conventional farm animals. Instead she kept cats: black cats and white cats; cats that were a mixture of the two; ginger toms and tortoiseshells; cats with a hint of Siamese in them, others whose appearance offered little clue as to their origins; sleepy cats and aggressive cats; cats who were wary, and cats who were complacent; cats who never left the house, and cats who were the scourge of all the mice in the barn.

Cats, cats, cats – an uncounted and uncountable number who came and went, bred and died. The home of these feline anarchists was called – and even now I gag at the name – "Cuddles Farm Cat Sanctuary."

Yet as ramshackle as the place was, as much as its very name cloyed, it was still my best bet at the time, and I waited anxiously while my aunt considered my offer of work in exchange for bed and board.

'Yes,' she said finally, as I stood there, still holding my suitcase in my hand. 'Yes, I suppose there are a few little jobs you could do – if you are up to them.'

'I'm a quick learner,' I promised.

'All right, since there's nobody else to look after you – and as a favour to your Aunt Catherine – we'll give it a month's trial.'

'Thank you, Auntie.'

'You can take the spare room at the top of the stairs,' Aunt Peggy said briskly. 'Don't bother to unpack, just leave your case there. Don't worry about bedding, either – you can put that on later.'

'All right, Auntie.'

'It's time to feed the cats. I'll show you where I keep the food, then that'll be your job from now on. And when you've finished the feeding, you can take a tin of creosote and give all the woodwork on the barn a coating. Not frightened of heights, are you?'

'I sometimes suffer from vertigo,' I admitted.

'You'll soon get over that. There's a couple of slates come loose close to the chimney stack. When you can find the time, go up and have a look at them.'

I was in! I considered myself very lucky indeed. Perhaps I would have felt a little less self-congratulatory if I'd known that, at the same time I was metaphorically patting myself on the back, an old adversary of mine was – literally – packing his size ten boots into a suitcase in preparation for his journey to Norton, a town only four miles from Cuddles Farm.

3

I'd been living with Aunt Peggy for about three months when I ran into him. He was standing outside Norton Market. He had a packet of crisps in his hand, and was pulling them out individually and holding them up to the light – as if searching for a flaw – before popping them into his mouth.

My first instinct, I admit, was to turn and run, but common sense told me that it would only draw attention to me.

I'd do better, I argued, to keep on walking, in the hope that I'd get past him before he'd finished interrogating his snack.

I kept my eyes fixed on the ground, and counted the gaps between the paving stones.

Ten … eleven … twelve … Just about enough to draw me level with him, I thought. Yes, from the corner of my eye I could see his shiny black boots and the start of a blue serge trouser leg.

Fifteen … sixteen … seventeen … I was well past him now – out of danger.

'Look who it is,' a familiar voice boomed behind me. 'The laddie who doesn't check his bike lights often enough.'

I stopped in my tracks, and turned around.

'I … I didn't see you there, Constable Fliques,' I stuttered.

'That's *Sergeant* Fliques,' he said, pointing to the stripes on the sleeve of his uniform. 'Didn't see me, hey? Funny, I could have sworn you'd noticed me half-way down the street.'

'I thought it *might* have been you – only I wasn't sure,' I lied.

'And you decided the best thing to do was to try and slip past me unnoticed, did you?'

I hung my head, and said nothing.

'Not a bad plan,' Fliques conceded. 'Not bad at all. But you should have known it would never work with me.'

Why was he there? I wondered. What possible reason could he have for being in a provincial backwater like Norton?

'You're starting to think that I'm here because you're here, aren't you?' he asked. 'You strongly suspect that I've followed you. Isn't that right?'

'Err … no. No, of course not, Sergeant Fliques,' I said, although that was exactly the conclusion my panic-stricken brain had just reached.

'You're getting paranoid,' Fliques said, ignoring my denial. 'Nasty thing, paranoia – can't get rid of that with a Vicks vapour rub and a couple of aspirins.'

'No, I suppose not,' I said inadequately.

'I moved to Norton for promotion,' Fliques told me. 'It's as simple as that. But,' he added ominously, 'I don't deny it's a bonus finding you here.'

He subjected another crisp to his scrutiny, whilst I stood there embarrassed, shifting my weight from one foot to the other. As he fed the crisp into his mouth, I wondered if I dared leave – then rapidly realised that I didn't.

'Well, well, well,' Fliques said, crunching his latest victim. 'Just fancy meeting you purely by chance. The laddie without the properly functioning bicycle lights – the laddie whose auntie got herself killed.'

He waited for me to speak.

'That's right, Sergeant,' I said, with some reluctance.

'What's right?' he countered cunningly. 'That your auntie got killed? Or that you haven't got any lights on your bike?'

'That my auntie got killed.'

'They that live by the club shall die by the club,' Fliques said.

'Pardon, Sergeant?'

'Famous for it, your auntie. She played bridge at every club in the Brighton area. And look how she met her end – her bridge partner finds out she's planning to leave town without even saying goodbye, and is so furious he rushes straight over to her house—'

'Will Tom go to prison?' I asked anxiously.

Fliques glared at me. 'You're interrupting my story, and it's never a wise move to interrupt me in my flow.'

'Please, Sergeant,' I begged.

I really *did* want to know, because Tom's fate was the one aspect of the whole affair I felt guilty about.

Fliques gave me a look only slightly less hostile than the one he'd bestowed on his crisps, then seemed to relent.

'Tom's *already* in prison,' he said. 'But he won't be there for long. His brief made quite a thing about the dance your auntie led him, and the judge was very sympathetic. Three years, he drew. With good behaviour, he should be out in eighteen months. Can I go on with my story now?'

'Yes, sir. Sorry, sir.'

'Where was I?'

'Tom was so furious over what he'd found out that he rushed right over to Auntie Jacqueline's house—'

'That's right. He was in such a hurry he didn't even take anything with him. But help was on hand. Right there in the trophy case was the Brighton and Hove Challenge Cup 1975-76.' Fliques chuckled. 'Lucky for him they came first instead of second, wasn't it?'

'Why's that, Sergeant?' I felt compelled to ask.

'I've seen the Runners' Up Cup. It's a tiny little thing. Clubbing her to death with that would have been like trying to knock down a brick wall with a toffee hammer. But the Winners' Cup,' he licked his lips with relish, 'there was a blunt instrument worthy of the name. With the Winners' Cup in his hands, he could crush her skull as easy as this …'

Fliques placed what remained of his packet of crisps in one hand, and brought the palm of the other down on it with some force. The crisps crunched – sickeningly loudly. He held up the result for me to see. Bits of crushed potato chip dribbled out of the bottom of the packet.

'Mustn't go littering the pavement,' Fliques said, quickly balling the bag up in his hands. 'But you do see what I mean about it being very lucky for him they came first?'

'They nearly always came first,' I said, and then, before I could stop myself, I added, 'They cheated.'

'Cheated, did they?' Fliques said thoughtfully. 'That tells me a lot. But what it doesn't tell me is how he knew she was planning to leave town.'

'I thought he got an anonymous call,' I said.

Fliques eyes hardened. 'Do you, indeed? Now where would you get that idea from?'

I shrugged. 'That's how these things usually happen, isn't it?'

'Yes, and you're right – that's how it happened in this case,' Fliques agreed. 'But who was the anonymous caller?'

'If you knew that, he wouldn't be anonymous,' I pointed out.

'Exactly. That's just what I was thinking. And then I asked myself, who exactly knew she was leaving town?'

'The people she sold the house to, the building society, her boss—'

'Precisely. But how many of them also knew about her private life? How many of them knew just how jealous her bridge partner was?'

'You've got me there,' I admitted.

'No, I haven't,' Fliques said. 'Not yet.' He walked over to the nearest rubbish bin, and deposited what was left of the crisp packet into it. 'I'll be watching you, laddie,' he said threateningly. 'If I was you – which I wouldn't be at any price – I'd make sure I had my bike working perfectly.'

And without another word, he turned on his heel and marched off down the street.

4

It took me very little time to realise that inside Aunt Peggy's round, little body there lurked two entirely different persons. The first – the one she presented to the world at large – was of the Cat Lady, a harmless eccentric who ran a sanctuary for any stray moggie she happened upon. Whenever I showed a visitor into our living room – doorman being one of the numerous jobs my aunt had thrust on me, so that now she hardly had to leave her chair – that visitor would inevitably discover Aunt Peggy sitting with a cat ensconced on her lap.

'Such sweet little things, pussies, aren't they?' my aunt would say. 'They're almost human, the way they understand you.'

'What's his name?' the visitor would feel obliged to ask.

It didn't matter what cat she was holding at the time – whether it was Dimples or Big George or Blanche Dubois, she always gave the same answer.

'He's called Mickey.'

They were all Mickey to her.

And as soon as the visitor had left, Aunt Peggy would revert to her second persona. The cat, which would have settled down comfortably on her chubby knees by then, would find itself cast aside like the stage prop that it actually was, and my aunt would pay absolutely no attention to any of the animals until the next time someone came calling.

****

Though the cats had no individuality as far as Aunt Peggy was concerned, they soon became distinct characters to me. There was one, a sleek grey tom, who would sit for hours gazing at the barn wall, as if he were contemplating the mysteries of the universe. I christened him Plato, and it was not long before he was answering to his name. Then there was Shere Khan, a tiny tabby who refused to accept the limitations of his size and padded around the yard with all the ferocity and confidence of a man-eater. And we must not forget the Critic, a half-breed Siamese who expressed his disdain for most aspects of life by puking up fur balls at regular intervals.

I do not mean to over-romanticise the cats. Like all animals – with the possible exception of mutants like Lassie, Champion the Wonder Horse and Skippy the Bush Kangaroo – they thought of themselves first, and my place in their world view was primarily as a source of food. Still, they did occasionally rub up against my leg or purr to show their appreciation – which was more thanks than I ever got from Aunt Peggy for all the cooking, ironing and cleaning I did.

Yes, I liked the cats. They were, I suppose, the only real family I'd had since Mother died.

5

Why then, if my aunt cared so little for cats, did she go to the expense of feeding so many of them? It was a complete mystery to me.

In fact, the whole set up was a mystery. A cat sanctuary, as it is commonly understood, is a place which takes in unwanted cats and tries to find homes for them. Cuddles Farm didn't work like that – not at all.

Picture the scene. A car pulls up in front of the farm, and two people get out. One is a man, big, red-faced and jovial. The other is a woman, small, serious and intense. The woman is carrying a cat basket, in which – surprise, surprise – temporarily resides a black kitten.

My aunt, who has somehow found the energy to get off her chair, meets them at the front door.

'Yes?' she says – as if she has no idea why these people might be calling on her.

The woman looks down at the cat box, and then up at Aunt Peggy. 'This is a cat sanctuary, isn't it?' she asks, plainly puzzled.

'In a manner of speaking,' Peggy replies.

'Well, we've brought you a cat to sanctuaryise,' the man says.

Peggy switches on her Cat Lady face, and looks down at the kitten, which is pressing its own face against the grille.

'He's a beautiful little pussy,' she says, in a voice which is pure syrup. 'Are you sure you want to give him up? I mean, I wouldn't, if I was you.'

'It's the dog, you see,' the woman says helplessly.

'Doesn't your naughty little doggie like sweet fluffy little kittens?' Aunt Peggy coos.

'On the contrary, he loves them,' the man says. 'He's eaten two of them since Christmas.'

'Cyril!' the woman hisses. 'This is serious!'

'Sorry, love,' says the man, duly chastened.

The woman turns to Peggy. 'We'd love to keep Sooty, but we can't, and that's why I've brought him here.'

'And I'd love to take him, but I just can't,' Peggy says. 'The place is full to bursting, and I can hardly afford to feed the pussies I've already got.'

The woman puts the cat box on the ground, and opens her hand bag. 'I would be willing to make a contribution to the sanctuary,' she says.

Peggy's piggy eyes flash with greed.

'How much?' she asks.

'Fifty pounds,' the woman says.

'Fifty pounds!' Cyril explodes. 'Have you gone completely off your chump, woman?'

'Would you rather get rid of the dog?' the woman asks sharply.

'Fair enough – fifty quid it is, then,' Cyril says, defeated.

'Would that be acceptable?' the woman asks Aunt Peggy.

'I'll have to think about it,' Peggy replies – but I can see her hands are itching to grab at the bank notes that the woman is holding out.

'I'd like to visit Sooty now and again, just to see how he's getting on,' the woman says. 'That would be all right, wouldn't it?'

My aunt's eyes fill with regret. 'I'm sorry,' she says, 'we can't allow that. It's against company policy.'

Thus – as a result of a policy laid down by a company I've never heard of until that moment – we lose both the kitten and the fifty pounds.

Here's another scene from sanctuary life: a woman appears at the farm with two small – very excited – children.

'They've been on at me for months to get them a cat, and I've finally given in,' she explains to Aunt Peggy.

But even as she's speaking, she's looking around her with a concerned expression on her face.

When she'd imagined the sanctuary, her expression says, what she'd been seeing in her mind's eye was large pens in which the cats were contained. It had never even occurred to her that all the cats would be allowed to roam freely.

'Are all these cats feral?' she asks.

'Some of them are Feral, but we've also Persians and Siamese,' my ignorant aunt says. 'I'd go for a Persian if I was you – they're the easiest to catch.'

'All the cats have been properly vaccinated haven't they?' asks the woman – who is sounding increasingly dubious about the whole project.

'In a manner of speaking, yes, they have,' Peggy tells her.

'Do you mean they haven't?'

'Not as such.'

'In that case, I'll leave it,' the woman says awkwardly.

'Please yourself,' Aunt Peggy replies, with a show of indifference.

****

My aunt is probably coming across as a very stupid woman, and indeed she was. She should have learned from her sister Catherine's example – and *what* she should have learned is that if you are playing a part in order to hide what you're *actually* doing, then you must play the part up to the hilt. Catherine was every inch the crazed evangelist, but anyone who got close to Peggy soon realised she was no Cat Lady. That said, Peggy still had a good run for her money, and even I – living in the middle of it – didn't work out exactly what was going on until a few days before Peggy's tragic accident.

6

In Sussex, I had been no more than average height for my age, but once in Cheshire I began to sprout up, some months gaining nearly an inch. My voice grew deeper, too, and my face was losing some of its childish chubbiness.

For the first time in my life, I found myself drawn to mirrors. Never a day went by without my spending a few minutes gazing at my reflection which, with equal confusion in its eyes, stared back at me. It was partly an exercise in vanity, I suppose, but I had a deeper purpose beyond that. I was trying, with all the desperation of a rootless, unloved orphan, to read my family history in a face which was rapidly becoming more adult.

Did I look like Mother? I wondered, looking critically at the image in the silvered glass. Was I carrying her legacy anywhere other than in my mind?

Search as I might, I could find little resemblance. The eyes were undoubtedly the same – a deep enigmatic blue – but that was as far as it went. Her nose was petite: mine had been borrowed from Michael Douglas. Her jaw was as delicate as china: mine the kind that strong men clench when surrounded by spear-waving natives.

Nor was I the only one to notice my maturing features. Examining myself in the hallway mirror one frosty December morning before setting off for school, I sensed that someone was watching me, and turned to find Aunt Peggy standing in the living room doorway.

'Did I forget to do something?' I asked, thinking that could be the only reason my aunt would have gone to the trouble of raising her fat rump from her comfortable chair.

Aunt Peggy made no reply, but instead stood perfectly still, her eyes fixed on my face.

'More logs for the fire?' I suggested.

Still my aunt said nothing. For perhaps a minute we were frozen, she apparently mesmerised by my face, me by the intensity of her scrutiny.

'I have to go, Auntie,' I said finally. 'I'll be late for school, otherwise.'

'You've got his looks, all right,' Aunt Peggy said, as if she hadn't heard me.

It was so unusual for my aunt to speak to me – other than to issue instructions – that, for a moment, I was pole-axed.

'Oh yes,' Aunt Peggy continued dreamily, 'you've got his looks. And you'll break a few hearts before you're finished – just like he did.'

He?

Him?

My father! She was talking about my father!

Mother had never felt called upon to mention him, and I'd felt no curiosity myself at the time. But circumstances had changed. My father was no longer someone who could be defined simply in negative terms – the man who hadn't played football with me, who hadn't carried me on his shoulders or taught me how to swim. I had his nose and his jaw – it was time to find out something about him.

'What was my father like, Auntie Peggy?' I asked.

The dreamy expression was wiped from my aunt's face, and was replaced by a look which was half-defensive, half-confused.

'I … I think there are some things we shouldn't go into, don't you?' Aunt Peggy stuttered. 'I mean, you might not like the truth when you hear it.'

'I've got a right to know,' I protested.

'Besides,' Aunt Peggy said, twisting the left cuff of her pink cardigan nervously in her right hand, 'I couldn't tell you even if I wanted to. We had an agreement, Catherine, Jacqueline, Sadie and me – a sort of pact of silence.'

'You only promised you'd never talk about Mother's death,' I pointed out. 'It's my father I'm asking about now.'

The cuff of the pink cardigan was now twisted so tightly that it had begun to function as a tourniquet. Or perhaps there were other reasons why the blood had drained from my aunt's face.

'My father,' I persisted. 'Not Mother's death – my father.'

'You can't separate the two,' my aunt said. She laughed – almost hysterically. 'Yes, that was the problem – you couldn't separate the one from the other.'

'I don't understand.'

'It would have different if they'd been cats, wouldn't it?' Aunt Peggy said. Her eyes had glazed over and her voice was dull – mechanical. Though her plump little body was still in the hallway, her mind was somewhere else entirely. 'Cats don't know any better, do they?' she continued as if she'd been programmed. 'They don't mean any harm – it's just the way they are.'

'You're not making any sense!' I shouted at her.

My words seemed to penetrate whatever world of memories my aunt had been floating in and burst the bubble of fantasy which had enveloped her. Her eyes cleared and she was once again the lazy, greedy Aunt Peggy I had come to know so well.

'You're going to be late for school,' she said shakily.

'Tell me about my father before I go,' I demanded, folding my arms across my chest.

My aunt wobbled up the hall with a speed close to that of a charging rhino, and grabbed the blue and white vase which lived on the hall table.

'Go to school!' she screamed, brandishing the vase in front of me. 'Go to school or, so help me, I'll break this over your head.'

She meant it. I backed along the hallway, groping behind me for the door handle.

'And don't you dare ask me about him again,' Aunt Peggy shrieked after me. 'Don't you ever dare!'

7

Had the electoral boundaries not been changed just prior to its completion, the school entrusted with my education would have been called Councillor Albert Arkwright High, in honour of the Red Alderman who once attempted to have the town declared a socialist republic. Judicious gerrymandering, however, had swept the Tories into power locally, so it was to the Margaret Thatcher High School – known locally as Snatchers – that I dragged myself reluctantly each morning.

Actually, I soon found there were compensations in going to school – or one compensation, at least. Half-way through my first year, I discovered an interest in girls – and from their shy glances and giggles, I could tell that some of them had discovered an interest in me, too.

It was a liberating experience, but it was also a confusing one. Mother and I had discussed women at great length, but never *girls*, and when I considered the advice she'd given me on women, I found it totally inadequate for dealing with my new situation.

'*Always be a little gentleman,*' Mother had told me again and again. '*I know it's not fashionable these days, but I've never been one to follow fashion.*'

But the simple truth was that girls didn't expect you to open doors for them, or offer them your seat on the bus. Believe me, I know – because I tried it. What girls liked was being punched – as long as the blow was light. What girls really appreciated were hastily scribbled notes which, when smuggled across the classroom to them, would make them blush.

After the way Mother had brought me up, I didn't think I could bring myself to hit a girl, even lightly. And as for the letters passed across the classroom, I simply had no idea what to put in one.

Even if I did get over the first hurdle – the courtship dance – what was I expected to do when I went out on a real date? Still more important than what I was *expected* to do, what would Mother have thought I *should* do.

I desperately needed someone to confide in.

But who?

There was only really my aunt, and she'd been absolutely no use on the question of my father. Besides, how could I bring myself to put my faith in someone who pretended to love cats, but, in fact, had no time for them? And if that particular slice of hypocrisy were not enough to make me distrust her, there were also the Night Callers.

****

The Night Callers never arrived before midnight, by which time my aunt assumed that I, exhausted by waiting on her hand and foot, must have fallen asleep. And maybe sometimes I did miss a visit, but I saw enough of them to realise that these unsavoury-looking men who kept Aunt Peggy company during the hours of darkness were not exactly model citizens.

I'm not quite sure how many of them there were – it could have been up to a dozen – but they always followed the same pattern. However dark the night, they always drove their battered Ford Cortinas and coughing Metros up the dirt track which led to Cuddles Farm with their headlights switched off. They would be met at the door by Aunt Peggy, and taken into the living room where – from the evidence of the mess I invariably found in the morning – many cigarettes were smoked and much whisky drunk.

Occasionally voices would be raised, and the sound of an argument would drift upstairs.

'Two hundred and fifty quid, lady! You've got to be joking.'

'That's the market price. Take it or leave it.'

'I'll bloody leave it.'

'Then pick up your cat and get out.'

His cat?

Yes, that was the point! Each of the Night Callers brought a cat with him – and left without it!

And what happened to these little moggies once the business downstairs was completed? Were they given the freedom of the sanctuary? No, they were locked in a windowless storeroom at the back of the house – a storeroom, moreover, to which only Aunt Peggy had a key.

'I'm keeping it there until it settles in,' my aunt explained when the first cat turned up shortly after my arrival at the farm.

'But how will keeping it in a dark room, all by itself, help it to settle in?' I asked.

'Mind your own business,' Aunt Peggy said.

'It'll make a mess.'

'If it does, I'll clean it up.'

If I had learned that the cats had organised a Turtles tribute band called the Purrtles, I would have been more shocked than I was at that moment – but not a lot!

Aunt Peggy? Cleaning up?

Doing an unpleasant task herself, when it could so easily have been handed on to me?

I wanted to know the reason behind this strange behaviour – but an orphan dependent on the charity of others soon learns not to ask unwelcome questions.

****

Not all Aunt Peggy's nocturnal visitors left cats – some took them away. These Night Collectors, as I came to call them, were a better class of unsavoury than the depositors. They drove BMWs and Rovers, and wore suits which were gaudy but expensive.

I remember leaning from my bedroom window, and listening to Aunt Peggy talking to one of them at the front door.

'Since you're new at this game, I'll give a few tips,' my aunt said. 'Best thing is to lock it up by itself for a while. A day's usually enough. Oh, and if I was you, I'd deal with it yourself, rather than leaving it up to one of your lads.'

'I will,' the man replied. 'I don't trust my lads as far as I can throw 'em – they're all a bunch of crooks.'

My aunt chuckled.

Why? I wondered, from my position on the windowsill.

'It's not too messy if you use rubber gloves,' Aunt Peggy informed the collector.

'What if I'm in a hurry?' the man asked.

Aunt Peggy laughed, nastily. 'If you're in a hurry, you can always use the knife,' she told him. 'I do, sometimes.'

The knife? Rubber gloves? It was all beyond me then. But I knew enough not to trust the delicate problem of my adolescent yearnings to someone who could laugh as nastily as my aunt.

8

I had just turned thirteen when these adolescent yearnings of mine transformed themselves into something harder, and sex began to raise my ugly head – and the ugly shaft to which it was attached.

It would happen at the most inconvenient moments. On the school corridor, in the High Street, while pushing a trolley around the supermarket, I would suddenly feel the limp little thing in my underpants take on a life of its own.

I wasn't safe anywhere. I had an erection in the Religious Knowledge class once. In the Religious Knowledge class, for God's sake – right in the middle of the teacher's explanation of one of the bloodier parts of the Old Testament.

There was only one place I was sure to be safe from the serpent in my loins, and that was at the bridge table. Yes, after four long years of playing the game in my head, I had finally found my way to a game with real players.

I started modestly enough as a reserve for the school team, which was otherwise made up entirely of Sixth Formers, but it wasn't long before my obvious ability shone through, and I was universally acknowledged to be the best player the school had ever had. And from there it was but a small step to the town's most prestigious bridge club – and into the arms of Mrs Cynthia Harrap.

Mrs Harrap was in her late thirties, which, in my eyes, made her approximately as old as God's grandmother. Yet despite her great age, she was still a stunning woman. She was a blonde – though not a natural one, as I was later to find out – with big, sensuous eyes and a wide, inviting mouth. Her legs were long, her waist only slightly thickening as middle age set in, and her breasts, while not the huge mounds of some of my adolescent wet dreams, were firm and rounded. She was charming and witty and kind, and, on looks alone, deserved to be married to a Paul Newman or a Steve McQueen.

Archie Harrap, her husband, had none of the Hollywood star qualities, but had probably been quite a good-looking man in his youth. In middle age, however, he had allowed his stomach to bulge and his chins to multiply, and his hair – perhaps in protest at the way he had treated the rest of his body – was already starting to desert him. None of which mattered of course – '*You must never judge anyone by their appearance, Bobby,*' Mother used to say – and I'm sure we could have got on well together if he hadn't been such a crashing, insensitive bore.

'Find a gap in the market, and plug it – that's what you have to do, Bobby,' he advised me, one night at the bridge club, when, despite my best efforts to avoid him, he had managed to force me into a corner. 'I've got a boat on Lake Windermere and a cottage in Wales – both of them paid for – and how do you think I managed that?'

'By finding a gap in the market, and plugging it?' I asked.

'By finding a gap in the market, and plugging it,' he repeated. 'When I started out with my luxury customised brass knockers and door handles, most of my business associates thought I'd gone off my chump. 'You'll never sell them,' they said. But let me tell you, those are the very people who are queuing for my knockers now – and there's an eighteen-month waiting list.'

'How interesting,' I said, hoping my tone would be enough of a hint that I was lying.

'Clem Watkins, who owns the chain of Watkins' Butchers, has got all his handles shaped like pork chops. Tompkins, the long distance haulier, has his shaped like wagons. Even my own wife is one of my customers – and what do you think she commissioned?'

'I've no idea,' I confessed.

'What's the first think you think of when you think of Cynthia?' Harrap demanded.

Breasts that could smother you! I thought. Long wonderful legs that could lock behind your back and nearly break your spine!

'I don't know,' I told him.

'You're a bit thick, aren't you, lad?' Harrap said. 'Hers are made to look like playing cards, spread out like a bridge hand.'

'Ah yes,' I said, as the thought of Cynthia's breasts and legs did its work on the beast within my underpants.

'So what do you do to earn a crust?' he asked.

'I'm still at school,' I replied wearily.

'You may well be, but it's never too early to start thinking about earning your first million,' Harrap said. 'Why, when I was your age, I was already breeding rabbits and selling them to the local butcher.' He paused. 'You've got that cat sanctuary, haven't you?'

'Yes.'

'Well, there you are then – you should sell a few of the moggies off for scientific research.'

'I couldn't do that,' I told him.

'There's no room for sentimentality in this world,' Harrap said. 'It's dog eat dog, and if you don't watch yourself—'

I don't know what exactly I might have said next – though I'd probably have broken Mother's cardinal rule about being polite to everybody – but fortunately, at that very moment, Mrs Harrap appeared on the scene.

'I'm ready to go home now,' she said.

'Right-ho,' her husband agreed.

She smiled at me. 'Good night, Bobby.'

Then, in a movement that was so quick I almost missed it, she glanced down at my crotch and her smile became much wider – and much more amused.

'Good night, Mrs Harrap,' I said, feeling myself reddening.

The Harraps turned towards the door, then Mrs Harrap turned back.

'I've just had an idea,' she said.

Archie Harrap chuckled. 'You're always in trouble when a woman starts having ideas, Bobby,' he said. 'And what is this idea of yours, my love?'

'You're away next week, aren't you?' Mrs Harrap asked.

'That's right,' Harrap confirmed. 'I'm attending the biggest brass novelty trade fair in Europe, Bobby – and not just as a delegate, but as a keynote speaker.'

'So I was thinking of having a bridge evening at home on – say – Wednesday,' Mrs Harrap continued. 'Would you be free to partner me, Bobby?'

'Well, yes, I suppose so,' I all-but stuttered.

'It sounds like a good idea to me,' Mr Harrap said. 'I'm all in favour of anything that keeps you out of mischief while I'm away.'

Did it ever enter his head that the bridge might be just an excuse – no more than a thin cover?

I don't think so. Nor, if I'm honest, did it ever enter mine. The Mrs Robinson scenario was one I'd often thought about, but then, since my willy had asserted its freedom, there were very few fantasy situations I had *not* contemplated. And fantasy is, after all, by definition, mere imaginings. So I took Mrs Harrap's invitation at face value, and promised to go to her house the following Wednesday night.

Ah, the innocence of youth!

9

'I'm sorry I'm late,' I told Mrs Cynthia Harrap in the hallway of her luxury stockbroker-style detached residence located at the better end of Norton, 'but I was stopped by the police.'

'Stopped by the police!'

Oh yes, Les Fliques had waved me down en route.

'We'll just make sure your machine's in proper working order, shall we, Bobby?' he'd asked.

'It was a sergeant I know,' I explained to Mrs Harrap. 'He wanted to check my brake blocks.'

'Hmm,' Mrs Harrap said. 'I must, say, it seems a very trivial matter for a sergeant to be bothering with.'

But then she didn't know Les, did she? To him, a crime was a crime, be it murder or faulty brake blocks – and each and every one of them commanded his full attention.

'I really am sorry,' I said. 'Especially since it's the first time you've invited me round.'

'Doesn't matter,' Mrs Harrap assured me. 'The girls and I have been having a really good natter.' Her eyes flashed mischievously, as she led me into the lounge. 'Women's talk, you know – comparing our love lives and things like that. Isn't that right, girls?'

The "girls", Ms King and Mrs Zimmerman, who were both in their fifties, giggled. I, for my part, looked around me, open-mouthed. I'd had very little experience of visiting other people's houses, and the open-plan lounge came as something of a shock. It had two long sofas in white leather, and a thick-pile carpet which – like the velvet curtains – was a deep claret colour. But it was the walls which really caught my attention. They were completely covered with artefacts – masks, beads, bracelets, spears, clubs and scores of objects I couldn't even begin to identify.

'Impressive, isn't it?' Mrs Harrap said. 'See that straw doll? It's a fertility fetish from Central Africa.'

I discovered that my hand, which seemed suddenly to have a will of its own, was pointing to a short, thick object which looked just like a … like a …

But surely, it couldn't be.

'What's that?' I asked before I could stop myself.

'That,' said Mrs Harrap, hooding her eyes, 'plays a very important part in the coming-of-age ritual on certain South Sea islands.'

****

Ms King and Mrs Zimmerman played a fairly competent game of bridge, but by half-past ten Mrs Harrap and I had accumulated so many points on our side of the sheet that there seemed little to be gained by starting a fresh rubber.

'Same time next week, girls?' Mrs Harrap asked. Then, turning to me, she said, 'You wouldn't mind staying behind to help me tidy up, would you, Bobby?'

'It would be my pleasure,' I said like a little gentleman – like *Mother's* little gentleman – but I couldn't help noticing the sly looks that the three women exchanged.

While Mrs Harrap was showing her guests to the door, I replaced the cards in their boxes, emptied the ashtrays and loaded the glasses into the dishwasher. The whole operation took me perhaps a couple of minutes. And that was it. Try as I might, I couldn't find another thing to tidy.

I walked over to the wall to re-examine the object which was so important in the coming-of-age ceremonies. It still looked like a penis to me.

'Well, that's that,' said a voice behind me.

I turned to face Mrs Harrap – and my eyes nearly popped out of my head. She was wearing a green blouse with a revealing neckline that night, and somehow, in the time she'd been seeing her friends out, the top two buttons had come undone, thus revealing more of Mrs Harrap's ample cleavage than I'd ever seen before. My eyes passed the image on to my brain, and my brain – with horrendous efficiency – dispatched it by express messenger to my groin.

'You're just like him,' Aunt Peggy had said – meaning my father.

Well, maybe it was all in the genes. It was certainly all in *my* jeans. I sat down quickly – though I never usually did that in the presence of a lady – and placed my hands on my lap in an attempt to hide the volcano which was erupting under my zipper.

'You remember my husband said he'd be away tonight?' Mrs Harrap asked, sitting down opposite me.

'Yes,' I squeaked.

I cleared my throat and tried again.

'Yes, I do remember that,' I growled in a voice my pulsating penis should have been proud of.

'The biggest brass novelties trade fair in Europe,' Mrs Harrap said with contempt. 'I sometimes think he should have himself cast in brass – or parts of him, anyway. At least then he might put up a decent showing in the bedroom.'

'This isn't happening,' I told myself. 'This can't be happening.'

'How old are you, Bobby?' Mrs Harrap asked, sitting down and leaning forward, so that the edge of one large brown nipple was just visible.

'Thirteen,' I croaked.

'You're big for your age,' Mrs Harrap said huskily. 'Handsome, too. But I expect the girls at school have already told you that.'

'Yes. No. I mean I …'

I searched the archives of my memory for guidance. If only Mother had anticipated this. If only, instead of advice on health and hygiene, she'd taken the time to give me a quick run-down on horniness.

'Come upstairs with me,' Mrs Harrap said. 'I've got something I want to show you.'

'Help me, Mother!' I prayed silently. 'To Hell with, "Honesty is always the best policy." Screw, "Your lies will always catch you out." What do I do now?'

Mrs Harrap stood up, took my hand, and pulled me reluctantly to my feet. 'Come on,' she said. 'I promise you'll enjoy it.'

I followed her upstairs, noticing, as I climbed, how short her skirt was and how inviting her legs looked.

'Help me, Mother,' I pleaded. 'Tell me what to do.'

And then, a strange thing happened. Just when I thought she'd abandoned me, Mother came to the rescue after all.

It wasn't with a direct message – a voice from Heaven.

It wasn't even by planting an idea in my mind for me to find, as I felt she'd done so many times before.

No, it was vaguer than that. It was a little like the flashback I'd had when Aunt Jacqueline threatened to tell me how Mother died – but nowhere near as frightening.

****

There are no black figures to menace me this time, but merely the door to a room which I know – don't ask me how – to be in the hotel in Cornwall where we spent that last tragic holiday.

The doorknob is within reach. I turn it, and the door starts to open.

'I thought you'd locked that door, Jennie!'

A voice – a man's voice – which I recognise, yet, in some strange way, do not associate with Mother's bedroom.

The door is half-way open, but Mother is suddenly standing in the gap, hurriedly pulling her favourite silk dressing gown around her and blocking my view of the room.

'Bobby, I thought you were asleep,' she says. 'Go back to your own room for a few minutes until Mother's dressed, then we'll go to the ice cream parlour.'

****

The picture dissolved, and I was back on the stairs of Chez Harrap – my heart beating furiously, Mrs Harrap's rear end swaying suggestively before me.

Mother wouldn't mind! I told myself joyfully. Cheating was wrong, and so was lying. But this was all right!

We entered the bedroom. Mrs Harrap closed the door behind us and stood with her back to it, cutting off my escape.

Not that I wanted to escape.

Not now I had received Mother's message.

'Yes, you're a very handsome boy,' Mrs Harrap said. 'You know why we're up here, in the bedroom, don't you?'

'Yes,' I gasped.

'I don't want to force you to do anything you don't want to,' she said, 'and if, at any point, you feel uncomfortable, we'll stop immediately. Do you understand that, Bobby?'

I nodded.

Mrs Harrap stepped away from the door.

'You can go now, if you want to,' she said. 'I won't be angry if you do, I won't hold it against you later, and I most definitely will not tell anyone else. No one is going to laugh at you and call you a sissy – because no one will ever know you've been up here.'

'I … don't … want … to go,' I said in a strangled voice.

'Then come here.'

She put her arms around my neck, and kissed me passionately.

My first real kiss – and at the lips of such an expert.

Stage One over, she pushed me gently away and walked to the bed.

'I'm going to take my clothes off now,' she announced calmly. 'You want me to, don't you?'

'Gurg!' I told her.

'Does that mean yes?'

I nodded my head like a woodpecker on amphetamines.

The blouse came first, then the bra. Mrs Harrap's breasts, released from their twin hammocks, swung free. She took off her skirt, and I saw that she had a small mole on the curve of her belly. She lowered her panties and revealed to me her exciting, jet-black pubic hair.

The pressure in my jeans was becoming unbearable. Mrs Harrap, completely naked now, lay down on the bed, and turned towards me.

'Wouldn't you like to get out of your clothes as well?' she asked me.

Shoes, socks, shirt, jeans, were all discarded in a moment. I pulled down my shorts, liberating my penis from its prison of elastic and cotton and giving it the opportunity – at last – to slip into something more comfortable.

****

I took to sex as naturally as I'd taken to bridge. From the beginner's class that night – missionary position – I soon advanced to complicated plays, many of them involving some of the more interesting objects displayed so prominently on the Harraps' lounge wall.

I was never in love with Mrs Harrap, but she gave me more pleasure lying down – as well as sitting, hanging upside down, and standing on my head – than I'd ever imagined possible. And though I never really thought about it, I suppose I assumed we would go on like that for a considerable time into the future.

But Fate had other plans for me.

10

The Finger of Fate – or rather the Fist – came rapping on Aunt Peggy's door one afternoon towards the end of the summer holidays.

'Well, go and answer it, then,' my aunt said, looking around the room for a cat to start stroking.

As I opened the front door, I was expecting to see the vicar or some family in search of a pet. Instead, I was confronted by a man with eyes as quick and mesmerising as a mongoose's.

'It's round the back, Sergeant,' I said.

'What is?' Fliques asked.

'My bike.'

'I'll check that later. I've no time at the moment.'

What? Could this be true – Les Fliques with not enough time on his hands to persecute me for my failures in cycle maintenance?

'Well, if there's nothing else, Sergeant ...' I said hopefully, beginning to close the door.

'It's not you I'm after this time,' Fliques barked, inserting his large boot into the decreasing gap between the door and the jamb. 'I want to see your auntie.'

My auntie? What could he possibly want to talk to Aunt Peggy about?

Me! It had to be about me!

I wondered which of my numerous crimes – as defined by the Fliques Criminal Code – he'd uncovered. A couple of weeks earlier, I'd accidentally cycled through a red light. Just the night before, after a particularly steamy session with Mrs Cynthia Harrap, I'd smoked my first cigarette.

Oh, my God, Mrs Cynthia Harrap. Fliques had found out she was having it off with a minor, and she was already in custody. I felt so *guilty*.

'Auntie Peggy's in the front room,' I stuttered.

'Is she now?' Fliques asked, as if that, in and of itself, was a crime. 'You'd better take me to her then, hadn't you?'

Aunt Peggy had had time to find a cat – a ginger tom who had earned the name Tennessee by spending most summer afternoons sleeping on the tin roof of the outside privy – and as we entered the room, she was lovingly stroking it.

'This is Sergeant Fliques,' I announced.

My aunt looked him up and down, from his shiny boots to the point of his bullet head.

'You're a policeman,' she said unnecessarily.

'That's right, madam,' Fliques agreed. 'I'm a policeman. Or, if you would prefer it, I'm a copper, a pig, or the Filth. It's whichever you feel more comfortable with.'

'Comfortable with?' Aunt Peggy repeated, obviously alarmed.

'I should have thought, madam, given some of your known associates, that underworld slang would be what you're most at home with,' Fliques explained. 'I've found that there's not a great deal of respect for the forces of law and order among the criminal classes.'

'Known associates?' Aunt Peggy echoed, seemingly unable to do anything but repeat her visitor's words. 'Criminal classes?'

Fliques sat down, uninvited, in the chair opposite her.

'You can go, Bobby,' he said, and for once, he sounded almost friendly.

I didn't go far – out of the kitchen door and then, on all fours like one of the moggies, round to the front of the house.

'Do you know what cat burglars are, madam?' I heard Fliques say through the open living room window.

'Cat burglars?' Aunt Peggy laughed, as though the whole idea was, of course, completely absurd.

'Cat burglars,' Fliques repeated flatly.

'Those horrible people who go around stealing cats, do you mean?' my aunt asked. She laughed again. 'Or do they actually steal *from* the cats. Is that it?'

She was trying to charm him. She'd have had more success charming a king cobra with a hangover.

'I mean neither of those things, madam,' Fliques said. 'By cat burglars I am referring to persons who engage in the act of forcible entry into properties not their own for the purpose of removing goods which also do not belong to them, thus contravening sections 9 and 10 of the Theft Act of 1968. Have I made my meaning clear?'

'Well, yes,' said Aunt Peggy, sounding much subdued.

'And are you familiar with any such persons?'

'Certainly not. How could I be? I hardly ever leave the farm. My pussies need me all the time.'

Oh yes, Auntie, the pussies need you, all right, I thought. You haven't raised a hand to help them since I moved in.

'The Manchester police picked up a well-known drainpipe artist yesterday,' Fliques continued. 'They caught him *in flagrante delicto*, as you might say. And do you know what he had in his pocket?'

'I haven't a clue,' Aunt Peggy said haughtily.

'No, madam,' Fliques agreed. 'How could you have? But you see, what we found in his pocket did give *us* a clue.'

Fliques fell silent. Having baited his trap, he was now content to wait until his prey went for it.

Secure in my hiding place under the windowsill, I pictured my aunt nervously twisting the cat on her lap into knots. I was really quite enjoying myself.

'What did you find in his pocket?' my aunt asked, finally giving in to the inevitable.

'Your address, madam.'

'What does that prove?' Aunt Peggy asked, not in her Cat Lady voice, but as she spoke to the Night Callers when she was arguing about money. 'I mean, he might just have got it out of the telephone book, mightn't he?'

'Perhaps, madam. But we also found this.'

I wanted desperately to see what "this" was, but the risk of raising my head above the windowsill was just too great.

'What does it look like to you, madam?' Fliques asked.

'Like a hand-drawn map,' Aunt Peggy said, through gritted teeth.

'A map of what?'

'Of how to get to Cuddles Farm.'

'And just what would a well-known jewel thief be doing with that in his possession?' Fliques asked.

'I don't know,' Aunt Peggy admitted. 'I mean, I've always been such a respectable person, haven't I? You've only to ask the vicar.'

'If you'd collared as many clergymen as I have, you'd think twice before using one of them as a character witness,' Fliques said. He paused for a moment. 'I've been a policeman for a long time, and I've developed a nose for smelling out villains. And you, madam, are a real villain if I ever sniffed one.'

'I think you'd better leave,' Aunt Peggy said angrily.

'Oh, I'll leave,' Fliques told her. 'But I'll be back – don't have any doubts about that.'

11

The midnight raid was swift and sudden. One moment Aunt Peggy and I were alone in the front room, the next the place was full of evil-looking men wearing "bovver" boots and glowing with malicious intent.

'You can't come bursting in like this,' Aunt Peggy protested, looking strangely vulnerable without a prop-cat on her knee. 'I mean, an Englishman's home is his castle, isn't it?'

'And castles sometimes get stormed,' Sergeant Fliques pointed out.

'Have you got a search warrant?' my aunt demanded.

'Certainly, madam,' Fliques said, taking out a piece of paper which might have been a warrant – but could just as easily have been his laundry list – waving it briefly through the air, and returning it to his pocket.

'You could have knocked, at least,' Aunt Peggy complained. 'I mean, it wouldn't have taken much of an effort to knock, would it?'

'Didn't want to disturb you unnecessarily,' Fliques told her, and the seven or eight coppers he'd brought with him all nodded their heads, as if to agree that they really didn't want to be any trouble.

The sergeant's eyes swept the room then homed in on the whisky bottle and two glasses which were sitting on the table.

'Has Bobby started drinking hard liquor?' he asked. 'Or are you expecting company?'

'What's all this about?' my aunt snapped, ignoring the question.

Fliques took out his notebook, and opened it with some ceremony. 'We have reason to believe—'

His affirmation of faith was cut off mid-way by a loud howl from one of the other policeman, who had gone quite white.

'Pull yourself together, man,' Fliques said harshly.

But it's not always that easy to pull yourself together when something else is doing its best to pull you apart.

The constable lifted his right leg in an effort to dislodge the cat which had attached itself to his trousers, but with no success. If anything, the moggie only dug its claws in further.

'Use your hands, you fool!' Fliques bellowed.

The constable did as instructed. No doubt it was the pain which made him forget to put his foot back on the ground first.

Hands around the cat, he rocked for a second then toppled backwards. The room was not large, and there were a lot of policemen there. It would have been a miracle indeed if the cat-savaged constable had managed to avoid cannoning into at least one of his colleagues.

He didn't avoid it. The top of his head caught the chin of the man behind him. The new victim's eyes crossed, then he, his unintending assailant and the moggie, were all in a downward plunge. A third officer, stepping smartly to the side, barked his shin on the coffee table, hopped on one foot briefly, then gave way to the forces of gravity and joined the waving pile of arms and legs on the floor.

The cat, well-satisfied with his handiwork, detached himself from the first constable's leg and padded smirkingly across the room.

'Good Mickey,' Aunt Peggy said, with what – for once – sounded like genuine affection.

'Get up, and start searching,' Fliques said angrily. 'And you two,' pointing to a couple of constables who had somehow managed to avoid injury, 'can bring in our mystery guest.'

The "mystery guest" was a tall man in his mid-thirties. He was dressed in an expensive, though flashy, blue suit. Heavy gold bracelets hung from his wrists. His arrival seemed to instantly put Fliques in a better mood.

'This is Harry Bowers,' the sergeant announced, playing the master of ceremonies to perfection.

'Pleased to meet you, Mr Bowers,' Aunt Peggy said, although she'd seen him often enough before.

'And Harry's line is …?' Fliques asked.

'His line?' my aunt repeated.

'His occupation. What he does for a living.'

'How would I know?'

'Do you want to do the mime for us, Harry?' Fliques asked jovially.

'Get stuffed!' Bowers growled.

But nothing would have dampened Fliques' spirits at that moment.

'Harry is a villain,' he told us. 'To be more precise, he's a fence. We caught him at the end of the drive. What were you doing there, Harry?'

The big man shrugged. 'I got lost.'

'You got lost!' Fliques echoed contemptuously. 'I'll lose you, Harry – in Strangeways Prison.'

One of the constables who'd been searching another part of the house returned to consult his leader.

'There's a room at the back that's locked, Skipper,' he said.

'Is there?' Fliques asked. 'Is there indeed?' He turned to my aunt. 'Have you got the key, madam?'

'Of course. Well, I would have, wouldn't I?'

'Then we'd both better go and take a look at it,' Fliques said. 'You, too, Bobby – I want you to see for yourself how little things like riding your bike without lights and inciting people to murder can be just the first step on the path to serious crime.'

****

If Fliques had expected to find the storeroom full of jewels, he was disappointed. In the old days, when the smallholding was a going concern, the shelves of the store must have been crammed with produce. Now, like Old Mother Hubbard's cupboard, most of them were bare.

Fliques' eyes fell on the cat in a cage on the floor. 'What's that?' he asked.

'It's a cat,' Aunt Peggy replied.

'I can see it's a cat, madam. Why is it locked up?'

'It's new. It's just settling in,'

Not true. The cat – called Elvis, because he liked to play dead – had been with us for over a year, and was one of my favourites. The reason he was in isolation was not because he'd just arrived but because he was about to leave – with Harry Bowers.

'I don't approve of keeping animals in cages,' Fliques said. 'People, yes, but not animals.' He glanced despondently at the row of empty shelves. 'Search this place thoroughly,' he told one of his constables, though without much hope in his voice.

As successes go, the search was about on a par with the maiden voyage of the *Titanic*.

'I know there's something here,' Fliques ranted, as his men emptied the sugar jar and examined the contents of the rubbish bin. 'I just know there is.'

In the end, he was forced to concede defeat with his usual grace.

'You can go,' he told Harry Bowers, 'but don't let me catch you on my patch again. And as for you, madam, I may not have found anything this time, but that doesn't mean I've given up. I'll get you in the end, you know.'

'Get me?' Aunt Peggy asked complacently. 'You haven't got a cat in hell's chance.'

****

'What did he mean about you inciting people to murder?' my aunt asked, when Fliques had finally stormed off.

'It's just his sense of humour,' I told her, praying that she didn't notice the catch in my voice.

But Aunt Peggy's mind had already moved on to other matters.

'He's making a nuisance of himself, that policeman, isn't he?' she said. 'I want him off my back, so I think I'm going to have to phone your Aunt Catherine.'

'Aunt Catherine. But she lives somewhere in darkest Wales – what can she do?'

'Our Chief Constable writes to her post box,' Aunt Peggy said.

'I don't understand.'

'He's one of her "special" correspondents. A lot of people write to her, but only a few are special.'

'Special? In what way?'

'And the ones who are special,' my aunt continued, ignoring my question, 'will do almost anything she asks them to.'

'Why?' I asked.

'I've said enough,' my aunt replied. 'If truth be told, I've probably said too much. So just take it from me – we'll have no more trouble from that sergeant.'

****

There is a big difference between knowing something for certain and being able to prove it, so even without the intervention of the Chief Constable, Les Fliques' investigation was going nowhere. He knew the *who*, you see – Aunt Peggy. He knew the *why* – greed. What he didn't know was the *how*. And it was the *how* that I thought I'd finally worked out.

If I was right, then the evidence Fliques needed had been under his nose all the time he was searching the house. If I was right, Aunt Peggy was not only a criminal, but also a cruel, evil woman. If I was right, she had to be punished.

'*Always make sure you've got your facts straight before you go making accusations,*' Mother used to say.

Very well, then – before I could condemn Aunt Peggy, it was first necessary to carry out a little investigation of my own.

12

I proceeded with caution, as Les Fliques might have said in his road safety lecturing days.

My first requirement was access to the storeroom. That was impossible when a cat was locked in there, because at such times Aunt Peggy kept the key on a ribbon around her fat little neck. But she didn't carry the key when the isolation cell was empty – therefore she must be hiding it somewhere else. It took me less than half an hour to find that the place she'd chosen was the bottom of her knickers' drawer.

Stage Two of my investigation was more complex.

'I want a voice-activated tape recorder, please,' I told the assistant in Norton Hi-Fi.

'I don't think we've got any in stock,' he said doubtfully. 'Not much call for them round here. I expect I could get you one – but it won't be cheap.'

'The price doesn't matter,' I told him, fingering the thick wad of pound notes which Mrs Cynthia Harrap had been only too glad to lend me.

The equipment arrived a week later. I smuggled the tape recorder into my room, and installed the microphone in the store while my aunt was snoring noisily on the sofa.

Now all I had to do was wait for the next cat delivery.

****

I did not have to wait long. The cat turned up the next Thursday evening. It was a scrawny, pale tom, with part of one ear missing, and was accompanied by a scrawny, pale man, who looked like he'd lost part of his brain in the same fight. As usual, once business had been satisfactorily completed Aunt Peggy took the cat to the storeroom, and locked it in.

School, the next day, was sheer hell. I couldn't concentrate on my lessons. I couldn't even think about bridge or Mrs Cynthia Harrap. There was room for only one thing in my mind, and that was the store room back at Cuddles Farm.

'You should have stayed at home,' I told myself a hundred times. 'If you'd stayed at home, you'd have known for certain by now.'

My mind raced, but time crawled. The clock at the front of the classroom seemed to be ticking off the minutes at half its normal speed. The teacher wrote on the whiteboard in slow motion. When my fellow pupils spoke, they stretched out their words with the sole purpose of prolonging my agony.

And I itched.

God, how I itched.

The final bell rang at last. I ran to the bike shed and leaped on my machine like the Lone Ranger used to leap on Silver. My feet hit the pedals, and I began to pump furiously. In the driveway, small children scattered, and teachers behind the wheels of middle-sized, sensible family cars slammed on their brakes and made a note to speak to me first thing on Monday morning.

Out on the open road, I knew no fear. Buses missed me by inches, lorry drivers paled and hit their horns in frantic, desperate warning.

I was a Titan. I was a Fury. I demolished any speed record there was – or ever could be – for covering the route between school and Cuddles Farm.

The bumpy dirt track to the farm did nothing to slow me down, and I was almost flying when I hit Aunt Peggy's back yard. I squeezed the brakes hard and the back wheel skidded, but I was already free and running towards the house by the time my bike clattered noisily to the ground. And then I saw the pale tom with the missing ear!

He was huddled tight against the wall under the kitchen window. What a change had come over him in the few hours he'd been at the farm. He'd seemed a plucky little thing the night before. Not unfriendly – just spirited. Now his eyes were wide with fear.

My own needs could wait. The frightened moggie came first.

I approached him slowly.

'It's all right, Van Gogh,' I crooned. 'Don't you worry, little pussy, it's all right.'

His fur stood on end, and he extended a threatening claw.

'I know you must feel a bit rough now,' I told him, 'but it will pass. I promise it will pass.'

The cat looked wildly to the left and to the right, then made a hysterical dash for the barn.

I didn't try to follow him. What would have been the point? Who could blame him if – after what I suspected he'd been through in the last few hours – he was in no mood to accept the assurances of a complete stranger.

I entered the house weighed down by the knowledge that it looked as if my theory about Aunt Peggy's racket was absolutely correct.

'How could I have been so stupid?' I asked myself angrily. 'If only I'd worked out what was going on earlier, I could have saved so much suffering.'

'There's the washing up from my lunch to be done,' Aunt Peggy called from the living room. 'And I want you to fix that dripping tap in the bathroom before you start making tea.'

'Yes, Auntie,' I said wearily.

But instead of starting my tasks immediately – as I usually did – I went straight up to my bedroom to listen to the tape recorder.

13

The tape had been running. With trembling hands, I rewound it.

'I don't want to be right,' I told the tape recorder. 'Please, please, don't make me right!'

I pressed the play button. There was just a hiss at first, then Aunt Peggy spoke.

'*Have you done what I wanted yet, Mickey*?' she asked. '*No, I can see you haven't.*'

'*Meow*,' the cat said plaintively.

'*Be a good little pussy and give your Auntie Peggy what she wants,*' my aunt wheedled.

'*Cough!*' went Van Gogh.

'*I don't care which end they come out of, as long as they come,*' Aunt Peggy told him.

'*Retch!*' Van Gogh replied.

'*Normally, I wouldn't rush you,*' my aunt said, all sweet reasonableness, '*but this time I'm in a hurry. The creep's coming back for his money this afternoon, and I have to see the diamonds before I pay him.*'

'*Gag!*' the cat commented.

'*Listen, you little bastard,*' my aunt said, losing her patience, '*we can do this the easy way or the hard way. The easy way is to shit them out. The hard way – for you – is that I slit your throat, slice open your belly, and root around inside until I find the jewels. It's a bit messy, but when you've done it as often as I have, you get used to it. So it's your choice, Cat.*'

If Aunt Peggy was so ready to use the knife, how much more willing would the people she did business with be to use it?

Would Harry Bowers wait for hours for the cats to perform their natural functions – or would he, once the animal had served its purpose as a carrier, do what my aunt was threatening to do to Van Gogh?

I thought of all the cats who had been spirited away from Cuddles Farm under the cover of darkness …

... Oscar ... Rudolph ... Kennedy ... Snow White ... Romeo ...

There was so many of them, and long before I had finished going through the list, I felt tears streaming down my face.

14

I should have thought about the rice jar first, but it never occurred to me that Aunt Peggy would hide anything in a room which, since my arrival, she'd rarely visited. So it was not until three o'clock in the morning – having searched her bedroom while she was watching television, and the rest of the house after she'd gone to sleep – that I finally reached the kitchen. And then, of course, it was obvious.

'We never use this rice, Auntie Peggy,' I'd said to her on more than one occasion. 'Shall I throw it out?'

'No, keep it,' my aunt had always replied. 'It might come in useful one of these days.'

And it had had come in useful – as a hiding place for jewellery when it was between cats!

I spread a newspaper carefully over the work surface and began pouring the rice onto it. The first ring, buried about a third of the way down the jar, took me by surprise, and before I could stop it, it fell free, bounced twice and landed on the floor with a terrifyingly loud clink.

My heart started pounding, and my breaths came fast and irregular. Frozen to the spot, I strained my ears for the sound of any movement from my aunt's bedroom.

Down the stairs came the reassuring sound of Peggy's fat-lady snores. I relaxed again – a little.

I spooned the rest of the rice slowly onto the newspaper, and not until the jar was completely empty did I stop to look at my haul. There were three rings and a small brooch which was edged with precious stones. I was holding a small fortune in my hands.

I spent some time examining the jewellery, and only when I was satisfied that I would remember every detail of it did I replace it – and the rice – back in the jar. That job successfully completed, I checked the floor and work surface for tell-tale grains of rice and, finding none, I screwed up the newspaper and placed it in the bin.

There was nothing more for me to do that night. I crept back up to my bedroom and grabbed a few hours' sleep.

My appearance in the yard early the following morning, weighed down with tins of food and plastic feed bowls, created something of a sensation. The cats knew as well as I did that this was not their normal feeding time, but saw no point in looking gift horse-meat in the mouth, and, as I crossed the threshold of the barn, I was being followed by a long line of slavering felines.

The cats arranged themselves in a semi-circle around me, and looked on hungrily as I dumped tin after tin of meat into the plastic bowls.

'Have you noticed anything different about what I'm doing today, Mr Spock?' I asked as I worked.

The cat I'd questioned blinked an affirmative response.

'What about you, Mae?' I said to a slinky tortoiseshell.

Miss West's responding purr indicated that she had.

'I'm giving you all extra rations,' I said, for the benefit of the slower cats. 'It's a sort of celebration.'

Or a sort of wake, because, though they didn't know it, this was to be the last time I would ever feed them.

As I piled the bowls high, other cats – who'd been hunting on the very edges of their kingdom, or else involved in amorous adventures beyond the paddock – began to arrive, and by the time I had completed my task, every cat on the farm, including the recently-abused Van Gogh, had congregated in the barn.

I placed the bowls on the floor.

'On your marks!' I said, going through, for one final time, the ritual which had given me so much pleasure.

Two or three of the newer cats put a tentative paw forward.

'Wait for it!' I ordered.

Tentative paws were withdrawn.

'And … go!' I told them.

Within a second, I was surrounded by a sea of rubbing, swaying fur. I made my way to the barn door. I had not intended to stop and turn around, but I couldn't help myself.

'Goodbye, little friends,' I said to the scores of rapidly bobbing heads.

I stepped outside and closed the door behind me. From my pocket, I took out my bike padlock. It was a big, heavy thing, the sort Les Fliques had advised us to buy – had *ordered* us to buy – during his lecture on road safety and crime prevention, back in my primary school days.

I slipped the padlock through the barn door hasp, and clicked it into place.

'Try and cut through that, Auntie Peggy,' I said aloud.

She could cut through it, of course, given time – but time was the one commodity I intended to rob her of.

I ran through my time projections in my mind. She would have about five minutes to do something. The first thirty seconds would be spent in shock. It would take her at least the next two minutes to discover that all the cats were locked up in the barn. She'd waste another couple of minutes looking for the hacksaw blades I'd already transferred to the saddlebag on my bike. And then, as the last, precious moments ticked away, she'd realise that, however much she hated the idea, there was only one course of action left open to her.

15

The call box was located at the edge of Norton, on the road which led – eventually – to Cuddles Farm. It was empty, which was only what you would expect so early on a Saturday morning. I stepped inside and dialled a famous three-digit number.

'Emergency,' the operator said, with reassuring calm. 'Which service do you require, please?'

'The Polis,' I told her in my best Irish accent.

There was a click, and then a new, wearier voice said, 'Norton Central Police Station.'

It was just possible that Les had taken the day off – but, knowing him as I did, I didn't think it likely.

'Oi want to speak to Sorjeant Fliques,' I said.

'Your call will be processed by the duty—'

'Tell him it's about the jools at Cuddles Farm,' I interrupted.

Fliques was on the line in seconds. 'Who is this?' he demanded.

'Oi'm not prepared to give moi name, sor.'

'Is that you, Bobby?' he asked.

'Shut your gob and listen, sor,' I said.

God, but that felt good.

'I'm listening, Bobby,' Fliques told me.

'I've got some information that might be of interest to youse, sor ...'

****

It was nearly half an hour before a black police car, with Les Fliques at the wheel, sped past my phone box hiding place. I already had the money ready, and I pushed it into the slot and then dialled Cuddles Farm.

'Yes?' my aunt answered, in a sleepy voice.

'The police are on the way,' I said.

'Police?' Aunt Peggy repeated. 'If this is a joke, Bobby, you're in a lot of trouble.'

'It's no joke,' I assured her. 'You've got five minutes – maybe less.'

'But your Aunt Catherine promised me that she'd—'

'You'll hear their sirens any second now,' I said.

'Cats!' my aunt screamed. 'Where are all the bloody cats?'

I hung up, to give her time to realise that she had no choice but to do what I'd planned she should do. Though it was still early, my work for the day was complete.

I decided to go for a bike ride.

****

It was a pleasant early-autumn morning, and the country lanes I followed were deserted. I enjoyed the feel of the sun on my neck, and the crisp air blowing against my face. A rabbit scuttled across the road, a hedgehog balled itself up at the base of a tree. Overhead, a flock of birds circled in preparation for their long journey south.

I dismounted by a bramble patch, and picked a handful of blackberries. They were sweet and juicy.

In some ways, I had to admire Aunt Peggy. The cat couriers had been a brilliant idea, because known criminals often got stopped by the police and had both their persons and their cars searched. But what policeman would also think to search the insides of the cat the criminal happened to have with him?

Yes, it had been clever – but it had also been very, very wrong. Moggies like Van Gogh must have suffered terrible discomfort when they were forced to swallow the jewels, and even more when they had to regurgitate them. And they had been the lucky ones. Cats like Charlie Chaplin – with his comical walk – and Wurzel – the scruffiest animal on the farm – had come to far worse ends, their throats cut by vicious men who only cared about the contents of their stomachs.

It was too horrible even for me to think about – and I knew Mother would have shared my horror.

'*Always be kind to dumb animals,*' I heard her voice say from the other side of the brambles. '*They're God's creatures, just the same as we are.*'

'Indeed they are, Mother,' I agreed.

'*And make the punishment fit the crime,*' Mother continued. '*Always make sure the punishment fits the crime.*'

I nodded. I was sure that in this case, that was exactly what I'd done.

16

Aunt Peggy died shortly after that, and so I went to live with Aunt Catherine.

PART FOUR: The Queen of Hearts

1

'God called me here,' Aunt Catherine said.

I looked around me.

To my left, the bay curved like a twisted lip, coming to a natural artistic conclusion at the run-down fishing port from which, every morning, a few dispirited boats would set out onto the hostile sea.

To my right lay the town. Boarding houses lined the front – inelegant peeling Victorian dwellings with names like "Sea View" and the "Atlantic Hotel". Immediately behind them – almost seeming to grow out of them – was the sharp hill on which most of Llawesuohtihs was built. As far as the eye could see, rows and rows of narrow terraced houses clung to the incline, confidently pessimistic that one day it would rain a little too hard, and they would slither helplessly down into the oily water.

My vantage point for this spectacular panorama was a crumbling platform which jutted out to sea on legs a spider would have been ashamed of.

"The World Famous Llawesuohtihs Pier", the sign announced at the entrance.

In what world was it famous? I wondered.

All in all, I decided, Llawesuohtihs was a very backward place. Even the name was unpronounceable to anyone not born under a cloud of drizzle and within the sound of bleating sheep.

'Yes,' Aunt Catherine said complacently. 'God called, and I answered that call.'

It seemed to me that if He'd sent her to a place like this, God couldn't have liked her very much.

'Your aunt has been a great, spurting fountain of strength for me,' said the man by her side.

Like all the great double acts in history – Holmes and Watson, the Lone Ranger and Tonto, Batman and Robin – my aunt and her mentor,

Pastor Ives, made an incongruous pair. Tall, gaunt Aunt Catherine habitually wore the long, flowing dress of a severe Victorian governess, but with her scrawny neck and a beak of a nose, she looked more like a reject from a chicken factory conveyor belt. Pastor Ives, by contrast, was a small, bulging man with a milky complexion and a topping of silver hair. He always dressed in white suits, and wore a pair of gold glasses with lenses as thick as bottle glass.

They made a ridiculous pair, yes, but it would be a mistake to underestimate them. Together, they made a formidable team, and, almost without help, they had managed to build the Church of Christ the Consumer into the most boring and completely incomprehensible mission in the whole of Wales.

'The Pastor asked you a question, Robert,' my aunt said harshly. 'Haven't you been listening?'

'Of course I have, Auntie,' I replied.

As a matter of fact, I hadn't. Instead, I'd been scanning the bleak seafront, expecting, at any moment, to see the figure of my old friend, Sergeant Fliques, resolutely marching towards us. But I needn't have worried – it would be months yet before Les came to hound me over what I'd done to Aunt Peggy.

'I was asking you if you understood the tremendous challenge of our mission,' Pastor Ives said.

'Not really,' I admitted.

'People have the wrong idea about our Saviour,' he told me. 'Christ was never against consumerism. Had there been a Sainsbury's in ancient Palestine, His holy feet would have been the first across the threshold, and He would have filled his basket with special offers, just as He filled His net with souls.'

'I didn't realise that,' I said, trying not to laugh.

'That's the point,' Ives said, drenching me in enthusiasm and spittle. 'Most people don't realise. Take another example. Had video shops existed in those far-off days, He would have rented a tape – as regularly as clockwork – every Friday night. Except, of course,' he chuckled, to indicate that as a modern, broad-minded churchman, he was comfortable enough with his faith to be able to poke mild fun at it, 'except, of course, on *Good* Friday, when He was otherwise engaged.'

'And He would have bought a Chinese take-away to eat as He watched it,' I said, as my contribution to the theological discussion.

'Perhaps, being from the Middle East, He would have a kebab rather than a chop suey,' Ives said, but he was obviously pleased with me. 'And that's the message we have to get across,' he continued, serious once more. 'Christ is relevant to ordinary people's lives.'

'It is as hard for a rich man to enter the gates of Heaven as it is for a shopper to pass through the check-out at Asda on a Saturday morning?' I suggested.

Pastor Ives frowned – and I realised I had gone too far.

'I'm not sure you quite understand,' he said. 'God wants us to spend. It is through new, improved washing powders and miracle cleaners that He manifests His wonders in the world.'

'The boy understands, well enough,' Aunt Catherine said, fixing me with her sharp little eyes, 'but his heart is hardened. The sins of his mother, his Aunt Jacqueline, and his Aunt Peggy, cling to him as tightly as does the price sticker on a bottle of Fairy – which is as kind to hands as the Lord is to souls who see the light. Yes, the sticker of sin is firmly fixed upon him, but we will scrub and scrub until we have succeeded in stripping it away.'

The wind had changed direction, and now it carried on it the stench of the fish-canning factory. Drizzle prickled against my face, that particularly Welsh drizzle which always manages to make itself feel wetter than rain elsewhere. Out at sea, heavy grey clouds merged with choppy grey water, and robbed me of a horizon.

It looked as if I was in for a jolly few years.

2

If there's one thing I'm especially proud of in my life – apart from my skill at the bridge table – it's the way I've behaved to the women who were part of it. To all of them, without exception, I have shown a sense of duty and responsibility which would have made Mother proud of me. I cleaned Aunt Jacqueline's house until it was as bright as a new pin. I fed Aunt Peggy's cats, and I fixed her roof despite my vertigo. Almost single-handed, I created the Shelton Bourne Trust to please Sadie. I even helped Rosalyn, my late fiancée, to produce those frightful stories her equally frightful newspaper was always demanding. Yet, on balance, I think it was Aunt Catherine who got the best value for her money.

God, how she worked me during my time in Wales, both as her personal servant and in the role of general building contractor to the Church of Christ the Consumer. I'm not complaining, you understand. In fact, I was glad to have the opportunity to do something which would pay Aunt Catherine back for the kindness she'd shown in taking me in.

And, as Mother used to say, '*Hard work never hurt anybody.*'

Still, I must admit that there was one job which really irritated me, because – unlike painting the house or re-hanging a door on the Mission – it seemed completely pointless.

And what was that job?

My monthly trek to Abernuffa.

The first of these expeditions to what could hardly have been called the centre of the universe – even if the universe in question was a pretty dull one – took place shortly after my arrival in Llawesuohtihs.

'We're both going to Abernuffa today,' my aunt announced one Saturday morning.

The name meant nothing to me, but Aunt Catherine was wearing her best governess dress – the one which made her look like a cockerel on stilts – and so she obviously attached some importance to the visit.

'Why are we going there, Auntie?' I asked.

'To shop.'

'But couldn't we shop here?'

'No, we couldn't,' my aunt told me. 'Not without drawing attention to ourselves.'

****

It was a slow, wearying journey from Llawesuohtihs to Abernuffa. The bus, a geriatric single-decker, coughed its way up the hills, breathed a sigh of relief when we reached the crowns, and seemed to go into a panic every time we began a descent. We stopped at innumerable slate-and-flint villages to drop off mail and pick up passengers who looked as if it would be news to them that the Hindenburg had crashed. Only after an hour and a half's bone-rattling travel did we see a sign which announced that Abernuffa welcomed careful drivers.

We may have wasted time by going to Abernuffa at all, but not a minute was squandered once we arrived. My aunt marched resolutely from the bus station into the near-by branch of Boots, and, once inside, headed straight for the hair brushes. She stood for perhaps a minute examining the array of brushes, then picked one up and stroked it against my cheek.

'What does it feel like?' she demanded.

'It tickles,' I giggled.

'Yes, yes,' my aunt said impatiently. 'But does it feel to you like it's human hair?'

'I suppose so – but very spiky human hair.'

'Always get them like this,' my aunt told me, 'real bristle, not plastic – and always in black. Do you understand?'

It didn't seem too difficult to grasp. I nodded my head.

My aunt paid for the brush.

'Do we need anything else?' I asked.

'Not from here,' Aunt Catherine replied.

From Boot's, we went to Hughes' Bros., and again immediately homed in on the hair brush section.

'You choose one this time,' my aunt said.

Anxious to please, I selected a brush similar to the one we'd bought in Boots, and handed it to her.

Aunt Catherine stroked it against her chin.

'Yes,' she said, 'this will do nicely.'

And a minute later, she was the owner of a second brush.

After Hughes Bros., we visited Marks and Spencer, the Welsh Handicraft Store, Griffiths and Son, and the Dylan Thomas Gift Shop. We bought brushes at all of them. Only then did my aunt seem satisfied.

'From now on, it will be your responsibility,' she told me. 'For just as the fork-lift truck in Tesco's can shift whole crates of Campbell's Concentrated Soup from one shelf to another, so has the Lord lifted this burden off my shoulders and placed it on yours.'

'What burden, Auntie?'

'Buying the brushes.'

'But you've just bought six,' I gasped.

'And I shall require six more next month and every month,' my aunt said, with a dangerous edge to her voice. 'Six new brushes, from six different shops. Have I made myself clear?'

Clear? Yes. But I couldn't honestly say she was making any sense.

****

On the way back to Llawesuohtihs, I did my best to solve the mystery of the hair brushes.

Perhaps she gave them out as prizes to her Sunday school class, I thought – but the class was not that large, and after a few months, surely every child in it would have been given at least one brush.

And the prize theory wouldn't explain why she went all the way to Abernuffa for them – and bought them all from different shops.

Maybe someone had told her that in the event of nuclear war, hair brushes would be in short supply, I speculated, and she was stockpiling them secretly to avoid a panic. But no, that was ludicrous – even for my aunt.

The answer to the mystery, as it turned out, was both simpler and more puzzling than any of my speculations – she needed new brushes because she used the old ones up.

I discovered the first of them in the kitchen bin, a week after our trip to Abernuffa. Initially, I was sure it couldn't have been one of the brushes we'd bought – not in that condition – but closer examination revealed that it was, indeed, the brush I'd selected in Hughes' Bros.. Another four turned up in the bin over the next few weeks, so that by the time I made my first solo trip to Abernuffa, Aunt Catherine was down to her very last brush.

How did she do it? I wondered as the old bus groaned its way into yet another oppressive hamlet. What could *anyone* possibly do to a hair brush to make it go completely bald in such a short time?

3

It was towards the end of November that I finally had a visit from my old friend, Les Fliques. I'd spent an uneventful day in the Owen Glendower High School – an institution which was a tasteful blend of Victorian ostentation and 1970s cheese-paring utilitarianism – and was just leaving for home when I noticed him standing by the gate.

He was dressed in civilian clothes, and though the air was cold enough to freeze the tail-feathers off a sparrow, he was sucking a stick of Llawesuohtihs souvenir rock.

'Just checking the name really does go all the way through, as the manufacturer claims it does,' he said, by way of a greeting.

'You could always just break it in two,' I suggested.

'That's not my way, laddie, and you know it,' Fliques replied. 'Slow but sure, that's my method – slow but sure.'

'Are you down here on holiday, Sergeant Fliques?' I asked.

'It's *Inspector* Fliques now,' he said. 'And no, I'm not on holiday. I don't take holidays. But,' he conceded, 'I am on leave.'

'And what brings you down to Llawesuohtihs, Inspector?' I asked.

'You, laddie,' Fliques told me. 'I'm checking up on you.'

'There's nothing to check up on. Even if I wanted to misbehave, there's no way to do it in a dump like this.'

Fliques chuckled. 'Don't underestimate yourself. I've come to have great respect for you over the years. What you did to your Auntie Jacqueline was smart enough, but that stroke with your Auntie Peggy was bloody brilliant.'

'I don't know what you're talking about, Inspector,' I said.

Fliques shook his head, wonderingly. 'Of course you don't. Then let me explain it. It's Saturday morning, and I get an anonymous call from a supposed Irishman about some jewellery hidden in Cuddles Farm – your Irish accent, by the way, is bloody awful. Now I've had some trouble with Cuddles Farm, because I've already pulled one search warrant, and come up with nothing. Besides, somebody's putting pressure on the people from the top floor to take me off the case.'

'Really?' I said, thinking that did he but realise it, the somebody in question was not a mile from where we were standing.

'Really,' Fliques repeated. 'Anyway, the upshot is that if I'm going to get another warrant, I need some very solid information. And the caller knows that as well. So what does he do?'

'I've no idea, Inspector.'

'He gives me such a detailed description of the goods that I can say for certain they've been nicked from a big house in Cheadle Hulme. And that's enough to convince the magistrate. Still following me, are you?'

'Yes, Inspector.'

'You leave it for a while before ringing your auntie—'

'Not me.'

'All right, have it your own way. The anonymous caller leaves it a while before ringing your auntie. And what does he say when she picks up the phone?'

'I've not a clue.'

'"The cops are coming, Auntie," he says. "They should be there any minute." Now Auntie knows we'll have no trouble finding the jewels where they're hidden at the moment. So what does she do? She looks around for a convenient moggie.'

'A convenient moggie?'

'So she can stick the jewels down its throat – as you well know. Anyway, there are no cats to be found – they're all locked up in the barn, and she hasn't got a key. "What am I going to do?" she asks herself in a panic, because – you must remember, Bobby – she's been told I'll be arriving any minute. "I'll hide them among the weeds in the vegetable garden," she thinks. No, that won't work because the police are bound to go over the whole place with a fine-toothed comb. "I'll flush them down the bog," she decides. Pity to throw so much money down the toilet, but it's better than being nicked. And then she remembers – she's got a septic tank. "Oh, why didn't I have mains drainage installed when I had the chance," she moans. Because she knows, you see, that I'll sift through a ton of shit if I have to. So what choices does she have left? She could always give herself up, but knowing your auntie like we do, that doesn't seem likely, does it?'

I tried to picture Aunt Peggy holding out her hands for the cuffs.

'No,' I agreed, 'that doesn't seem likely.'

'Not Diamond Peggy,' Fliques said. 'That wasn't her way at all. So in the end, as you well knew – as you'd *planned* it – there was only one thing she could do, wasn't there? "It worked with the cats," she thinks as she pops the first ring in her mouth, "so it's worth trying myself." Down goes one ring, then another, and finally a third. But the brooch doesn't go down – the brooch gets stuck. But you couldn't have known that for certain, Bobby. You couldn't have been *sure* she'd have choked to death by the time we arrived.'

No, but at the very least, I'd have made sure that she got a taste of her own medicine before she was arrested.

'Even if you could prove any of this, Auntie Peggy still died by her own hand,' I told Fliques.

'And your Auntie Jacqueline died by the hand of her lover. I know.' Fliques took another suck on his rock, and examined the result. The name of the town was still clearly visible. 'Can't see any grounds here for prosecution under the Trade Descriptions Act,' he said disappointedly.

'Can I go now, Inspector?' I asked.

'In a minute,' Fliques said. 'You are aware that Cuddles Farm is being run as a proper cat sanctuary now?'

'Yes, as a matter of fact, I am.'

'The new owner is a Mrs Cynthia Harrap. Did you know that?'

'Yes.'

'Are you acquainted with the lady, by any chance?'

'We met a few times,' I said cautiously.

Fliques laughed. 'Oh no, Bobby, I'm not going let you get away with that. Your relationship was much more intimate than is implied by "met a few times".'

How did he know? I wondered as my stomach did somersaults. How did he bloody know?

'I don't know what you're talking about,' I protested.

'She was your bridge partner, wasn't she, so you must have spent quite a lot of time together.'

'Yes, we did,' I admitted.

'So what made her take over the farm?'

'I think she decided she needed a new hobby,' I said.

Fliques' eyes narrowed. 'And what exactly happened to her *old* hobby?' he demanded.

'He moved away to darkest Wales,' I thought.

But aloud, I said, 'She'd filled up one stamp album, and didn't see the point in buying another one.'

'Yes, it's true what they say,' Fliques mused, 'philately will get you nowhere.'

'You just made a joke, Inspector,' I said.

'Yes, I didn't, didn't I?' Les Fliques said, sounding almost as surprised as I was. He took a final – possibly contemplative – lick of his stick of rock before speaking again. 'I like you, Bobby, I really do. You're a lad of spirit, and if it wasn't for you I'd probably still be a sergeant. But before I've finished, I'll find a way to nail you.'

'There's gratitude for you – as we say in Llawesuohtihs,' I joked nervously.

'Your Welsh accent's nearly as bad as your Irish one,' Fliques said cuttingly. 'I'll be around for a couple of days, asking questions about you. I'm staying at the ...' he consulted his black police notebook, '... at the Land of My Fathers Commercial Hotel. Come and see me if there's anything you want to get off your chest.'

He turned and walked back towards the centre of town, sucking on his rock again. I was about to move off myself, when he suddenly wheeled round and froze me to the spot with his piercing eyes.

'Was there ... was there something else, Inspector?' I called across the ten-yard gap which now separated us.

'Just one thing,' he shouted back. 'Purely as a matter of interest, Bobby, how long do you think *this* auntie's going to last?'

4

My involvement with Aunt Catherine's famous post box was due to a combination of geography and cardiology. My aunt's terraced house was located half-way up Gregynog Street. To the left, the road plunged recklessly down to the sea. To the right, it clawed its way up a small mountain. The post office was located to the right, making getting there a fair pull even for a healthy youth like me. For my aunt, who suffered from angina, it was almost an ordeal.

'So why don't you let me go instead,' I suggested, when she first mentioned her difficulties.

'I wouldn't think of it,' Aunt Catherine replied. 'My letters are far too important to be entrusted to you.'

She remained adamant about going herself for quite some time, but one day in early spring, when the burning pains in her chest were particularly bad, she gave way. 'But mind you bring them straight back to me,' she said.

'I will, Auntie,' I promised.

I set out determined to complete this task with the speed and efficiency I'd demonstrated in all the other things my aunt had assigned me. At first, everything went smoothly – no aeroplanes crash-landed on me as I climbed the hill, not a single fissure suddenly opened in the ground to swallow me up. It was only when I reached the post office that I hit a problem – in the form of a white-haired man in a heavy tweed jacket who was arguing with the only counter clerk on duty.

'Why can't I use this stamp?' the white-haired man demanded.

'I've told you a dozen times, Mr Jones,' the clerk said wearily, 'it's Mauritanian.'

'It's still a stamp, isn't it?' the customer asked.

'Not really.'

Mr Jones looked round in search of support, and his eye fell on me.

'Does it look like a stamp to you?' he asked.

'Well, yes, but—'

'He thinks it's a stamp,' Jones said, swinging back to the clerk.

'All right, it is a stamp,' the clerk admitted. 'But it's only legal in its country of origin.'

Realisation was beginning to dawn on Jones' face.

'Are you saying that if I go to Mauritania, I can use this stamp to post a letter to my niece in Cardiff?' he asked.

'Yes,' the clerk replied, with obvious relief.

'How long will it take me to get there?' Mr Jones asked.

'I don't know,' the clerk said. 'You'll have to check at the bus station. Now if that's all, sir …'

But it wasn't all. Mr Jones had a number of other urgent enquiries to make. If the cost of postal orders was going up, did that mean the pound was worth more – or less? Was it true that the government had yet again turned down his request to have a stamp issued commemorating his granddaughter's birthday? What was the Post Office going to about the poor reception he was getting on BBC2?

'He only comes in once a month, thank God,' the bedraggled clerk told me, three-quarters of an hour later. 'Now, let's see. It's P.O. Box 32 we're looking for, isn't it?'

There were eight letters waiting to be picked up.

'That's rather a lot, isn't it?' I asked.

'About average, I'd say,' the clerk replied. 'Sometimes she gets a few more, sometimes a few less, but normally she gets around eight a day.'

Was I tempted to open one of the letters as I rushed down the hill? Of course I was!

I was dying to know why so many people would write to an ageing widow living in the back of beyond.

And, of course, I wanted to know what the difference was between Aunt Catherine's ordinary correspondents and the "special" ones who Aunt Peggy had told me would do anything for her.

Oh yes, the temptation was there, all right – but so was my early training.

'*You should never, ever, read other people's letters,*' Mother used to say. '*That's as bad as spying on them.*'

So though my fingers itched to slit open one of the envelopes, the letters stayed safely in my pocket.

Aunt Catherine was waiting for me on the doorstep, with an anxious expression on her face.

'You've been a long time,' she gasped.

'There was a queue at the Post Office,' I explained.

'I was worried,' Aunt Catherine croaked. 'Those letters …' She placed a hand on her scrawny chest. 'I … I don't know what's worse for my angina – climbing up that hill, or fretting over you doing it.'

I'd never heard my aunt talk this way before. Imagine it – three whole sentences without her once resorting to one of her infamous supermarket images! Anxiety can do all kinds of strange things to people – and it had almost turned Aunt Catherine into a human being.

'Let's go inside, Auntie Catherine,' I said. 'You look as if you could use a cup of tea.'

'A cup of tea,' my aunt repeated, in a tone which suggested that what I'd just offered her was as strange and alien as a trip to the planet Venus.

'It'll do you good,' I told her.

'Yes,' Aunt Catherine agreed, pulling herself together a little. 'A cup of tea would be very nice.'

I led her into the kitchen, and sat her down in her favourite chair.

'Are all those letters to do with the work of the Mission?' I asked, playing on the fact that my late return from the Post Office had, for once, caused my aunt to drop her guard.

'No,' Aunt Catherine said, obviously still a little dazed and incautious. 'No, they're business.'

Business? I thought. What sort of business could my aunt possibly be involved in?

'Is that why you've got your computer,' I prodded, 'because you need it for your business?'

My aunt's eyes hardened. 'Computer? What computer?'

'The one you keep in the spare room upstairs.'

'How do you know about that?' my aunt demanded.

Why was she making such a fuss about it?

'You left the door to the spare room open once,' I said. 'I saw it as I walking past.'

Aunt Catherine relaxed. 'No, the computer is not for business,' she said. 'I have it for my lists.'

'Lists? Lists of what?'

'Of memberships,' my aunt said, almost dreamily. She began counting them off on her fingers. 'The Church of God the Rambler, Chepstow;

The Holy Sinners of Reading; God the Astronaut, Chipping Sodbury; The Second Coming Reserved Exclusively For Bradford, plc ... endless organisations, all striving, in their different ways, for salvation.'

She wasn't lying – not about that. When I finally got around to checking, that's exactly what I found – lists, endless lists, giving the names and addresses of a wide assortment of individual crackpots and the clearly lunatic organisations to which they belonged.

'Do you ever write to any of these people?' I asked.

'No.'

'Then why keep the lists at all?'

'Because it is a comfort to me to read the names, and to know that all over the country there are people spreading God's message.'

The old hypocrite. The lists weren't there to give her comfort – she kept them so she could do cross-referencing, and thus determine who was to be one of her "special" correspondents.

5

The Mission Hall was a corrugated-iron structure with a curved roof. From the air, it must have resembled a beached whale. From the ground, it just looked like a mistake.

It had been erected – hurriedly – at the start of the Second World War, to house the Home Guard. Adolf Hitler, back in Berlin, immediately realising its importance to Britain's strategic defence, had done his best to bomb it – but had failed. Instead, one of his misguided bombs had destroyed Probert's fish and chip shop, an act of destruction which inflicted far more damage to the town's morale than could ever have been achieved by blowing up a few old bank clerks and insurance agents who were playing at soldiers.

Just after the War, it had been purchased by a shady character from London, who claimed he wanted to use it as a store for his "novelty" goods. It did not take long for word of just how novel the goods were to spread around the town. The place was stormed by the Zionist Chapel and Townswomen's Guild Combined Shock Troops, and its entire contents were either burned or dumped into the sea. The smell of rubber hung over the town for several days, and prophylactics – singly or in packs of three – proved a hazard to shipping for several months after that.

After its flirtation with commerce, the building stood empty for several years. By the time Pastor Ives took it over, the weather had almost completed the task at which the Luftwaffe had failed, and whenever the wind blew in from the sea, the Mission creaked and groaned alarmingly. And then its saviour appeared on the horizon – a young man eager to please his aunt, a hardy lad willing to devote his weekends to tightening bolts, replacing panels and slotting in new supports.

'You are doing God's work, Robert,' Pastor Ives told me one day, as I was fixing a leak in the roof. 'The Mission may not seem much, but appearances are deceptive. Some of the finest products in the world are stored in places like this before they see the light of day in the supermarkets. This mission,' he waved his hand expansively, 'is God's warehouse. It is from here that my flock will be transported to the shelves of Paradise.'

The inside of God's warehouse had to seen to be believed. In many ways it was quite conventional. There was a font near the door, and rows of standard pews stretched from the back of the hall to the front. If you ignored the fact that the altar – dominated by a large cash register – had once served as a counter in Williams' High Class Drapery, you could have been excused for believing that it was a perfectly ordinary chapel.

Except for the walls!

The walls were plastered with captioned paintings, all of them the efforts of the good Pastor Ives.

And what subjects he chose: God gazing down lovingly on a young couple (closely resembling Adam and Eve) who are just about to sign a hire purchase agreement; Moses, exhorting his followers on to land of milk and honey – and the January sales;   Christ on the cross – immaculately turned out in His designer loincloth and Pierre Cardin crown of thorns – over which hung the caption, "He died that you might spend."

They were garish, yet at the same time skilfully executed, and, despite myself – despite the stomach churning it induced – I sometimes couldn't stop myself staring at them.

Yet even though it was a hideous place, I grew quite fond of the old Mission. It's impossible, I think, to spend as much time patching and mending as I did, without developing some affection for the object of your labours. And it's strange to reflect that without the deaths of Aunt Jacqueline and Aunt Peggy, I'd never have been there to fix it, and one night the wind would have blown a little too hard, bringing the whole edifice crashing down.

God moves in mysterious ways, His wonders to perform.

6

My reader may have noticed that thus far in my narrative of my life with Aunt Catherine, I have not mentioned my twin obsessions – bridge and sex. The reason for this is very simple – I was not getting much of either of them!

My aunt was, of course, the obstacle in both cases.

'Cards were your Aunt Jacqueline's downfall,' she told me, more than once. 'Had it not been for cards, she would have been alive today.'

'Yes, auntie, you're right,' I agreed – because, after all, what she'd said was quite true.

'They are truly the Devil's instrument,' my aunt would continue. 'I'd sooner give up my Flash and use an ordinary liquid cleaner than harbour a card player under my roof.'

Thus, although there was a bridge club in town, I never dared to cross its threshold. True, I did manage the occasional guilty game at school, but it was poor stuff, giving me the kick of rot-gut cider when what I really needed was the headiness of champagne.

And sex? From my Auntie Catherine's perspective, sex was even worse than cards.

'I once gave in to your Uncle Reginald's filthy demands,' she confided in me. 'But never again! And he was a better man for my refusal.'

Yes, Auntie, I thought – so *much* a better man that he ended up hanging himself in the outside privy on his allotment.

What I needed, I decided, was safe sex, by which I meant sex my aunt didn't find out about – because if there was even a hint that I was immersing myself in that particular pit of slime, I'd be out of the house before I could say coitus interruptus. Yet safe sex was not an easy thing to find in Llawesuohtihs, and after the unfortunate incident with Glynis and Elaine, I pretty much gave up looking.

****

Elaine was a pretty little redhead, a year above me in school. I first noticed her one lunchtime, when I was playing bridge. And *what* I noticed about her was that she was watching me, not the game. So it came as no surprise to me when she approached me the next day.

'Daddy's always going on at me to learn to play bridge,' she told me. 'He says it's such a useful social skill. Will you teach me?'

Most kids in Llawesuohtihs would have died rather than call their fathers "Daddy", and as for social skills, wasn't that some way of fiddling money out of the Social Security?

But Elaine's background was different to that of most of the rest of pupils. Her family lived on a small private housing estate, well out of town, where the men drove Range Rovers and wore chunky sweaters when they went out for "a quick half of bitter" at Sunday lunchtime.

'Will you?' Elaine asked me. 'Will you teach me?'

I could tell from the way she was looking at me that bridge was the last thing on her mind, but I smiled warmly, and said that, of course, I'd give her all the lessons she needed.

The pretence broke down during our first session. Soon we were into heavy kissing behind the bike sheds, and hurried fondling in empty classrooms. I couldn't really say it was satisfactory. Like the lunchtime bridge, it was better than nothing, but nowhere near enough.

'I want to go further,' I told Elaine during a quick mutual grope in the deserted Biology Lab, three weeks after our affair had begun.

'Me, too,' she said, gazing down at the bench. 'But where could we do it?'

'Your house?'

She looked embarrassed. 'You'd be seen,' she said. 'Our neighbours always notice when people from the town come onto the estate.'

I didn't quite like the way she said "people from the town", but when you're as close to the object of your desires as I was, you don't take offence easily.

'Well, maybe we could do it at my house,' I suggested.

'When?'

Yes, when?

The short answer was when I could be absolutely sure that my evil-doings would not be detected by Aunt Catherine's finely-tuned sin-antennae – and I didn't have a clue if such an opportunity would *ever* arise.

****

Glynis was, as Aunt Catherine might have said, an entirely different kettle of golden-battered cod fillets to Elaine. She worked in Visconti's Ice Cream Parlour, Llawesuohtihs' excuse for a social centre. She was a big girl – in all the best possible ways – with wild eyes and a wide, inviting mouth.

She was good for trade, the manager said, because the customers enjoyed her banter.

Like hell they did! It was not her banter but her boobs that the lads who crowded into Visconti's came for. Every time she bent over to place a fudge sundae on one of the tables, the place would go quiet. One day, we all knew, her low-cut blouse would give up the struggle and set those gorgeous breasts free. One day, some lucky lad would find himself being served a *knocker*bocker glory.

Glynis did not resent all the attention. On the contrary, she seemed to revel in it, and it was rumoured that she could be generous – very generous – if she took a liking to you.

I was no more impervious to Glynis' charms than the rest of the boys, but my relationship with Elaine was still developing, so while I might look, I had no intention of touching. But it was Glynis who made the running – Glynis who ambushed me in the alley outside Visconti's one night, pushed me up against the wall next to the dustbins, and pressed her body against mine.

'I's fancied you for a bit, hasn't I?' she said throatily.

'Has you?' I asked, in a state of shock.

'Yes, and you fancies me, doesn't you, boyo? I feels it in your trousers.'

I glanced nervously up and down the alley. We were on our own for the moment – but how long would that last?

'I really don't think we should …' I began.

But actions speak louder than words, and Glynis' action was to reach down for the zip in my trousers.

'Glynis …' I gasped.

Getting a hardened penis through the fly hole of a pair of underpants can be quite a tricky business, but she seemed to manage it with ease.

'There's better, isn't it?' she asked.

Better – but crazy. We couldn't do this – not in a bloody alley.

Her experienced hand moved up and down my shaft – stroke … stroke … stroke – a fingernail now and again pricking me lightly for the sake of variety.

'Glynis …' I said again, since this was, apparently, the only word I had left in my vocabulary.

I should have walked away. I knew back then that I should. But it's very hard to walk away when some nymphomaniac has your knob in her hand.

Stroke … stroke … stroke … stroke … stroke.

'Where does you live?' Glynis asked.

'Pardon?'

'Your address, like?'

Where *did* I live? Come to that, who was I? I was experiencing some difficulty in relating my normal life to what was happening just then.

'Well?' Glynis demanded.

'159 Gregynog Road,' some tiny, sane corner of my mind instructed my mouth to say.

'That's down from the Post Office, isn't it?'

Stroke … stroke … stroke … stroke … stroke.

'Yes,' I gurgled. 'Down from the Post Office.'

Stroke … stroke … stroke … stroke … stroke …

Ahhhhhhhh!

With practiced efficiency, Glynis returned the lion to his cage, and zipped up again.

'That was just a taster, like,' she said. 'I'll give you the full Banana Split some other time, but right now, I's got to get back to work.'

I watched her walking down the alley, swaying her hips in a way she must have copied from a vamp in some old silent film. I'd just had a very pleasant – but somewhat shattering – experience, and for the sake of the lads inside the ice cream parlour, I could only hope she'd wash her hands before she served any more Raspberry Surprises.

****

Only a few days after Elaine and I had decided to consummate our relationship – and even a shorter time since Glynis had spilled my seed in the alley next to Visconti's – my aunt announced both that she was giving a lecture in Abernuffa the following Saturday, and that my presence would not be required. As is often the case when the reverse is about to happen, it looked as if luck was running my way.

'Come round about half past two,' I said to Elaine during the school break the next day.

'Shall I use the back door?' she asked conspiratorially.

'There isn't one,' I told her. 'Or, at least, there is, but it only opens onto the garden.'

Elaine sniffed. 'You don't live in a back-to-back terraced house, do you?' she asked.

'As a matter of fact, yes.'

She sniffed again. 'Oh well, I suppose it's not your fault,' she conceded graciously.

7

Though it seemed to take forever, the great day finally arrived. At twelve o'clock my aunt left the house, and at two-thirty there was a knock on the front door, and I opened it to find Elaine standing there.

'Would you like a drink of something?' I asked as we grappled with each other in the hallway, 'or would you like to go straight upstairs?'

'We could just go straight upstairs,' Elaine said breathlessly.

God, but we were eager to get at it.

If only we'd been a little less eager, one of us might have noticed that we'd neglected to close the front door properly.

****

Stage One, the kissing and cuddling, was rushed through at breakneck speed, and it was only a few minutes before we were taking each other's clothes off.

What cute little breasts she'd got, I thought as I carelessly threw her bra over my shoulder.

How great it was going to feel to have those slim legs wrapped around me, I told myself as I lowered her onto the bed.

I'd waited a long time for this. Now it was finally going to happen – and nothing could go wrong.

'So this is what you gets up to behind my back, boyo,' said an amused voice from the doorway.

I turned round fast enough to give myself a whiplash fracture.

'Glynis!' I spluttered.

'The front door was open,' she said, starting to unbutton her blouse. 'I's not on duty until six, see, so we's got plenty of time.'

I glanced frantically at Elaine, and then back at Glynis.

'But I … we … that is …' I protested.

'I's done threesomes before,' Glynis said, dropping her skirt carelessly to the floor. 'They's good fun. An' from the look of your John Thomas, he's well up to the job.'

Elaine, her face turned bright red, had climbed into bed and pulled the sheet protectively up to her chin. If she thought threesomes were good fun, she was doing a good job of hiding it.

'You'll enjoy it once we gets started, girl,' Glynis said, removing her bra. 'I can do some lovely things with my tongue, I can.'

The colour drained from Elaine's face.

'Oh, my God,' she said faintly.

This was positively the worst day of my life, I thought. If I lived to be a hundred, nothing more horrendous than this could possibly happen.

Something more horrendous was about to happen. From downstairs came the sound of the front door opening.

'Why didn't you shut it properly?' I hissed at Glynis. 'That could be anybody coming in.'

'I did shut it properly,' she said huffily – though the attack of huffiness didn't stop her stripping her panties off.

If she'd closed it behind her, then it must have been opened with a key, and the only people who had keys were me and …

'Robert?' a voice called from the hallway.

'My auntie!' I said frantically. 'Get dressed! Get dressed!'

The girls stayed exactly where they were, Glynis through indifference, Elaine because of a temporary attack of paralysis.

'Please!' I begged, as I attempted to cram both my legs into the left leg of my jeans.

'Fancy bein' frightened of your auntie,' Glynis said scornfully. 'My mam don't care what I do, as long as I doesn't leave a stain on the carpet.'

I was having as much trouble getting both my legs into the right leg of my jeans as I'd encountered when I'd tried it with the left.

'Put your bloody clothes back on,' I pleaded.

'You oughts to be ashamed of yourself, actin' like this at your age,' Glynis told me. 'How old is you, anyway. Eighteen? Nineteen?'

'Fifteen,' I said, finally succeeding in getting one of my legs in the right hole.

'Fifteen! You can't be. You looks a lot older than that.'

'He is, honestly,' Elaine contributed from the bed. 'He's only in the Fifth Form. I'm in the Lower Sixth.'

'I'm sure she really wanted to know what year you were in,' I told Elaine as I made a hysterical grab for my shirt. 'Why don't you tell her about your hobbies, as well? I bet she'll be fascinated. And it's not as if we're in a hurry, is it?'

'I's eighteen,' Glynis mused, as if that fact alone was enough to stop me being my real age.

'Wonderful,' I said, fumbling with my shirt buttons. 'Glynis is eighteen. That's the best news I've heard today. Now, for Christ's sake, get dressed.'

'I certainly will,' Glynis said, reaching for her bra. 'I's no cradle-snatcher. Never was, and never will be.'

'Robert!' my aunt called again.

'I won't be a minute, Auntie,' I called from the top of the stairs. 'I'm just tidying my room.'

'Well, hurry up,' Aunt Catherine said impatiently.

Back in the bedroom, Glynis was almost dressed, and even Elaine was making some effort.

But did that really improve my situation?

From my aunt's perspective, weren't two clothed girls in my room nearly as bad as two naked ones?

I looked around for a hiding place. The wardrobe was big enough for one of them. The other would have to crawl under the bed. But how the hell was I going to talk them into it? I imagined myself trying.

'You'll find it quite comfortable in the cupboard, Glynis. And Elaine, I'm sorry you have to be the one who goes under the bed, but with boobs like hers, Glynis simply wouldn't fit. How long will you have to stay there? Not that long. I know for a fact my aunt's going to the early service tomorrow morning.'

No, that wouldn't work. I walked over to the window in search of inspiration, and found it in the shape of the coalhouse roof.

'I've got a way out,' I said excitedly.

'A way out?' Glynis repeated, sounding distinctly unenthusiastic.

'Yes. You could climb down the drainpipe onto the coalhouse. From there, it's only a short drop to the ground.'

'You must be bloody mad,' Glynis said.

'And what do we do once we're there?' Elaine asked. 'I mean, it is the garden of a back-to-back terraced house, isn't it?'

'This is no time for snobbishness,' I snapped. 'We'll work out what you do next once you're in the garden.'

'No chance,' Glynis said.

'I agree,' Elaine chipped in.

'Be reasonable,' I pleaded. 'Elaine, you'll probably be in as much trouble as me if this comes out. And as for you, Glynis,' I added with a touch of cunning brought about by fear, 'do you want it to get all around the town that you've been cradle-snatching?'

'Jesus Christ, no!' Glynis said.

'You've got a point,' Elaine concurred.

8

Aunt Catherine was sitting at the kitchen table.

'The meeting hall was double-booked,' she complained.

'Was it another church which wanted to use it?' I asked.

'No, it was not another church,' my aunt replied. 'It was the Licensed Victuallers Association! And the manageress – like the handmaiden of Satan that she is – let those purveyors of evil have it in preference to us.'

'Bad luck, Auntie,' I said. 'Would you like a nice cup of tea?'

'Of course I would like a nice cup of tea,' Aunt Catherine said irritably. 'I have been wanting a nice cup of tea since I first stepped through the door. And you have kept me waiting.'

From overhead came the sound of feet scraping against tiles.

'What was that?' my aunt asked.

'Birds,' I said hastily. 'Seagulls. There have been hundreds of them hanging about all day.' I needed to distract her. 'So tell me, Auntie,' I continued, 'what was your talk going to be about?'

'I was going to talk about raising funds for Africa,' my aunt said. 'You don't realise how lucky you are, living here. In many parts of the Dark Continent, there are no Kwik Saves or Safeways, as we know them.'

'Aren't there, Auntie?' I said. 'Tell me more.'

I needed to keep her talking, you see, because although she couldn't see it from where she was sitting, Elaine and Glynis had arrived in the garden. They'd obviously decided to take matters into their own hands, and instead of staying hidden they were heading for the back wall.

'Many Africans live in mud huts,' my aunt told me, 'and do their washing in the river – without the benefits of soap powder.'

'How terrible,' I said.

Elaine tried to reach the top of the wall, and fell far short. Glynis disappeared from my view for a moment, then re-appeared pushing the wheelbarrow. Elaine stood on it. She still wasn't tall enough. She pointed to something outside my range of vision, and Glynis vanished again.

'Is it any wonder they worship false idols when they do not even have the price of a tin of Huntley and Palmer's Tea Time Assorted in their pockets?' my aunt droned on.

'No,' I said. 'I don't suppose it is.'

Glynis returned with an old watering can, and placed it on its side in the barrow.

'That won't hold!' I screamed telepathically. 'That won't hold!'

My message went unheard. Elaine stepped on the watering can and, when it collapsed, fell arse over tit onto the lawn.

'We must encourage the poor black heathen to spend towards Jesus,' my aunt said.

'Oh God,' I prayed silently, 'even if you *are* the god Aunt Catherine thinks you are, help me now. Don't let her turn around. Don't let her see what's going on in the garden.'

Elaine had stood up, and dusted herself off. She didn't look any the worse for her fall. Glynis had replaced the watering can with a couple of seed boxes and, standing on them, already had one leg cocked over the wall. Then she was gone – and a few seconds later, so was Elaine.

'Never again,' I promised myself.

I had nearly disgraced myself in Aunt Catherine's eyes, and I needed to stay in her good books, at least for a while – because I was rapidly running out of aunts.

****

The rest of the details of the girls' odyssey were related to me later – rather coldly – by Elaine.

Having landed in the garden of 146 Llandaff Street, Glynis had walked boldly up to the back door, and knocked loudly.

'We's girl guides,' she announced to the surprised householder who answered the door.

'But what are you doing in my back garden?' the man demanded.

'We's on one of them whatsit tests,' Glynis told him.

'Initiative tests,' Elaine supplied.

'That's right,' Glynis agreed. 'We was supposed to be hikin' in the Brecon Beacons, wasn't we? Only we seems to have got lost. So if you'll just let us go through your house, like, we'll try again. Right?'

'Right,' said the man, who, according to Elaine, was looking a little shell-shocked by this time.

'And if you tells anybody about this,' Glynis said to Elaine, as they stepped out into the street, 'I swears to God I'll cut your heart out.'

'That goes double for me,' Elaine replied. 'With knobs on!'

****

In a way, I'm glad Glynis' intervention ended my affair with Elaine even before it had really got started. She'd never have satisfied me. I still yearned for the womanly embrace of Mrs Cynthia Harrap, you see, and even if Elaine had been willing to take up Glynis' suggestion of a threesome, it could never have been as good as the beautiful music Mrs Harrap and I used to make together. Or, to put it in terms my aunt would understand, I didn't want to swap my memories of Miracle Cynthia for two packets of ordinary women.

9

The regular work of the Mission was not enough for someone of Aunt Catherine's enthusiasm. She lectured at WIs, she taught Sunday school classes. And here, too, I was able to help her.

Take the Sunday school classes as an example. It was my job to go to the hall an hour before the class, take the heavy, old-fashioned board and easel out of the closet, and pin up the week's visual displays; that done, I would cover the whole thing up with a large cloth.

A few minutes later, the children would come shuffling reluctantly in, and take their places. And finally, my aunt would make her impressive entrance.

She was formidable in action, her scrawny neck thrust aggressively forward, her claw-like fingers scraping through the air as she made her point. I enjoyed all her stories, but perhaps my favourite – by virtue of its sheer ludicrousness – was The Good Shopkeeper.

'Jesus was asked, "Who is my neighbour",' she'd announce, 'and this is what He said. "There was once a man who was set upon by other men to whom he owed money. They stripped him financially naked and left him lying on the floor – for they'd re-possessed his three-piece suite, which was made of genuine leather and had real brass studs all along the top …"'

The children would sit perfectly still while she told the tale, their small hands clutching tightly at their small knees. Some appeared mesmerised, others merely terrified. But hypnotised or fearful, a look of complete incomprehension filled the eyes of each and every one of them.

'Who, then, was the man's neighbour?' Aunt Catherine would ask at the end of the story.

The children would stare back blankly.

'Was it the woman in the building society, who passed by on the other side of the counter?'

No response.

'Was it the bank manager who would not give him an overdraft?'
Silence.

'No, of course not. It was the Good Shopkeeper, wasn't it? He was the one who gave the man credit.'

Not a head nodded in agreement. The children remained as frozen as they had been since the beginning. But that was about to change, for now we were reaching the climax of the proceedings. My aunt would walk over to the board and easel, grip the cloth firmly, and whip it off so dramatically that even veterans flinched, while those children new to the game would actually scream.

There it would be for all to gaze on – the whole story revealed in Pastor Ives' lurid watercolours.

'See!' my aunt would demand. 'See the man set about by creditors! See the bank manager! See the Good Shopkeeper!'

I do not wish to portray my aunt's teaching as ineffective. It was far from that. Though the children have since grown into adults, I'm sure some of them feel a spasm of unease whenever they see the particular brand of corned beef that the Prodigal's father opened on his son's return home, and that even now they can't hear the *put-put* sound of a Japanese motorbike without thinking of Christ's entry into Jerusalem.

10

I looked back on my time in Norton – with the cats and Mrs Cynthia Harrap – as the golden period of my life. So it was only natural that, on occasion, I should wish it had not been necessary for Aunt Peggy to meet with her unfortunate accident. Yet what was done was done – as Mother used to say – and though I could scarcely be said to be happy with Aunt Catherine, I was quite prepared to tolerate it until I was old enough to strike out on my own.

It's very important that you appreciate this last point. I really *would have* stayed with Aunt Catherine until I turned eighteen – and I in no way sought what was about to happen.

Ernest Fellstead of Tunbridge Wells was the catalyst. If only he'd bothered to seal his letter properly, events would have taken an entirely different turn. But we can't really blame him, I suppose. How could we possibly expect him to make a decent job of gumming down the envelope flap when his hands were probably trembling nineteen to the dozen?

I noticed the flap of Ernest's Fellstead's letter was loose the moment I picked it up at the Post Office.

'*The fact that you could read it doesn't make it any less private,*' Mother's voice said in my ear.

True – but try to understand my position, Mother. Every day, I went to the Post Office and picked up seven or eight letters – business letters – for my aunt. Wasn't it natural that I should want to know what kind of business a half-mad widow with no apparent skills could be involved in?

'Read me! Read me!' the letter screamed from my pocket.

'You've carried hundreds of letters without yielding to temptation,' I told myself as I began the sharp descent to my aunt's house. 'Don't give in now.'

'What about your aunt's "special" correspondents?' the letter jeered. 'Wouldn't you like to know about them?'

I had already reached 203 Gregynog Road. I did not have to hold out for much longer. I fixed my gaze firmly on the horizon – the usual grey clouds hanging gloomily in the air, further depressing an already miserable sea – and kept walking.

'*Good boy*!' Mother encouraged.

'Last chance!' the letter warned.

I stopped and looked up and down the street. There was no one around. I reached into my pocket, pulled out the envelope, and removed the letter from it.

The paper was cheap and blue-lined, the writing shaky – and the message a revelation:

"Madam Cathy,

You set my pulse racing, my blood boiling. You are the queen of my heart, and though I know it can never be, I yearn for you nightly. Were it not for your precious gifts, which I hold to my cheek as I lie in bed, I could not go on.

Your affectionate slave

Ernest Fellstead (Mr)

P.S. I enclose a postal order for more of the same. I can't get enough of you!"

Madame Cathy?

Precious gift?

I knew then, as I had known after Sergeant Fliques' raid on Cuddles Farm, that I couldn't let matters rest there.

****

I assumed that the key to the computer room – like the one to Diamond Peggy the Cat Abuser's store – was hidden away, but I had no idea where, and as I stood in the living room and watched Aunt Catherine make her way down the street, I tried my best to get into her head.

Would she keep the key in her knickers' drawer, as Aunt Peggy had done? I hoped not – because that was the last place I wanted to look.

Was it in one of her precious packets of soap powder, then? No, she would have considered that practically sacrilegious.

My eye fell on the bookcase – and on Pastor Ives' magnum opus, *The Holy Trinity: Three for the Price of Two*. I removed the book from the shelf, and found the key sitting snugly behind it.

11

A large, old-fashioned oak desk dominated the computer room, and each of the objects which had been placed on it had – as in the pages of an Agatha Christie novel – its own special significance.

'We must apply our little grey cells,' I said to myself, in a Belgian accent which Les Fliques would no doubt have ridiculed.

At the corner of the desk was the IBM computer on which Aunt Catherine stored her list of lunatic religious organisations. Next to it lay one of the hairbrushes I had bought in Abernuffa the previous Saturday – and which was already half-bald.

Beyond the hairbrush was a tube of lipstick – *bright red* lipstick. Strange, since Aunt Catherine never used make-up.

'Except for business purposes,' I muttered to myself.

A pot of thick liquid was the next object for my attention. It looked like glue – and it was sticky enough to the touch – but it had the faint odour of fish paste.

There was only one more clue to exercise my grey cells – a curling iron with a few strands of hairbrush bristle clinging to it – but even without the letter which Aunt Catherine must have been working on just before she'd gone out, I already had a fair picture of how the racket worked.

I read the letter anyway.

"Dearest Walter," my aunt had written,

"I, too, long for our bodies to become one, but that can never be. Instead, I will plant a kiss on this paper and imagine it is your lips."

A bright red lipstick smudge followed.

"There is more," the letter continued. *"I will pick up this paper and imagine it to be your proud knight. Then I will place it between my legs, at the very entrance to the citadel I ache for you to storm, and I will keep it there until the juices of my passion have left their mark."*

The sticky patch below smelled faintly of fish paste.

"And more!" my aunt wrote. *"Some of the thatch from that heavenly mound in which you yearn to rub your strong, masculine nose, shall be yours, too".*

A strand of bristles – hot from the curling iron – had been sellotaped underneath.

The tone changed a little in the last paragraph.

"Dear, dear Walter, I do not know how I would survive without your kind gifts. But if, perhaps, you could make your next postal order a little more substantial, I would be forever in your debt."

There was – as my aunt had said – more. In the top desk drawer, I found a number of the kind of magazines which are only sold in adult bookshops.

'Are these just what you advertise in, Auntie?' I said aloud. 'Or are they your style primers, as well?'

In the middle drawer were letters to – and from – my aunt's clients. They were a mixed bunch, some wanting to feel Aunt Catherine's stiletto heel pressing down on their cheeks (Aunt Catherine! Stiletto heels!), others going into grisly detail about the way in which they would punish her for her disobedience. And to give her credit where it was due, my aunt had done a good job of replying, matching the tone of her own letters perfectly to theirs.

How did I feel about what I'd discovered? I was amused rather than outraged. Mother had not disapproved of sex, and it seemed to me that Aunt Catherine was doing very little harm.

So what if she took small amounts of money under false pretences? The people she was taking it from *wanted* to be fooled. It could even be argued that she was performing a public service – or a pubic one, anyway – by providing a safe outlet for all the perverts and deviants who wrote to her.

Thus, I didn't condemn her for her little racket at all – and she would have been quite safe if it hadn't been for the pile of letters in her bottom drawer.

Some of these letters were angry, others pleading, but all of them carried the same message:

"What I'm paying you is crippling me," one said. *"The children haven't had a holiday in three years."*

"My wife wanted to know where all the money had gone," another man wrote. *"And when I wouldn't – couldn't – tell her, she left me."*

"Show me a little mercy," a third begged. *"If you don't, I swear I'll kill myself."*

But mercy was not Aunt Catherine's strong point. However touching the plea, each poor victim received exactly the same form letter by return of post.

"Dear _____

Whilst I find your personal situation distressing, I am afraid it would be unfair to give you special consideration over my other clients.

You have only two alternatives. Should you send me your usual charitable contribution next month, you can rest assured it will be put to a good cause. Should you fail to do so, however, I am sure your pastor at _____ *will be most interested to see some of the letters which you wrote to me, and I still have in my possession."*

****

I knew now how she chose her "special" correspondents. Understood, too, how she'd been able to put pressure on Chief Constable Hampton – a member of the Law and Order Tabernacle – to pull Les Fliques off Aunt Peggy's case. Every time she got a new client, she'd check his name and address against the lists on her computer. If there was no match, then she'd enter into a normal business relationship, as she had with Walter and Ernest Fellstead (Mr). But if she did find a match – if the writer was a member of a religious congregation, with a position to keep up – then she had him by the short and curlies.

It only took a moment of weakness to answer Madame Cathy's advertisement in a dirty magazine, and yet the poor soul who'd done it could find himself paying for ever.

Who knew the damage Aunt Catherine had done over the years – how many lives she'd ruined?

What a revenge on men in general for the filthy demands Uncle Reginald had made on her before he hanged himself in the privy!

What a magnificent way of living out the doctrine of Christ the Consumer – a doctrine of unlimited, insatiable greed!

'What should I do, Mother?' I said.

But I had no real need to ask. I knew what Mother would want me to do – what she would have done herself, if she'd still been alive.

12

Aunt Catherine died shortly after that, and so I went to live with Aunt Sadie.

PART FIVE: The Queen of Spades

1

Aunt Sadie was standing on the platform, just as she'd promised she would be. It was seven years since I'd last seen her, but I recognised her immediately.

'I'm sorry I didn't come to the funeral,' she said, standing on tip-toe to kiss me. 'But, you know, it would have been hypocritical of me to turn up. I really loved your mother, but as for the rest of them ...'

I have described Aunt Sadie before – her corn-coloured hair, deep blue eyes and translucent skin – but now I took in some details which the eyes of childhood seemed to have missed. She was wearing a light, summery dress which, though not immodest, did nothing to hide her figure. Her legs were long and slim, her waist was narrow, her breasts firm and pointed. If I'd tried to conjure up a beautiful – sexy – woman in my imagination, I could not have done any better.

Aunt Sadie laughed. 'Have I changed that much?' she asked.

I realised I'd been staring at her, and blushed. 'You haven't changed at all,' I said.

She linked her arm through mine, and led me towards the barrier.

'I can see I'm going to have a shameless flatterer living under my roof,' she said.

'It's not flattery,' I blurted out. 'You really are beautiful.'

She laughed again. 'I suppose I don't look bad for a woman pushing middle age,' she conceded. 'Of course, part of the reason I've taken such good care of myself is that you simply *had to* in my line of business.'

'What exactly was your job in France?'

'Entertainment.'

'Singing and dancing?'

'Something like that,' my aunt said. 'The car's over there.'

It was a TR6 – old, but in immaculate condition. I put my cases in the boot, and climbed into the passenger seat beside my aunt. Sadie, I soon appreciated, was a good driver who, while not exactly aggressive, certainly took any advantage she could to get ahead.

'We'll have to get you driving lessons as soon as you're old enough,' she said as we shot past a heavy gravel lorry. 'It'll give you a bit of independence.'

Soon, we had left the town behind and were out in open countryside.

'I hope you'll like Shelton Bourne,' Aunt Sadie said. 'I hope you'll like the cottage, too. I fell in love with it the first time I saw it and that was – oh, ages ago. When I came back from France, and saw it was for sale, I couldn't believe my luck.'

'When *did* you come back from France?' I asked.

Aunt Sadie frowned. 'Over a year ago – but surely, you knew that already, didn't you?'

'No.'

'That's funny. I wrote to your Aunt Catherine and said that now I was established in England again, you could come and live me with if you wanted to. Didn't she even mention the possibility to you?'

Of course not! What master would ever give up a willing slave voluntarily? What did it matter to Catherine that I might have more chance of happiness in Shelton Bourne than in Llawesuohtihs? Someone had to collect her mail, repair the Mission and set up her lectures, didn't they?

'Look – here's your new home,' Aunt Sadie said, pulling up.

I looked – but I didn't believe. It was an old thatched cottage, with leaded windows. Until that moment, I'd thought that such places only existed on the lids of biscuit tins. I got out of the car and walked to the gate. To my left was a rose garden, and the sweet smell of the flowers drifted across and enveloped me. To my right was the rock garden, with a small stream cascading gently over the washed stones.

'You do like it, don't you?' Aunt Sadie asked anxiously.

'It's beautiful,' I said.

Everything seemed beautiful that day.

Aunt Sadie led me into her oak-beamed living room.

'You sit down over there, and I'll make a pot of tea,' she said. 'Then we can talk.'

Imagine that – an aunt of mine who made pots of tea herself. And when the tea arrived, it tasted both delicious and delicate. I told my aunt so.

'Flattery again,' she said. 'Well, actually, I do have it blended specially for me. It costs a little more, but then that's true of most of the good things in life.' She hesitated, as if she was reluctant to say what was really on her mind, then forced herself to speak. 'It's time to lay down the house rules,' she told me.

'I'll earn my keep,' I promised.

'Earn your keep?'

I shrugged. 'You know – the cleaning, the cooking, the repairs.'

'You'll do no such thing,' Aunt Sadie said hotly. 'As far as household chores go, we'll split them. I like cooking, and I don't mind doing the laundry. But I can't stand washing up so, if you don't mind, that'll be your job. We'll share out the cleaning between us. Does that seem fair?'

'Very fair,' I said, hardly able to believe my luck.

'But there are other matters I'm going to have to be firm on,' my aunt said ominously. 'You're still at school, so I'm not having you staying out until all hours of the night during the week.'

'Aunt Sadie, I—'

'Weekends are a different matter,' my aunt added hastily. 'Then, you can go and come as you choose. But if you want to entertain any friends here – and you want me out of the house – you'll have to let me know in advance.' She smiled uncertainly. 'Have I started turning into the wicked stepmother already?' she asked.

'No,' I said happily, 'not at all.'

2

We ate our first dinner together on the patio. It was a warm summer evening, and the air had that balmy quality, peculiar to England, which almost makes it worth putting up with a filthy climate for the rest of the year.

Sadie, on top of all her other accomplishments, was an excellent cook, and after years of eating new, improved, mighty-meaty beefburgers at Aunt Catherine's house, it was a pleasure to cut into a real filet mignon.

'In the kind of entertaining I did in France, a good meal played an important part,' Sadie told me. She laughed. 'Sometimes, if the meal was heavy enough, it was the only part.'

'What do you do now, Aunt Sadie?' I asked, because, for some reason I couldn't quite explain, it made me feel uncomfortable to talk about her time in France, and I felt the urge to change the subject.

'What do I do now?' Sadie repeated. 'I suppose you could say I'm semi-retired – but I'm very active in the local preservation society.'

As I would learn later, almost everyone in Shelton Bourne was involved in the preservation society. The villagers were off-comers, by and large – retired stock brokers and people of that ilk – rootless city folk who had embraced the rural tradition with a missionary zeal.

'There's a lot of work to be done on preservation,' Sadie said ominously. 'The vultures are hovering already.'

'The vultures?'

'The property developers. This is prime land, close to the motorway. They'd love to get their feet in the door, and if we don't fight back, they will. We've already beaten off one attack by that swine Cypher.'

Cypher. The name of Shelton Bourne's arch-fiend was new to me then, but as time passed I was to find out more about him than I ever wanted to know.

Sir Llewellyn Cypher – Lew to his many low friends in high places – was a construction magnate and architectural philistine. His skyscraper blocks loomed darkly over the landscape as monuments to ugliness. His shopping centres were nightmares in pre-cast concrete. Almost single-handed, he had converted the Georgian hamlet of Wentwell into Wentwell New Town – Went Wrong New Town to its inhabitants – an urban jungle of flyovers which flew over other fly-overs, and underpasses which passed under other underpasses.

Had Cypher owned the Sistine Chapel, it was said, he would have plastered the ceiling, installed neon lighting, and sold it to a fast food chain. If the Amazon rain forest had been his, he would have asphalted it as quickly as it could be burned down.

Where Cypher was involved, planning regulations were brushed aside. He employed an army of lawyers who even the shysters of the profession were wary about being seen with. He kept any number of local and national environmental officials awake at night, worrying over what would happen to their mortgage repayments if he ceased to be their friend.

It would be unfair to say he would resort to anything to get his own way – he drew the line at dirty tricks he had not yet thought of. He was, in every way, a formidable opponent – and when he eventually turned his attention to Shelton Bourne, he would bring into play his full repertoire of ruthlessness and corruption.

But that night on the patio, there was no hint of the battle to come. There were, instead, two people getting to know each other, chatting about this and that, eating good food, and – in Sadie's case – drinking a full bottle of wine.

The sun went down, and the rising moon cast a silvery glow over the remains of our feast. We listened to the chirp of the crickets, and the hoot of a passing owl. We watched the bats circling around the patio light. I felt as if I had come home at last.

Finally, towards midnight, Sadie stood up.

'You've had a long day,' she told me. 'I think you'd better get yourself off to bed.'

Only when she'd spoken did I realise how tired I was. I rose heavily to my feet, and started to collect up the dishes.

Sadie put a restraining hand on my arm.

'Leave that,' she said. 'You can start being Number One Washing Up Boy tomorrow. Tonight, your old auntie's going to spoil you.'

****

I'd been in bed for about fifteen minutes, and was almost asleep, when I heard the knock on the door.

'Come in,' I said.

The door opened slowly – almost reluctantly – and Sadie hovered on the threshold. She was wearing a long, slinky nightdress, and the hall light behind her cast her slim, beautiful body into relief.

'Just came to see if you'd settled in,' she said.

She slurred her words slightly, and I realised, for the first time, that she was a little drunk.

'I'm fine,' I assured her.

'You look very like him,' she told me.

'My father?'

'Very like him. I could have had him, you know.' She advanced uncertainly into the room. 'He wanted me – badly. But I couldn't have done it to Jennifer – to your mother. She needed him more than I did. Yet sometimes, I wish ...'

She was standing by my bed now. I longed to reach up and stroke her silky hair – to wrap my arms around her smooth, white neck and pull her closer to me.

But I didn't. My muscles tensed, my arms seemed glued to my sides, my whole body became as rigid as a corpse.

'Do you think ...?' she asked, her voice quavering with indecision.

'Think what, Auntie Sadie?' I croaked.

'Nothing. It's nice to have you here, Rob. It really is.'

She bent over and kissed me lightly on the forehead. And then she turned, and fled stumbling from the room.

3

It was autumn. The morning air was crisper than it had been when I first arrived in Shelton Bourne, and the lawn was heavy with dew. The days were growing shorter, too, and hedgerows which had seemed so drab in the full glory of summer were now ablaze with bright red berries.

Sadie and I watched the red admirals perching gracefully on the Michaelmas daisies, their wings spread to catch the weaker sunlight.

'They won't last through the winter,' Sadie said sadly. 'It's such a pity that beautiful things have to die.'

She had never spoken a truer word.

I was enrolled in the local secondary school by this time, and was doing as well as I chose to – which is to say just a little better than average.

Yet there was one school subject – albeit an extra-curricular one – which did catch my imagination.

Arts and Crafts!

Incredible, isn't it, that a non-joiner like me – a boy already dominated by two obsessions – should suddenly acquire a new hobby.

And I was good at it.

'You don't want to be going wasting your time on Maths and History and all that rubbish,' Mr Ferris, my metalwork teacher, told me. 'This is where your way lies – making jewellery.'

For it was to jewellery that I devoted my newly discovered talent. Brooches, bracelets, ear rings – lovingly and patiently, I made them all. And what did I do with them once they were finished? I gave them to Sadie, of course.

Not that jewellery-making was my only interest. I was playing bridge again. My partner was a retired solicitor called Martin Lord, and together, we did the local circuit. I would soon be a Club Master, the first step on a ladder of local, regional and national promotions which would eventually lead me to the title of Grand Master. Nothing could stop me – it was only a matter of time.

And sex? As my old friend Les Fliques might say, that requires means, motive and opportunity.

I had the means now. There need be no girls climbing over walls and pretending to be Girl Guides in Shelton Bourne – Sadie had made it quite plain that if I wanted to "entertain" girls at home, she would have no objection.

I had the opportunity, too. A number of girls, both at school and in the village shops, had hinted that they would like to get to know me better.

So all that was missing was the motive – I just didn't feel like it.

None of the girls really attracted me, you see. Oh, I suppose several of them were pretty enough – in their way. A couple of them could even have been called beautiful – at a push. But none of them had anything like Sadie's grace and charm. Thus, for the moment at least, I was more than willing to remain celibate.

4

Life was so full and happy that even the thought of the inevitable arrival of Les Fliques could not dampen my spirits. In fact, if truth be told, I was rather looking forward to it.

He came in late October, ambushing me at the school entrance, just as he had done in Llawesuohtihs.

He was holding a bag of roasted chestnuts in his hand.

'Very seasonal, Chief Inspector,' I said, cocky in my new security.

Fliques slowly munched the nut he'd just popped into his mouth, then said, 'Not trying to be funny, are you, Bobby?'

'Funny? About chestnuts?'

'About me being a Chief Inspector.'

'Aren't you?'

'I am not.'

If the sun had failed to set that evening, if winter had not followed autumn, I could not have been more surprised. Fliques' promotions between our meetings were a fact of life, a small, but important, part of an inexorable cosmic law.

'Maybe I'll be a CI by the next time,' Fliques said.

'There won't be a next time,' I promised him.

'What?' he said with mock-comic surprise. 'No more assaults with a deadly trophy? No more five-carat asphyxiations? No more heart attacks?'

'No.'

Fliques peeled a chestnut neatly with his teeth, and spat the skin back into his bag.

'Let's consider the last one,' he said. 'A slightly different modus operandi this time, wasn't it? You were miles away when your Auntie Jacqueline and Auntie Peggy died, but you were right there when your Auntie Catherine bought it ….'

****

Aunt Catherine is giving a demonstration lesson to Sunday school teachers from throughout the area.

'My method is to split the lesson into two parts,' my aunt says proudly. 'In the first part, I tell the story in a way which makes it relevant to the children. In the second part,' she points to the board and easel covered with the usual cloth, 'I reveal the same story in pictures.'

A quiet, spinsterish lady with a faint moustache raises a timid hand.

'Yes?' my aunt says sharply.

'I was just wondering … I mean … wouldn't it be better to show the pictures as you tell the story?'

'Certainly not!' Aunt Catherine replies, her voice thick with contempt. 'For just as we must put down the cash deposit before we can take away the television set, so we must listen to the story before we can have the pleasure of the pictures. Everyone knows that!'

'Oh, I see,' the spinster mumbles, looking both ashamed and humiliated.

'The Parable of the Talents,' my aunt announces grandly. 'It seems that a certain man was going away for a long holiday to Tenerife, where Thompson's had booked him into a five-star hotel which had a Jacuzzi in every bathroom. On the day of departure, he called his servants together. To one he gave two hundred pounds, to another one hundred pounds, and to the third fifty. Then he left.'

From the looks on the faces of the middle-aged ladies who make up my aunt's audience, it is plain that they would like to do the same.

'The first servant, on walking into town, saw there was a sale on at Rumblelows, and bought a freezer at a bargain price. The second, seeing special offers in Tesco, stocked the freezer with frozen food. The third, the unworthy one, did nothing with his money …'

On and on, my aunt drones. Many of the women in the audience have gone glassy-eyed, and most of the rest seem about to tear their hair out by the roots. Only the quiet spinster, apparently in an effort to compensate for her previous outrageous behaviour, pretends to be interested.

'Fling this useless servant out into the dark, the place of wailing and grinding of National Health dentures,' Aunt Catherine says, bringing her tale to an end. 'Now,' and she is looking at the spinster as she speaks, 'now, as anyone with even a little knowledge of how to teach would understand, is the time to reveal the display.'

The spinster sinks back as far as her hard wooden chair will let her, a mortified expression on her face.

My aunt marches over to the board and easel, whips off the cloth, and steps back.

'See!' she demands. 'See the good servants!'

An immediate change comes over the audience. Glazed eyes are suddenly wide. Mouths, previously set in a grim determination to stick this thing out until the end, flop helplessly open.

'See the freezer!' Aunt Catherine says.

'Big Hot Screws,' the quiet spinster reads aloud, not without a little malicious satisfaction.

'What?' my aunt asks.

'Inside: The Randy Sunday School Teachers Who Cum For Jesus,' the spinster answers.

Now, for the first time, Aunt Catherine looks at the board herself. The magazine cover from which the spinster has quoted has a photograph of a young woman carrying a Bible on it. She is wearing glasses but – regrettably – nothing else. And it is obvious from the angle at which the picture has been taken that the photographer is more interested in gynaecology than he is in religion.

Nor is that the only thing on the board. Radiating out from this central display are other examples of Aunt Catherine's trade.

'No!' my aunt croaks, as she sees a transparent envelope containing fake pubic hair.

'Urg!' she says, when she notices the sheets of paper smeared with lipstick and adhesive love juice.

'Aiee!' she cries, while examining the letters written to Madam Cathy, and samples of her blackmailing replies.

With her hand pressed tightly against her chest, she turns back to the audience.

'I can explain,' she gasps. 'I … I can explain … everything …'

Then her legs buckle beneath her.

Later, the doctor will say that she was probably dead by the time she hit the floor.

****

'You knew that your auntie had a cardiac condition,' Inspector Fliques said accusingly.

'So did a lot of other people.'

'And I suppose you'd say that a lot of other people could have mounted the display as well.'

'I set it up for the Parable of the Talents, then I went for a walk. The Mission wasn't locked. Anybody could have gone in and made the substitution.'

Fliques rummaged around in his paper bag for an uneaten chestnut, and came up with nothing but shells.

'Anybody could have called your Auntie Jacqueline's lover,' he said, 'or tipped me off about the jewels at your Auntie Peggy's farm. But it wasn't just anybody – it was you.'

'You can't prove that,' I told him.

'I can't prove it *yet*,' he admitted, 'but there'll be other chances. I know you better than you know yourself, Bobby, and I wouldn't give your Auntie Sadie more than two years maximum. And this time, you just might make a fatal slip. Then I'll have you.'

Fliques looked around for a litter bin, and then – there not being one in evidence – screwed up the paper bag and put it in his pocket. He turned his back on me and started to walk away, but I'd got used to his methods by now, and anticipated his sudden about-face.

'You'll be around for a few days?' I suggested. 'So if you were me, you'd make sure your bike lights were working properly?'

Fliques grinned. 'Right,' he agreed.

'By the way, Inspector Fliques,' I said, 'if you really want that promotion of yours, you could do a lot worse than drop a hint to your Chief Constable that you've been talking to someone who's been through my Auntie Catherine's correspondence.'

5

Shelton Bourne is perhaps most famous for its association with Digger Morton. It was there that Digger was raised, there that he was living in retirement at the time of his arrest and trial. Notwithstanding all his dastardly crimes, he was something of a local hero and in an odd sort of way he probably deserved his hero status, because he was, undoubtedly, an innovator – the man who turned the gentle art of piracy into something of a cold-blooded science.

The story goes like this. Digger had spent a hard day on the high seas, chasing – and failing to catch – a Spanish treasure galleon. That made it three that he'd missed since Sunday, so, all-in-all, it had not been a good week.

'Sod this for a game of buccaneers!' he muttered to himself as he sat in his cabin, a bottle of rum clutched in his hand, and his feet up on a crouching Negro slave girl.

There had to be a better way to make a dishonest living, he argued to himself. And then he had his idea. Instead of all this pursuit lark – involving as it did, endlessly mucking about with sails and swinging from ropes with a knife held between your teeth – why not make the victims come to him?

He chose as his new base a small island convenient for the main shipping lanes. The natives who already called it home objected to being supplanted, but by the judicious use of gunpowder and musket balls, Digger persuaded them that their souls – if not their bodies – should vacate the island, and soon he was master of all he surveyed. All he had to do now was to wait for the ships.

It was Digger himself who sailed out to meet the first one – a heavily armed English man-of-war.

'Help me, brother!' he shouted from his deliberately crude raft.

These were dangerous, pirate-infested waters, where even the British Navy was wary, but what threat could one man in tattered clothes possibly pose? A line was thrown down, and Digger climbed aboard.

According to his own testimony at the Chepstow Assizes, he was taken to the poop-deck, where the Captain happened to be at the time.

'Where have you come from, my good man?' the worthy officer asked.

'That island over there, sir,' Digger told him, pointing to a patch of greenery not three miles distant.

'And how long have you been a castaway?'

'We've been there for over a year, sir.'

'We? Are there other men with you?'

'No, sir.'

'You're not making sense.'

'It's not men on the island, sir – it's women.'

'Women?'

'Twenty of them, sir, ladies travelling to the New World, hoping to marry into the colonial nobility. Great beauties they are, all of them. But no man in his right mind would marry them now.'

The crewmen within earshot had stopped working, but the Captain didn't notice.

'Why will no man want to marry them?' he asked.

'Well, sir, the shipwreck turned 'em all a bit odd. They were very respectable before, but now they can't control themselves. Sex is the only thing that interests them.' Digger sank to his knees and hugged the Captain's legs. 'Please take me away, sir. There's only so much a man can stand. And they're on at me day and night.'

Some of the later captains who were victims of the scam refused to land. Not a wise move! Within seconds, they had a mutiny on their hands. Within minutes, they'd taken up permanent residence in Davy Jones' Locker.

Nothing like that happened with Digger's first victim. He was an English gentleman – by God – not a Frog or a Dago, and if there were damsels in distress, he'd jolly well go and rescue them, even if they were a little … err … strange in their habits. This, in its own way, was as unwise a decision as the ones taken by some of the Frogs and Dagoes he looked down his stupid English gentleman's nose at.

Actually, the only really wise course would have been to blow Digger out of the water as soon as he came into sight. But then it's always difficult to know these things in advance, isn't it?

As the ship sailed closer to the island, any idea the Captain may have had about trickery were dispelled by what he saw through his telescope. Three young ladies who – though he didn't know it – came direct from a successful appearance in Blind Mary's brothel, Nassau, were frolicking naked on the beach.

'I shall send a party of five men ashore,' the Captain announced to his First Officer.

The menacing mutters of the crew, half of whom were now on the poop-deck, disconcerted him.

'Or perhaps ten,' he hastily amended.

Most of the sailors seemed suddenly interested in cleaning their fingernails – for which purpose they had taken out their long seamen's knives.

'We will leave a skeleton crew of officers on board,' the Captain decided, 'and everyone else will go ashore. The men deserve a little leave.'

There were four longboats in all. The first, since it contained Digger himself, was allowed to land, but as soon as it touched the shore the pirates descended on it with such typical cries as 'Charge, me hearties,' and hacked the sailors to pieces.

The rest of the crew, finding their desire to visit the island had somewhat abated, turned their longboats around, and rowed rapidly back towards the ship.

'Cannons!' Digger roared.

Cannons quickly appeared from their hiding place between the trees at the edge of the jungle.

'Fire!' Digger ordered.

The cannon was a notoriously inaccurate instrument of destruction, but Digger's gunners were skilled at their trade and, more to the point, were motivated by the fact that they really liked to kill other people. They scored two direct hits, and soon the sea was full of driftwood and sailors. It was then that Digger's ship, the *Bloody Shovel*, appeared round the headland, causing the sailors in the remaining longboat to feel more than somewhat depressed.

'Ram 'em!' Digger screamed from the shore, and though the men on the *Bloody Shovel* couldn't hear him, that was exactly what they did.

By the time Digger boarded the man-of-war again, the officers had gone over the side, believing – correctly – that being eaten by sharks was preferable to falling into the hands of the pirates.

There was no reason why the scam shouldn't have worked forever. Who, after all, was left alive to reveal its mechanism? Yet with the passing of the years, Digger found he was growing bored with stabbing, shooting, skull-splitting and bloodletting in general. It was time to take his ill-gotten gains and retire, he decided.

He settled back in Shelton Bourne, a real local-boy-made-good. Since there were no living witnesses to his infamy – his last act as Captain having been to get his crew blind drunk on the deck of the *Bloody Shovel* and set the ship on fire – he could reasonably expect to live out his remaining days in peaceful respectability. And so he would have done, had not his craving for immortality made him commission one Daniel Defoe – already famous for his "true" histories of Robinson Crusoe and Moll Flanders – to ghost-write his memoirs. Morton intended the book to be published posthumously, and indeed it was – but post-humousness came quicker than he had anticipated because Defoe, calculating correctly that the rewards of informer were greater than those of ghost-writer, shopped him to the local constabulary.

He made a good death, the Chepstow Register reported.

'You may have found me,' he thundered from the gallows, 'but you'll never find my treasure – even though it's right under your noses!'

The crowd cheered him wildly, then munched on their baked potatoes as they watched him swing back and forth in front of them.

So Digger passed out of life, and into legend. His treasure became something of a local obsession. Several amateur historians made it their life's work, two of them publishing monographs on the subject. Generations of young children in the village had played an elaborate game called "Morton's Gold." The thriving Digger Morton Society met twice a month in the church hall. And the pub – always packed with tourists clutching metal detectors in the summer – went by the name of The Treasure Hunter's Arms.

Since I am not in the habit of going off at a tangent, you may wonder why, instead of talking about Aunt Sadie, I have devoted my efforts to describing the career of a notorious and long-dead pirate.

Or perhaps you think you already know.

Perhaps you assume that Morton's Treasure will have an important role in this part of my narrative – you may even assume that I find it.

If that is the case, you are half-right and half-wrong. I didn't find the treasure, although, in a way, it determined both my own future and my aunt's lack of one.

6

March came, and no sooner had the snow melted than Sir Llewellyn Cypher launched his spring campaign. The point of attack was a small parcel of land in front of the almshouse.

'It's a toe-hold, nothing more,' Sadie said. 'But it shows us which direction he's thinking of moving in.'

'It's the almshouse he really wants, you mean?'

'Exactly.'

The almshouse, I should explain, had long since ceased to have any charitable associations. It was now, in fact, two rows of twenty small cottages, the only part of the village where the original inhabitants existed in any force.

'Those cottages have large gardens as well,' Sadie pointed out. 'With all that land, Cypher could do whatever he wanted.'

'Is there any chance the people who are living in the cottages will sell?' I asked her.

Sadie shook her head. 'Not from what they've told me. They're mostly old couples. They were born in the village, and their dearest wish is to die here. But when they *do* die, who's to say what their children will do? Most of them don't live here – or even in the area – anymore. Why should they turn down a price which is well above market value?'

'It could be years before the process is completed,' I said.

'Ten years,' Sadie replied gloomily. 'Ten years at the most. And then the village will be ruined.'

I'd grown very fond of Shelton Bourne, but it was not for the love of rural England that I put my mind to creating a scheme which would protect the almshouse forever. I did it because I wanted to please Aunt Sadie.

****

The idea started to form in my head while watching him on *Joyspear*, the popular BBC chat show which was later to make me something of a celebrity. Cypher had agreed to appear on the programme mainly because his latest development proposal, the erection of a bowling alley and cinema complex on the site of an ancient Celtic burial ground, had caused something of a furore in the press.

'Balls to the Welsh!' had proclaimed one of the tabloids, following the headline with an article which, though written in simple vocabulary, left me confused as to which side it was on.

'Cypher 1, Celtic 0 – but suspicions of foul play!' trumpeted another, the newspaper for which, a few years in the future, my late fiancée Rosalyn would do such sterling work.

'It will be a great cultural and historical loss,' said one of the heavier dailies, showing by its choice of verb tenses that though it was choosing to protest, it considered the fight already lost.

'Sacrilege!' screamed *The Druids' Monthly*, though since it had an average circulation of only a hundred and fifty, its protest had little impact.

And so it was left to Cadbury Joyspear, the chubby Irishman whose salary accounted for about half the BBC's annual budget, to bring Cypher down a peg or two.

Joyspear's first guest, an octogenarian who'd gone round the world on a monocycle while playing *Rule Britannia* on a harmonica, had some novelty value, but it was plain half-way through his interview that the audience was waiting impatiently for the main event.

Joyspear looked sincerely at the camera. 'My next guest is perhaps the most controversial builder in Britain today,' he said. 'Will you welcome Sir Llewellyn Cypher.'

The audience clapped, and Cypher walked down the stairs. I'm not quite sure what I'd been expecting – a giant of a man, perhaps, with a concrete mixer of a mouth and a chin you could have driven rivets in with – but Cypher's appearance took me completely by surprise. Though he was quite tall, he was also remarkably thin. He had grey hair, combed straight back from his widow's peak, but sticking up in small tufts over each ear. His face was deathly pale, making the narrow eyebrows which snaked across his forehead seem blacker than they really were. He had eyes of the sort you feel are watching you in a thick, dark wood on a stormy night. His nose was hooked, his mouth small, and from his chin hung a pointed Mephistophelian beard. I shuddered and found myself glancing down at his feet, just to make sure they were not actually cloven hooves.

Joyspear uncrossed his legs and leant forward slightly, a sure sign to anyone familiar with his body language that he was sliding into attack mode.

'Sir Lew,' he began, 'it has been said that you're the Genghis Khan of the modern building industry. How would you respond to that?'

Cypher stroked his beard, and I felt the hairs on the back of my neck prickle.

'I can't respond to it,' he said. 'I've never seen one of Genghis Khan's car parks.'

Joyspear looked a little nonplussed. 'What I mean is, people think of you as something of a wrecker,' he said.

'That's nonsense,' Cypher replied. 'I'm not a wrecker, I'm a builder. I take perfectly empty tracts of land and stick huge concrete blocks on them.'

'Exactly,' Joyspear said, getting back on track. 'And some of the buildings you've erected, in what was once unspoiled countryside, have been pretty ugly, haven't they?'

'Yes.'

'I beg your pardon?' said Joyspear, who had not been expecting that answer at all.

'Yes, I've erected some pretty ugly buildings in what was once unspoilt countryside,' Cypher told him. 'If it will make your job any easier, I'll go so far as to say that I've erected some horrendously ugly buildings on what was once *beautiful* countryside.'

Was Cypher's apparent candour nothing more than a trap?

Joyspear looked as though *he* thought it was.

'Why do you do it?' he asked cautiously. 'Isn't it just as simple to put up an attractive building as it is to put up an ugly one?'

'No,' Cypher said. 'It's always harder to do things well than to do them badly. Anyway, why should I bother?'

Joyspear switched his expression to one of mild outrage.

'You surely have some responsibility to the environment ...' he began.

'If you want beautiful buildings, go to Athens,' Cypher interrupted him. 'Have you seen the Parthenon? It's a marvellous piece of work. And it will still be standing when all the rubbish I've built has long since fallen down.'

'You still haven't ...'

'It was built in the Golden Age of Greece,' Cypher said. 'Do you think this is another golden age?'

Joyspear loosened his tie slightly. 'Err … no,' he said. 'Not exactly.'

'This is an age when people grab whatever they can – and to hell with anyone else.'

'Including you?' Joyspear asked, fighting back.

'Especially me!' Cypher responded. 'I'm the most advanced man I know. I'm right at the top of the evolutionary scale.'

'But …' Joyspear protested.

'We've turned into a race of greedy, grabbing, sweaty materialists,' Cypher ploughed on. 'The ancient Greeks went to see great comedies and tragedies as a way of purging their souls. We stay at home and watch other people on quiz shows win prizes we wish we could afford ourselves.'

'I …'

'You get the architecture you deserve. This is an ugly age: I give it ugly buildings. And do you know why I can say that? It's because as long as I keep my prices low, nobody cares enough to try and stop me.'

Joyspear was famous for his coolness in the face of crisis. Now, however, he seemed to be in trouble. His face had gone as white as Cypher's, and the microphone on his lapel picked up the fact that his breathing had been reduced to short gasps. He looked like nothing so much as a man who suddenly discovers that his soul has been sucked from him while he wasn't looking.

Joyspear's director, no doubt to shield us from the sight of his rapidly crumbling star, had the camera sweep the audience – then probably wished he hadn't, because Joyspear was not alone in his discomfort. A number of men had twisted their ties into knots, and several of the women looked on the point of hysterics. Even the monocyclist, now back on camera, was fiddling nervously with his harmonica.

It wasn't so much Cypher's *words* which had produced this effect, it was his *presence*. The man generated an aura of naked, unashamed greed which was suffocating. Worse, he managed to suggest that he was nothing more than a magnified reflection of what is in all of us. He made me feel uneasy, nearly a hundred miles from the television centre – it must have been hell in the studio itself.

'Well, that … that seems to be all we have time for,' Cadbury Joyspear stuttered.

The camera panned round, accidentally revealing the floor manager, who was frantically signalling that the show still had several minutes to run.

'Yes, we have to go now,' Joyspear said off camera, in a shaky, yet determined voice. 'We'll be back next week, when my special guest will be … will be … someone else.'

The credits rolled. For a second, the screen went blank, then it was filled with a hastily slotted-in video of Queen singing *Another One Bites the Dust*.

'He's going to be a dangerous enemy,' I said.

Aunt Sadie made no reply. She was still staring at the television screen with an intensity which even Freddie Mercury, one of the most charismatic rock stars of the decade, didn't seem to merit.

'Auntie Sadie?' I said. 'Is anything the matter, Auntie Sadie?'

This time I did seem to get through to her.

'I'm sorry, Rob. What was that you said?'

'He's going to be a dangerous enemy,' I repeated.

'What power he has,' said Aunt Sadie, in what was more a statement than a reply.

7

I spent most of the night analysing and re-analysing my scheme to save Shelton Bourne from the evil clutches of Sir Llewellyn Cypher, and, finding no obvious weaknesses in it, I put it to Aunt Sadie over breakfast.

'It's very simple,' I told her. 'There are enough well-heeled conservationists living in the village to form a limited company and buy all the cottages in the almshouse.'

'But the old folks will never sell. They want to stay there.'

'That's the point – they can. That will be part of the deal. They get the money now, but they keep their homes until they die, at which point the cottage reverts to the company. And then you can lease it out again. It doesn't matter how long the lease is, because as long as the company controls the freehold, Cypher can't touch it.'

'Will people want to invest in a company which won't show a return for a long time?' Aunt Sadie asked.

'Do they want a drive-in discotheque and car-exhaust franchise on the edge of their village?' I countered.

'It just might work,' my aunt said.

****

It did work! Three weeks later, Shelton Bourne plc was registered at Company House. Aunt Sadie was its Chairperson and Managing Director.

I devoted even more of my energy to making the company work than I did to playing bridge. I spent hours arguing with retired colonels and ex-civil servants that it was in their own interest to invest in the company.

'If you want to know what it'll be like living near a discotheque,' I told them, 'just put a metal bucket over your head, and then get someone to hit the bucket with a large hammer.'

They nodded thoughtfully and then reached for their cheque books.

I gave over days and days to persuading the pensioners in the almshouse that they would be better off signing their property over to Shelton Bourne plc.

'You'll keep your home,' I said to one doubting old woman, 'but at the same time, you'll get some money.'

'So I could go and see my grandchildren in Australia!'

'Of course you could.'

By the end of June, we'd raised all the money we needed. By the middle of July, the houses were ours. I flattered myself that my contribution had been vital – my logic swaying the investors, my earnestness and transparent honesty convincing the old folks that they were in safe hands. Yes, whichever way I looked at it, a great deal of the credit had to go to me – which meant, of course, that if anything went wrong, I should shoulder a major part of the blame.

And things did go wrong – as they were bound to, when dealing with a demon like Sir Llewellyn Cypher.

8

The first whiff of the trouble ahead did not reach me until the middle of December, and had I not been such an obsessive bridge player, I might not have smelled it until even later. It was my partner, Martin Lord, who gave off the odour. He'd been a competent player up until then, but suddenly his game went to pieces. I carried him through a few matches without complaint, but when, in the last big pre-Xmas tournament, he failed to double the opposition's rashly bid six no-trumps – even though he held two aces and had the lead – I felt I had to say something.

'Are you ill, Mr Lord?' I asked him.

'Ill?' he replied, avoiding my eyes. 'Yes – ill with worry.'

Ill with guilt, too, by the look of him, I thought.

But apart from screwing up a few matches – which was annoying, but didn't really matter in the long term – what could he possibly have to feel guilty about?

'It might help to talk about it,' I suggested.

'You're a good boy, Rob,' Lord said, patting me affectionately on the shoulder, but still keeping well clear of any eye contact.

'Is it money?' I asked.

'Of course it's money,' Lord said, laughing hollowly. 'The result of forty years' hard work wiped out just like that.'

'Have you made some bad investments?'

'No, it was my broker who did that,' Lord said tiredly.

'But you must have agreed to them.'

'He didn't consult me. I trusted him completely, and he had power of attorney, you see. Known him for years, and he's always been such a sensible, conservative chap before, the sort who deals mainly in Gilts and Treasury Bonds. But the last few months, I don't know, he seems to have gone completely haywire. What could have possessed him to sink half my savings into a company prospecting for diamonds in the Lake District? And as for that scheme for laying a floating railway across the Atlantic Ocean …'

The stench of corruption was filling my nostrils by now. Martin Lord's guilty looks, the timing of his broker's going haywire – it was all starting to make sense.

'You sold your shares in Shelton Bourne plc, didn't you?' I said.

'I had to, just to stay afloat – which is more than the bloody transatlantic railway did,' Lord confessed. He put his hand back on my shoulder. 'I'm sorry, Rob. I know how hard you've worked on our behalf.'

'And who did you sell them to?'

'A company called B.L. Zebub. I think it's Belgian.'

It was, but it was also wholly owned by a Spanish company – Dia Blo S.A. – which was, in turn, a subsidiary of Llewellyn Cypher (UK) plc.

And the broker who was so profligate with my partner's carefully accumulated savings? By the time Martin Lord and I were having this conversation, that broker was already CEO of Llecyph Investments plc, a company created with the sole purpose of giving him his just reward.

****

Aunt Sadie and I turned our usual round of Christmas visits into interrogations.

'Yes,' Mr Paice at the Old Mill admitted. 'I have sold my shares. The bank called in a short-term loan my son had taken out on his business. No explanation – they just said they wanted their money back. I couldn't let him go to the wall, could I? And the shares in SB were the only way I could raise cash in a hurry.'

'Certainly I sold them,' Wing Commander Crabtree of Riseholme said defiantly. 'Got a damn good price for them, too. And there's no point in looking at me like that, Rob. I fought in the War for the right to sell my shares when I wanted to.'

'Well … err … yes, I did sell them,' Mr Holroyd of Hollywell House mumbled. 'And I'll tell you why, Rob, because I know I can rely on you not to repeat it. I've been seeing a certain young lady in London, and it appears that someone, somehow, managed to take certain pictures of us – pictures which my wife, Mrs Holroyd, might possibly misinterpret if she saw them.'

'You mean pictures of you in bed with her?' I asked.

'Not just in bed,' Holroyd said gloomily. 'On the tumble drier, in the chest freezer, under the sink – God, she was an inventive little minx.'

'And you were told that if you didn't sell your shares, the photographs would find their way to your wife?'

'Not in so many words, but that was what was meant.' Holroyd shuddered. 'Mrs Holroyd has many fine qualities, Rob, but the quality of mercy is not numbered among them.'

****

Our round of Christmas visits brought nothing but gloom. Cypher now had control of about 30% of our company, my aunt and I estimated, and if we didn't do something about it now, he could soon have a great deal more.

We held a meeting of the surviving shareholders just before the New Year. The village hall was still decked with streamers, and as I climbed onto the platform, the portrait of Digger Morton – edged with tinsel – glared down at me.

'Digger never gave anyone a second chance,' I told my audience towards the end of my speech, 'and neither will Sir Llewellyn Cypher. The village is a treasure chest for Cypher, and all he needs is a way to dig it up. Please don't help provide him with a spade.'

It was a little trite – I knew that even as I was saying it – but the effect it had on the retired businessmen and military dinosaurs who'd trudged through the snow to listen to me was electric. Mr Acland, who'd spent a career buried in the sombre world of discount undertaking, looked positively alive with enthusiasm. Colonel Todd was ready to hobble home, rummage through the attic for his sword, and lead the charge against headquarters.

'You've done a marvellous job, Rob,' Aunt Sadie assured me. 'After what you said, Cypher won't be able to get his hands on any more of our shares.'

And I nodded – almost complacently – unaware of just how powerful Cypher was.

Unaware of the enemy within!

9

In March, I learned that Professor Smallridge had crowned a lifetime of advocating a return to Olde England by sinking his money into a tin mine in Cornwall.

'And the beauty of it is, we'll be using methods of extraction which go right back to the Middle Ages,' he told me excitedly.

'But will it be economically viable?' I asked.

'What?' the professor replied, blinking uncomprehendingly at me.

'Will it be able to compete with the Malaysians?'

'Malaysians?'

It was pointless my saying more. I should have realised earlier that for a man who mentally dwelt in an age when maps of all the land masses beyond Europe showed nothing but a tentative coastline and fiery sea serpents, my question about the Malaysian tin industry had little meaning.

The tin mine failed, as it was intended to. Professor Smallridge lost a modest amount in comparison to the sum invested by the majority shareholder, but then Sir Llewellyn Cypher could stand the loss, and Smallridge could not. In order to avoid bankruptcy, the professor was forced to sell his shares in SB.

****

In April, Dr Mulroon confessed that he had sold his shares, too.

'I had to,' he told me as we sat together in his pretty, pretty living room.

'Had to?'

'I enjoy the company of young men, you see. I mean, I don't do anything improper, I just like to talk to them.'

'Your hand is on my knee, Dr Mulroon,' I told him.

'So it is,' he agreed, apparently surprised by the discovery.

'Take it off.'

Mulroon removed the hand, and crammed it awkwardly into his jacket pocket to prevent it wandering again.

'Anyway,' he continued, 'one of my young friends – a charming boy called Bunnie, such lovely pink hair – well, his mother needed an operation, you see. And I couldn't refuse, could I? I mean, I did try, but he got quite cross and started making all sorts of nasty threats.'

****

Sir Anthony Fitzsimmons, the village's only baronet, had a penchant for the horses.

'It's in the blood,' he boasted. 'My grandfather was a giant of the turf. Bet a thousand guineas – and that was real money in those days – without even blinking. He made an absolute fortune out of the nags.'

It was unfortunate for Shelton Bourne plc, then, that Sir Anthony himself was watered-down stock.

'Can't understand it,' he told me. 'Met this perfectly splendid chap over a few drinks at my club, and he said he had a certain winner in the two o'clock at Ascot. Knew for a fact it had been stuffed up to the eyeballs with pep pills. And then he was even decent enough to ring up his bookmaker for me.'

'But the horse didn't win, did it?' I asked.

'Bit of bad luck there – fell at the first furlong,' Sir Anthony admitted. 'But then this fellow said never mind, because he had the name of a sure thing in the three-thirty at Doncaster, and if I put my packet on that, I'd get all my money back and more. Well, I'd had a few drinks, and it started to seem like a pretty good idea.'

'And that horse lost, too?' I asked, fearing the worst.

'Well, yes. As a matter of fact, it came in seventh. But you can't blame this chap in the club for that. Horse had always done well before. Even the tipsters were surprised.'

But not, presumably, the horse's owner – Sir Llewellyn Cypher!

****

'You worry too much,' Aunt Sadie told me as we sat side by side on the patio, watching the swallows swoop.

'Of course I worry,' I said. 'This was all my idea, and now it looks as if it's doomed. Cypher's managed to con or bully nearly two dozen people since January, and now he's got forty-eight percent of the shares. Another three percent and he'll be in complete control.'

My aunt reached over, and ruffled my hair.

'Rob, we are happy together, aren't we?' she said.

'Of course.'

'And whatever happens, nothing can change that?'

'I don't think so.'

'Then stop trying to spoil a perfect summer evening by taking all the troubles of the world on your own shoulders.'

'I can't help it,' I said. 'It's the way Mother brought me up.'

Aunt Sadie sighed heavily. 'Ah yes, your mother. Always your mother. There are times when I'd have liked to ... I sometimes wish Catherine, Jacqueline, Peggy and I had never agreed ...'

She stopped abruptly.

'What is it?' I asked, alarmed by the edge to her voice.

'Drinks,' Aunt Sadie said. 'We need some drinks.'

Then she stood up and rushed through the French windows into the house.

She emerged again, a few minutes later, carrying a tray containing a whisky bottle, two glasses and a soda siphon.

'I think it's time you tried it,' she said, by way of explanation. 'After all, you are almost a man.'

'Okay, I will,' I agreed.

She poured two glasses, handed one to me, and sat down again.

'It's only the lame ducks who've sold their shares,' she said. 'The ones remaining are as solid as rocks. And without another three percent, Cypher can do nothing.'

'I'm not convinced,' I told her.

'I've got to go down to London for a couple of days soon,' Aunt Sadie said. 'While I'm there, I'll pop in on a few of my old friends in the City, and ask them exactly what Cypher might try, and what we can do to prevent it. Would that make you feel better?'

'Much,' I admitted.

'Right, that's dealt with,' my aunt said, draping her arm over my shoulder. 'Now let's not waste the evening. Let's pretend it's the last one that you and I will have together and—'

'Don't talk that way, Sadie!' I interrupted. 'I don't like it.'

My aunt gently stroked my hair.

'In this world, my dear sweet Rob, we all have to put up with things we don't like very much,' she said. 'Would it be so very hard to pretend – if you knew that by pretending, you'd be pleasing your old auntie?'

I grinned. 'You know how to fight dirty, don't you?'

'Yes,' my aunt said seriously. 'Yes, I do.'

'All right,' I conceded, 'we'll pretend it's our last evening.'

The unfamiliar taste of whisky left an exciting tang in my mouth. My aunt's skin felt soft and cool against my neck. Together we sat perfectly still – perfectly contented – and watched the sun set.

10

Aunt Sadie, in her own magical way, had managed to melt my mood of despondency, and as I drove her into Hoxwold to catch the London train, I was feeling on top of the world. True, there was the dark cloud of A-Levels hanging over me, but it did not hang as heavily as it did over my contemporaries – I was confident of doing reasonably well, and anyway, I'd never contemplated a university career. As for the other business – Shelton Bourne plc – I was sure that Aunt Sadie, who could do anything she set her mind to, would come up with a solution while she was in London.

I changed gear, and the back of my hand brushed against my aunt's knee. I turned to look at her. The sun shone on her hair, making it more golden than ever. She was wearing a simple white blouse which clung to her rounded breasts, and a lightweight summer suit. On the lapel of her jacket, she was proudly displaying the latest brooch I'd made for her.

I imagined my future. Playing bridge in exotic places – Nice, Hong Kong, Los Angeles. After the game was over, I would meet Sadie in a bar, and together we would walk into dinner. And I knew I would feel proud – so very, very proud. What man could not feel proud when he was beside such a beautiful woman?

I parked outside Hoxwold Station and saw my aunt to the train.

'I'll only be two days,' she said through the open carriage window, 'three at the most. You'll be all right, won't you?'

'Of course I'll be all right,' I told her. 'Before I came to live with you, I'd been looking after myself for years.'

My aunt smiled. Sadly, I thought.

'Try to miss me just a little bit,' she said.

'I didn't mean that I wouldn't miss you when I said I'll be all right,' I protested. 'I didn't mean that at all.'

The guard blew his whistle. Aunt Sadie leant forward, and kissed me full on the lips.

'And don't go breaking any speed records on the way back home,' she called as the train began to pull out of the station. 'Remember, you haven't been driving that long.'

****

I drove slowly along the country lanes back to Shelton Bourne, the top of the TR6 up, and a gentle breeze blowing through my hair. Crab apple and blue germander speedwell bloomed in the hedgerows. Starry-flowered greater stitchwort grew in clusters along the grassy banks. I pulled up and got out of the car. To my right lay a field of wheat, still a vivid pale green. To my left was a small wood, its floor carpeted with bluebells.

'Nature …' I said softly to myself, for no particular reason, '… beautiful, tranquil nature.'

A family of voles – a mother and four babies – emerged from the long grass. They scuttled around, confused to suddenly lose their protective covering, disorientated now that the springy ground had given way to unyielding gravel.

'Go back where you belong,' I told them silently. 'Go back to what you feel comfortable in.'

They were given no chance to follow my wise, unspoken advice. One second the voles and I were alone on the lane, the next – in a brown flash – we had been joined by a creature which must often have filled the voles' furry little nightmares.

How enormous the weasel must have seemed to the tiny creatures it towered over.

How powerful.

How invincible.

The mother vole could do nothing but squeak urgent messages of danger to her offspring. But she was too late – far too late. The weasel already had one baby in its mouth and was vigorously shaking it, while a second struggled ineffectually under its giant paw.

The survivors of the vole family scattered, disappearing into different parts of the vast, green jungle from which they had come. The weasel, content with its cull, made no attempt to follow. I climbed back into the TR6, and headed for the lovely village of Shelton Bourne.

****

I heard the roar of the monsters in the distance, but it was not until I'd almost reached the junction with the main road that I saw them. They moved as slowly as a funeral cortège, as inexorably as tanks trundling into battle. There were heavy dumper trucks, their headlights glinting malevolently. There were mighty bulldozers, worthy of the Juggernaut. There were pile-drivers, their huge steel pistons hanging in the air but ready, at a moment's notice, to slam down and pulverise whatever lay in their path.

None of them stopped in order to let me into the lane of traffic, even though there was now a queue building up behind me. I was not surprised. I might as well have expected a river in full flood – or a glacier grinding its way forward – to stop for my convenience.

On and on the monstrous procession lumbered, until it had all finally passed. The rear-guard was a yellow JCB digger, its mechanical arm raised menacingly high in the air, like the head of an advancing Tyrannosaurus Rex.

How enormous that JCB seemed as it towered over me and my tiny vehicle, I thought.

How powerful.

How invincible.

The procession rumbled through the village – rattling windows, spitting mud on the white-washed cottages, crushing curb stones as it mounted the pavements which fringed Shelton Bourne's narrow streets. The journey's end, as I'd always known it would be, was the land in front of the almshouse – Sir Llewellyn Cypher's toe-hold in the village.

When I'd passed the site on the way to Hoxwold only two hours earlier, it had been nothing but a piece of waste land, a place to walk dogs and pick early morning mushrooms. Now, it had been completely transformed. A high wire fence surrounded it as though it were a prison. Portable cabins squatted in one corner, with as much assurance as if they'd occupied the same spot for centuries. Where the sun had smiled kindly down on dew-tipped grass that morning, there was now a morass.

But horrifying as all these things were, it was the billboard which came as the greatest shock. It stood thirty feet high, and was a hundred feet long. At the top, it announced that the site was Phase One of the newest Cypher Shopping and Leisure Centre. Below, in colours garish enough to have pleased my old friend Pastor Ives, was an artist's impression of what the finished complex would look like.

The artist was undoubtedly mad, I decided – or else the architect who commissioned him was. Nobody but a madman – and an inspired one at that – could ever have conceived such a surrealistic nightmare of concrete and bare metal.

Ground had already been broken by the monsters which had arrived earlier, and a foundation shaft – already several feet deep – gaped like an open wound in the centre of the site.

'This simply can't be happening!' I said – although unless I was hallucinating, it undoubtedly was.

But it still made no sense. The picture on the billboard clearly indicated that the completed building would cover a much larger area than the land Cypher already owned. So the complex could not be completed unless he acquired the almshouse gardens – and he couldn't do that.

'Think it through,' I ordered myself. 'Treat it like a game of bridge, and consider all the options.'

Even if Cypher managed to take control of our company, he would inherit a binding agreement which said he couldn't take possession of the cottages until the present tenants had died. And how long would he have to wait before that happened?

'It'll take ten years,' Aunt Sadie had said. 'Ten years at the most.'

Say it only took eight years.

Say six.

Say, for the sake of argument, a flu epidemic would wipe out all the OAPs the following winter.

Even if this last case proved true – and it was highly improbable that it would – then the arrival of the heavy plant was premature, because it would have to sit around for at least six months before it could do *anything*.

Unless …

The thought which had just come into my head was too horrible to contemplate – but impossible to ignore.

The clock in the waiting room of Crick, Gatsby & Brock, Solicitors and Commissioners of Oaths, ticked off another minute as I shifted uncomfortably in my seat. I wondered how much longer I could stand the strain – the sheer bloody tension – of not knowing for sure whether or not my suspicions were correct.

Martin Lord, who was sitting next to me, put his hand on my shoulder. 'Try to relax, Rob.'

That was easy for him to say. He wasn't carrying the burden of responsibility that I was.

The phone on the receptionist desk rang, making me jump.

'Relax!' my bridge partner repeated.

The receptionist replaced the phone.

'Mr Crick will see you now,' she said.

I wanted to run down the corridor which led to Crick's office, but I forced myself to walk in step with Lord. We reached the right door, Lord knocked, and a plummy voice invited us to enter.

The man who stood up to greet us was small and rotund, with bobbles of cotton-wool hair perched precariously behind his ears. He was obviously delighted to see Martin Lord, and pumped his hand vigorously.

'How long has it been since we last got together, Martin?' he asked.

'Must be a good year,' Lord said. 'Perhaps even more than that, now I think about it.'

'We must go out to dinner somewhere soon,' Crick said, 'maybe that nice little restaurant down by the river.'

'I'd like that,' Lord agreed.

And all the time this was going on, a voice in my head was silently screaming, 'Cut the pleasantries, and let's get down to what's important!'

Crick invited us to sit down.

'Now, what brings you here today, Martin?' he asked.

'It was really Mr Brock we wanted to talk to,' Lord said, almost apologetically, 'but your receptionist told us he's no longer with you.'

'That's right,' Crick agreed. 'He resigned from the partnership – which between you and me and the gatepost was a good thing – and took a pukka job in London. So it looks like you're stuck with me. How can I help you?'

Lord cleared his throat. 'We'd like to see the papers relating to the sale of the almshouse cottages to Shelton Bourne plc' he said.

Crick tugged at the bobble of hair above his right ear.

'I'm not sure that's possible,' he said. 'Strictly speaking, we should only show them to officers of the company.'

'It's very important,' I said desperately.

Lord shot me a warning look. 'Rob has been in on the whole business right from the start,' he cajoled, 'and he is the ward of the CEO.'

Crick hesitated for a second, and then said, 'Well, since you used to be in the profession yourself, Martin, I suppose I could stretch a point.'

He stood up, walked over to an old-fashioned filing cabinet, and returned with a bright blue folder.

'You don't mind if I familiarise myself with it first, do you?' he asked, sitting down again and opening the folder.

He started to read through the top document, gently pulling at his hair as he did so, but by the time he'd got half-way down the first page, the pull had become a firm tug.

'Is anything wrong?' I asked, my feeling of doom growing stronger and stronger by the second.

'I don't understand this,' Crick told me. 'I know Jack Brock had certain personal problems when he was drawing up these papers – money worries and so on – but even so, this really is a very careless piece of work.'

'Careless?'

'Yes. Even from what I've read so far, I can see you could drive a large horse and cart through the holes in this agreement, especially the clauses relating to the right of tenure.'

'You mean, there's nothing to stop Shelton Bourne plc evicting all its tenants tomorrow, if it feels like it?'

'Exactly so. It really is a shocking piece of work. What can Brock have been thinking of when he drafted it?'

'This new job that Mr Brock went to,' I said. 'Who was it with?'

'It was some big multi-national company. I can't actually recall its name at the moment.'

'It wasn't Cypher International, was it?'

'Do you know, I rather think that it was … but how could you possibly have known that?'

'Oh, it wasn't too difficult to work out,' I said. 'Where else would Brock pick up his thirty pieces of silver after he betrayed us?'

****

The deed of covenant was a dead letter. Now the only thing which was keeping the old people in the almshouse from eviction was the fact that we still controlled the company – but we only controlled it by the skin of our teeth. List of shareholders in hand, I made a tour of the village.

I found Colonel and Mrs Todd of Benares House working in their garden. The Colonel seemed content with a little gentle hoeing, but his wife – a pith helmet crammed down firmly on her head – was attacking one of her shrubs as if it were a recalcitrant punkah-wallah.

'We'd never sell our shares, would we, Memsahib?' the Colonel asked his wife.

'Never!' the memsahib answered, making a fresh assault on the shrub.

There was an even more adamant response from Primrose Cottage. 'It's our duty to look after those poor old souls in the almshouse,' said Mrs Blake, who would never see eighty again herself. 'They'll not be turned out onto the street – not in my lifetime. And I intend to live to a hundred.'

Everywhere I went, I got the same response – the shares were a sacred trust and would never be relinquished.

****

It was almost dark when I opened the gate and walked through the rose garden to the front door. I was exhausted – but also reassured. Aunt Sadie had been right all along – the people who'd sold their stock were lame ducks, the shareholders who were left were solid as rocks. There was no possible way that Cypher could get his hands on the extra three percent he needed to take control of the company.

I opened the front door.

'I'm back,' I called.

I was greeted by silence. Of course, I thought, as I felt a wave of disappointment sweep over me – with all the feverish activity I'd thrown myself into, I'd quite forgotten that Aunt Sadie would be in London for two or three days.

I made myself a cheese sandwich, but though I hadn't eaten since breakfast, I was not hungry. The day had begun in disaster, and ended in triumph. I wanted to share that triumph with someone – and who else would I share it with but my beloved Aunt Sadie?

'*Try to miss me a little,*' she'd said, as she boarded the express train for London.

How could I *not* miss her? The air was filled with her perfume. The chair on which she normally sat looked achingly empty. At my feet lay the silk Persian rug on which she would stretch out, almost like a cat, whenever we lit the log fire. Everything which surrounded me was part of her – everything which surrounded me was part of *us*.

I wandered around the cottage distractedly for a while, and finally, more through boredom than through interest, I turned on the television.

The news had just started. I sat through two minor wars and one major famine before the news reader's expression shifted from serious concern to mildly salacious interest.

'Rumours persist that rock star "Cocky" Wadd has broken up with his long-time girlfriend, Olivia Anstruther-Ponsonby' he said. 'Tonight, Wadd was spotted dining at Filet Mekong, the fashionable French-Indochinese restaurant, with controversial film starlet Bazoom Bazooms, whose latest film, *Take me, take me, Dolphin-baby!* has still to receive a certificate.'

The newsreader's image faded out, to be replaced by an exterior shot of the Filet Mekong. Wadd, a young man with long greasy hair which spilled over the shoulders of his expensive dinner jacket, was adopting an aggressive stance.

'Why don't you … you know … just piss off?' he suggested.

The camera swung round to his companion, whose topography more than lived up to her name. Though I'd never heard of her before (we country mice lead such innocent lives!) it was immediately obvious to me that she was the perfect fusion of Hollywood glamour and pornography – the dumb blonde with a heart of gold and a turnstile on her bedroom door. In many ways, she reminded me of Glynis, the Welsh expert in threesomes.

'Do *you* have any comment to make, Ms Bazooms?' an off-camera voice asked the starlet.

Bazoom Bazooms wiggled. 'Cocky and me are just good friends,' she said. 'My real true love is Moby.'

'Moby?'

'My dolphin.'

Behind her, a new couple emerged from the restaurant. They had obviously not been expecting a camera crew to be lurking outside, and for a moment, it had a paralysing effect on them. The man, who was wearing a long, flowing cloak, had hair which stuck up in small tufts over each ear, and a pointed, Mephistophelian beard. I'd seen him on television once before – the night he'd reduced Cadbury Joyspear to a quivering jelly.

'That's Sir Llewellyn Cypher, the building tycoon,' the reporter said excitedly. 'But who's that with him?'

Bazoom Bazooms forgotten, the camera zoomed in on this newer sensation. Cypher was now almost in close-up. And so was the woman with him. She was wearing a black dress which revealed her beautiful shoulders and the shape of her firm breasts. She lacked the blatant sexiness of Ms Bazooms, yet not one man in a thousand would have chosen the starlet over her. I recognised her, as I had recognised Cypher, though I'd never seen her on television before. Oh yes, I recognised her, all right. The quality of the camera work was so good that I could even tell that the brooch pinned to her dress was the most recent one I'd made her.

12

Aunt Sadie arrived with a stack of gift-wrapped parcels, most of them – as usual – for me.

'I was rushed off my feet in London,' she said, throwing her arms around me and kissing me on the cheek. 'I've seen – oh, tons of people – and they promised they'll do all they can to help us fight Cypher.'

I unwrapped her arms from around my neck.

'Don't lie to me,' I told her.

Aunt Sadie backed away a little.

'You saw me on the news, didn't you?' she asked dully.

'Did you think I wouldn't?'

She shrugged. 'There was a good chance you'd miss it. It was only shown once, and then Lew used his influence to have it stopped.'

'How could you?' I demanded bitterly. 'What could possibly make you agree to sell your soul like that?'

'Money,' Aunt Sadie said. 'Lots of it.'

'And are you sleeping with him, as well?'

'Yes,' my aunt admitted. 'But that means nothing to me – it's just a sort of bonus I threw into the pot.'

'It was you who told him about the shareholders' weaknesses,' I said, wondering why I'd not thought of it before. 'Cypher got it all from you … Professor Smallridge and his crackpot Merrie England ideas, Dr Mulroon and his little boys, Sir Anthony Fitzsimmons' gambling habit—'

' … Mr Paice and his son's business, Mr Holroyd and his little tart in Bayswater …' Aunt Sadie recited. 'Yes, all of it came from me. Why don't we sit down, Rob?'

'I don't want to sit down. I'm not even sure I want to be in the same room as you.'

'Please.'

I sat down. I never could resist her.

Aunt Sadie sat opposite me, so that our knees were almost touching.

'You know how you feel about bridge?' she asked.

'What's that got to do with anything?'

'I feel the same way about money. When I was entertaining in France – hell, why not call a spade a spade? – when I was *whoring* in France, I told myself that when my savings had reached a certain level, I'd have enough. But you can never have enough.'

'And so you've sold your shares in Shelton Bourne to Cypher?'

'Not yet. We're still negotiating. But in the end, he'll have to come closer to my price – he really has no choice – and then I *will* sell.'

'Don't do it,' I pleaded. 'Think of all the old people. They trusted us, and because of that, they'll lose their homes.'

'I know,' my aunt said softly.

'It'll break their hearts,' I pressed on. 'It will kill some of them – literally – and in a way, they'll be the lucky ones, because the rest will be condemned to spend their few remaining years in misery.'

'I know,' Aunt Sadie repeated. 'I know. I'm very sorry for them.'

And I really believed she was. I searched desperately for some argument – any argument – with which I might persuade her to change her mind.

Money to her was what bridge was to me, she'd said. Would I give up bridge if she asked me to? Yes! Without a second's hesitation!

'If you won't do it for the old people, then do it for me,' I said.

'Haven't you understood a word I've been saying?' Aunt Sadie asked me – and there were tears in her eyes. 'I'm a gold digger. It's as simple as that. I love you more than anyone else I've ever met, but I can't keep those shares – not even for you.'

I couldn't bear to look at her beautiful, corrupt face any longer. I stood up and rushed into the garden, where we had spent so many happy hours together. The scent of roses filled the air, just as it had done when I first arrived at the cottage, and I could hear the stream trickling through the rock garden.

'Gold digger,' I said to myself.

It was rather unfortunate Aunt Sadie had used precisely that term – because it had started me thinking.

13

To my great regret, Aunt Sadie died soon after and, not having yet met Rosalyn, I went without a permanent woman in my life for quite a while.

PART SIX: Grand Slam

1

As the make-up artist's deft hands and light touch worked on my face, I asked myself – for probably the hundredth time – what I was doing there.

Stupid question, of course. I knew perfectly well why I was there – I was there because Wesley Heatherington-Gore had made the booking.

'I've got you a spot on the Cadbury Joyspear show,' he'd said, a happy, complacent grin filling his face. 'Clever, aren't I?'

'Clever?' I'd repeated, hardly able to believe what he'd just told me. 'And what am I expected to talk about on the Joyspear show?'

'Bridge, of course.'

'Oh, I see. You think I should use up ten or fifteen minutes of a prime time television show talking about the intricacies and statistical probabilities of a double finesse?'

'I don't see why not. It's jolly interesting.'

'It's jolly interesting to *you*, Wesley. To the average viewer, who expects to hear movie stars plugging their latest films, and footballers talking about the most exciting matches they've played, it will be a complete bore.'

A puzzled frown had appeared on Wesley's face.

'Are you sure about that?' he'd asked.

'I'm sure.'

'Well, then, maybe you could talk about your childhood.'

Another great idea! I could tell Cadbury Joyspear all about how I arranged for my aunts to die, and maybe – as a bonus – I could have Les Fliques arrest me on air.

'There are many aspects of my childhood I'd rather not discuss,' I'd said evasively.

A glum expression had come to Wesley's face and lingered there for at least half a minute – a personal record for him. Then his customary optimism had reasserted itself.

'I'm sure you'll think of something,' he'd said.

The problem was, sitting there in the make-up chair, I hadn't thought of anything yet.

'What's Joyspear really like?' I asked the girl who was working so diligently on my face.

'He's lovely,' she said, 'a simple, unspoiled Irishman who still can't quite believe his own success.'

She sounded as if she was reading a script – and she probably was.

'A simple unspoiled Irishman ...' I repeated.

'Yes.'

'... who has a PhD in the development of nineteenth century Transylvanian moral philosophy.'

The make-up girl froze.

'How did you know that?' she asked.

I knew it because I was a professional bridge player – and a professional bridge player never sits down at the table without finding out all he can about his opponents first.

'Help me out here,' I pleaded.

'I shouldn't ...'

'Don't send me into battle with a plastic sword.'

'If you weren't so cute, I wouldn't be telling you this,' the girl said, in a whisper. 'All Cadbury wants out of life is to be adored by his audience. If the audience likes you, then he likes you – because he'll be getting the reflected glory.'

'And what if the audience doesn't like me?' I asked.

'Then he'll get them on his side by tearing you apart.'

Great!

2

As I stood in the wings, listening to Joyspear interview his first guest – a man who had constructed a working model of Tower Bridge out of dried prunes – my mind inevitably reviewed the chain of events which had led to me having the opportunity to humiliate myself in front of millions of television viewers. And that, of course, meant I was thinking about the first time I met Wesley.

****

It was a warm Thursday afternoon in St-Jean-de-Luz, shortly after I'd made my hurried departure from England. It was not a happy time for me. I owned no more than a suitcase of clothes and the few hundred francs in my pocket, and I considered myself to be on the run. Not, you understand, that I thought Les Fliques, super-cop, could actually *prove* anything against me, but given the nature of the beast, I had decided it would be wisest to stay well clear of him.

It was in the casino that Wesley hi-jacked my life and annexed me to his restless spirit. I'd been playing blackjack that afternoon, and having won just enough to enable me to survive for the next few days, I'd cashed in my chips and was heading for the door when I felt the tap on my shoulder.

'Fliques!' my panicking mind screamed.

I swung round, and saw Wesley for the first time. He must have been about twenty-five or twenty-six then. He was chubby rather than fat, with a head like a football which was not quite fully inflated and cheeks as round and shining as apples. He had silky, fair hair, and when a lock of it fell over his eyes, which happened often, he would flick his head back as if a wasp had flown up his nose.

A buffoon? In some ways, perhaps, but there was a depth of experience in his eyes which was fascinating to a boy brought up by a conspiracy of aunts.

'Wesley Heatherington-Gore,' he said, holding out a podgy hand. 'I say, are you actually old enough to be in here?'

'What's it to you?' I demanded, fingering the passport I'd hired for the afternoon from a perpetual student I'd met earlier.

'No offence meant, old chap,' Wesley said, flicking back a strand of hair. 'Just curious – that's all. I've been watching you at the table, and you're really rather good. Do you, by any chance, play bridge?'

The magic word!

'Now and again,' I said cautiously.

'How about a drink?' he asked. 'You do drink, don't you?'

'Yes.'

The bar that Wesley had in mind – 'a place the fishermen use, absolutely charming if a little unhygienic' – was at the other end of the Promenade de la Plage, and as we walked along, Wesley told me all about himself.

'I received my education – if that's what you want to call it – at "Donners",' he said.

'Donners?'

'Donnington! You must have heard of it.'

'No, I don't think I have. Is it like Eton?'

'Not *quite* like Eton, no. I suppose, if you were being strictly accurate, you might say it was only a minor public school, but it was a jolly fine place. Anyway, the Officer Training Corps was run by the chaplain – an awfully bloodthirsty chap – and he was as keen as mustard on me entering the army. He said I'd be a general in no time at all. But there's no military tradition in our family, and anyway, I had my sights set on Oxford.'

'You went to Oxford University?'

'Well, no, actually. Just missed getting in, or so the Admissions' Tutor at Oriel told me. But there it is, so I thought to myself that if I couldn't go to Pater's old coll, the next best thing was to sit down and write a best-seller.'

'And did you?'

'Not yet. Haven't even put pen to paper, as a matter of fact. What I have been doing is collecting experiences for it.'

'What kind of experiences?'

'All sorts. I was a deck-chair attendant until the unfortunate incident of The Fat Lady Who Got Her Tits Caught in the Mechanism. I worked in a mortuary for a while, but that was deathly boring. And I once applied to

177

be a mercenary – it sounded less stuffy than the real army – but they said I needed experience killing people somewhere else, first.'

'So what are you doing now?'

'Considering my options … surveying the opportunities …deciding between various short-term career moves.'

We had reached the bar, which was on the Quai de l'Infante. Wesley seemed to be a regular, and the moment he sat down, the waiter brought him a large anise.

'And a beer for my friend,' Wesley said in a language which – on a good day – might have been charitably interpreted as vaguely resembling French.

Wesley took a generous sip of his own drink.

'Filthy muck,' he pronounced, 'but if your aim is to alter your brain chemistry, it's as convenient a reactive agent as any.' He leaned across the table conspiritorially. 'You're wasting your time in the casinos, you know.'

'I did all right today,' I said defensively.

'Chickenfeed, my dear boy. Why peck around for single grains of corn when there exists the possibility of getting your hands on the whole sack?'

'The whole sack?'

'Croupiers are professionals, and however good you are, it's never wise to go up against pros. What we're looking for is someone who *thinks* he's professional, but is no more than a gifted amateur.'

'That makes sense,' I agreed.

'And blackjack is the wrong game, because the mugs find out too quickly which way the wind is blowing. That's why I asked you about bridge. With bridge, they've always got the hope that with a couple of good hands, they'll re-coup their losses. Never do, of course, but it gives them the incentive to keep losing.'

'Are you saying we could make a living out of it?' I asked, intrigued.

'Of course we could, dear boy. Easy as pie. But we'll never find a serious game here. We'll have to go to Nice or Monte, and mix with the Arabs and Russians.'

He spoke as if the whole matter were settled – which, in fact, it was. It suited me very well to put more miles between myself and Fliques' investigation. Besides, there was something irresistible – unstoppable –

about Wesley. He was Mr Micawber with a public school accent – as free as a bird, as uninhibited as a puppy. He became my firm friend, and has the distinction of being one of the few people I got close to who didn't come to an unpleasant end.

****

'My next guest tonight is regarded as something of a phenomenon in the bridge world,' Cadbury Joyspear said. 'He was the youngest player ever to be awarded the title Grand Master and the youngest ever winner of the European Bridge League Mixed Pairs Championship. So would you please give a warm welcome to Rob Bates!'

The studio audience, like trained monkeys, applauded thunderously, and I wondered – almost hysterical now – if my legs would ever obey my brain and take me down the steps. If I'd known then what I know now – that as a direct result of appearing on *Joyspear*, I'd meet the woman who would eventually become my fiancée – I'd have had no trouble moving. In fact, I'd have been though the door and out into the street before Joyspear could say "platitude".

The applause was starting to thin, and I was still standing there.

'*If you don't believe in yourself, nobody else will, either,*' Mother's voice said, from somewhere high up in the studio lighting.

'Quite right, Mother,' I said, and took the first steps on the path which would lead to yet another violent death.

3

Cadbury Joyspear shook my hand warmly and vigorously, and offered me a seat on the couch.

'After an introduction like the one I've just given you – a real cracker if I say so meself – you'd better be good,' he said.

The audience chuckled at his wit.

I gave him a thin smile. 'You almost make that sound like a threat, Cadbury,' I said.

It was meant to be humorous – a merry quip – but instead I sounded as if I was stranded in a no man's land between terrified and aggressive.

'A t'reat!' the Great Man said to his audience. 'Now have you ever known me to be t'retening?'

'No, Cadbury!' the rows of white, round faces called back.

It was not going well.

'Rob and I were talking earlier,' Joyspear began. He paused, as if he had heard a heckler in his adoring audience. 'Yes, we were,' he said emphatically, addressing the imaginary heckler, 'because contrary to what some of youse up there seem to t'ink, my guests are not complete strangers to me when they walk down the stairs.'

But I was. I hadn't spoken to Joyspear at all, only to a spotty junior researcher with a clipboard.

'Now where was I?' Joyspear asked when the laughter had died down. 'Oh yes, we were talking about some of the adventures Rob had before he climbed to the pinnacle of the bridge establishment.' He turned to me. 'So why don't you tell us one of your tall tales, Rob?'

'The Russians?' I asked.

Joyspear nodded. 'That'll do for a start.'

'There were two of them,' I said. 'They called themselves Grand Dukes, although they must both have been born long after the Tsar took his trip down to the cellar from which he never returned …'

****

The younger one was called Dimitri, the older Alexei. We had arranged to meet them in the card room of their Monte Carlo hotel.

'I think we would be more comfortable playing in our suite,' Dimitri said, and though Alexei looked troubled by the suggestion, Wesley said it was a fine idea, and he was sure we'd be much more comfortable there.

We hustled them gently, settling for simple games when we could have bid slams, and over a couple of hours we built up a fair number of points on our side of the score sheet. As the play progressed, Grand Duke Alexei seemed to be growing more and more concerned – though I didn't think it was losing at cards that was bothering him. As for Dimitri, he looked blacker with each hand, and finally began muttering to himself.

I suppose I should have been able to read the signs, but having only been in the game for a few weeks, I was still a bit green.

And Wesley – Wesley, who had seduced me into the bridge racket in the first place?

He didn't read signs. He didn't anticipate. His particular genius was for getting us into a scrape and then – hopefully! – finding a way out of it.

It was when Grand Duke Dimitri picked up his fourth mediocre hand in a row that he lost control.

'By the Black Virgin of Kazan, I swear you are cheating!' he shouted.

'Not cheats, old chap,' Wesley said, taking umbrage. 'Not cheats at all. Just better players.'

The Russian's hand disappeared into his pocket, and when it emerged again, it was holding a large pistol.

'Now this is a powerful hand, my friend,' he said. 'This is a hand not to be argued with.'

'Please, Dimitri, not again,' Grand Duke Alexei said.

Again! The word bounced around in my increasingly panicked brain: "Again" … "again" … "again!"

'They are cheats,' Grand Duke Dimitri said. 'And they are probably Jewish Socialists, too. The world would be well rid of scum like them.'

'You cannot keep shooting people,' Alexei told him.

Of course he couldn't! It was wrong to shoot people – especially when one of those people was me!

'They are cheats,' repeated Dimitri, whose inbred brain seemed incapable of containing more than a single idea at any one time.

'Remember how much it cost us last time you killed someone?' asked Alexei. 'We simply cannot afford it, Dimitri.'

Not a moral argument against murder, then – only a financial one.

'I will pay the price – whatever it is,' Grand Duke Dimitri said. 'I will pay it gladly.'

He's really going to do it! I thought. He's going to pull the trigger! We'll be dead!

I searched around desperately for some way to escape our fate – and could come up with nothing.

'Would you mind if I look at my cards before you shoot us, old chap?' Wesley asked.

'What?' Dimitri replied – clearly as mystified as I was.

'Well, after all, if you're going to blow us to Kingdom Come, the least you can do is let us see what our last hand would have been like.'

'All right,' Grand Duke Dimitri agreed.

Wesley picked up his cards and gave them no more than a cursory glance.

'D'you know, if I'd been given a chance to play this hand, I'd have bid Seven No Trumps,' he announced.

Still keeping his weapon on us, Dimitri picked up his own hand.

'And it will be my lead?' he asked.

'No, old chap, it *would have* been your lead,' Wesley corrected him.

'What do you mean?'

'Dead men can't play cards, however keen they are.'

Grand Duke Dimitri put his pistol back in his pocket. 'You bid Seven No Trumps?'

'Yes.'

Dimitri was smiling broadly, as if the last few minutes had never happened. 'And I double,' he said.

'Oh what the hell, Re-double,' Wesley said.

The grin was so wide now it was almost cutting the Russian's face in two.

'I will lead with the Ace of Spades,' he said grandly.

We would have gone down under any circumstances, but the way Wesley played out the hand – throwing winners on winners, ducking when he should have taken the trick – we were positively annihilated.

****

'It had taken two weeks to build up our stake, and Wesley blew it on one hand,' I told Cadbury Joyspear. 'We walked out of the Russians' suite as losers – but at least we did *walk* out.'

182

The Irishman was laughing, and so was most of his audience.

'And if you'll believe that, you'll believe anyt'ing,' the jovial host said.

It was going to be all right, I thought – Wesley's insane idea had actually worked out.

'But that wasn't your only adventure, was it, Rob?' Joyspear asked, after taking a surreptitious glance at the sheet his researcher had provided him with. 'I believe youse were also involved in the trouble in Qagmire.'

'No so much involved, as caught right in the middle of it,' I said. 'And, as usual, it was all Wesley's idea …'

4

Things were going very well for us on the French Riviera, so well, in fact, that it was almost inevitable Wesley would decide it was time for us to move on.

'Just met this Emir chappie down in the bar,' he told me one night. 'Apparently, he's got hundreds of male relatives back home, and they're all just bursting to learn how to play bridge.'

'What's that got to do with us?' I asked cautiously.

'He wants to recruit a couple of bridge tutors. And who better than the famous team of Heatherington-Gore and Bates?'

'We're doing all right here in Monte.'

'We'd do even better in Qagmire.'

'France is almost our own back yard,' I argued. 'We're comfortable in it. We know our way around. The Middle East is a very different matter.'

'Nonsense,' Wesley said cheerfully. 'It's pretty much like here, except they've got more sand and they all wear tea-towels on their heads. We'd be living like kings in Qagmire – well, like emirs, anyway.'

'And if something went wrong …?'

'What could possibly go wrong, old chap?'

What indeed, Wesley? A revolution, perhaps? Thousands of armed fanatics running around all over the place, high on hashish and Anglophobia?

I didn't say that at the time, of course. I didn't even *think* it at the time. Any qualms I might have had about going to Qagmire were centred on more mundane matters – how would I feel about all the women being veiled? Would it be compulsory to eat sheep's eyes? – and it wasn't until eight months later, when it was already happening, that the idea of a popular uprising even occurred to me.

The first indication I had that anything was wrong was that Wesley came into my room in the palace – at four o'clock in the morning – and shook me awake.

Why the bloody hell was he carrying a couple of bed sheets in his hands, I wondered sleepily?

'Not laundry day,' I mumbled sleepily.

'No, not laundry day,' Wesley agreed. 'Thing is, the situation's turning rather unpleasant – chaps downstairs with rifles, shooting anything that moves. It might be a good idea to put these robes on and get out of here.'

We donned the robes and headed for the back door – which in a palace approximately the size of Oxfordshire is not as easy as it seems. Several times we nearly fell foul of the revolutionaries. Once, we hid in a cupboard which would not have comfortably accommodated two very intimate midgets. Once, we flattened ourselves against a wall while a hoard of blood-thirsty fundamentalists thundered along the passageway which connected with ours.

'Can't understand why they're all so annoyed,' Wesley whispered. 'The Emir's always seemed a fine fellow to me.'

When we finally reached the exit, we found it was blocked by the bodies of several Royal Guardsmen who looked as if they'd been involuntary donors in a now-abandoned intestine transplant.

'Frightfully un-British, all this, don't you think?' Wesley asked, turning slightly green.

'They're just like us, but with tea-towels on their heads,' I reminded him.

'Hmm, I think I might have got that slightly wrong,' Wesley admitted.

We shifted some corpses, scrambled over others, and were finally out in the street. The air was thick with smoke and the stink of cordite, the sky glowed from the light of a hundred merrily burning buildings. All around us, people rushed frantically in one direction, only to frantically retrace their steps seconds later.

'Can't help thinking there are better places to be,' Wesley said.

More by luck than judgement, we made it to the edge of the town, and from there to the sea. For the next four days we followed the coastline. We lived on dates and brackish water, hid while the sweltering sun beat down, and travelled only through the cool – very often chilling – darkness.

'Let's go to Qagmire,' I quoted sarcastically, during one of these hellish treks. 'We'll live like emirs there.'

'Matter of fact, we're living rather *better* than the Emir,' Wesley told me. 'The last time I saw him, his head was bouncing about on top of a pole.'

It was on the fourth day, just before dusk, that we were finally spotted. We'd been hiding in a small oasis, and were just getting ready to move out when we saw the nomads. There were twelve of them, each sitting comfortably astride his camel. They rode slowly towards us, the setting sun at their backs, rifles at the ready. Escape was impossible – we had no choice but to face them.

Since we had both had several months of intensive Arabic lessons by this point (if two men speak different languages but need to communicate, it is generally the one who *doesn't* own an oil well who is expected to make the effort), I had no worries about making myself understood at a relatively simple level. My only problem was that having a dozen rifles pointed at me seemed to have robbed me of the ability to make a coherent argument.

'Leave the talking to me,' Wesley said, sensing my dilemma.

'All right,' I agreed reluctantly. 'But just remember – they're not just us in tea-towels.'

'Of course not,' Wesley said huffily. 'Learnt my lesson over that, haven't I? I'll talk to them on their own level.'

The nomads had formed a semi-circle around the edge of the oasis. Their leader, who would have been a shoo-in for the role of Bad Guy in any spaghetti western, edged his camel a little further forward. Wesley and I abandoned the protective covering of the trees, and stepped out into the open.

'Greetings!' Wesley said in an Arabic which was even worse than his schoolboy French.

The nomad chief glared, but said nothing.

'We're a couple of humble desert dwellers, just like you, old chap,' Wesley continued.

'Humble desert dwellers!' I whispered hysterically. 'Tell him we're travelling loonies, or extra-terrestrials. Tell him anything you like. But for God's sake, don't try to pass us off as Bedouins.'

The nomad leader spat thoughtfully on the sand. His men slid back the bolts of their rifles. Even the camels looked at us contemptuously.

But Wesley, once in his stride, was not to be put off.

'Yes, humble desert dwellers,' he repeated. 'Camels doing all right, are they? Jolly good. May Allah bless your household, and all that sort of thing.'

The nomad leader looked from us to his men, then back at us. And slowly, his expression began to change; his eyes, which had been as hooded as a hawk's, started to widen; the corners of his mouth were twitching, as though he were finding it difficult to maintain his villainous expression. A gurgle – which sounded much like the noise an oil well makes when on the point of blowing – was being forced through his teeth. And then the gurgle spilled out, as loud, uncontrollable laughter.

The leader's amusement spread to his followers. How they laughed, these nomads, brought up without the advantage of regular exposure to *The Benny Hill Show* and *The Two Ronnies*. They slapped their sides, they rocked in their saddles. Had they been on horses, they would undoubtedly have fallen off. As it was, they only managed to keep astride their camels by clinging tightly to the humps.

The chief, as befitted his position, was the first to regain something of his composure.

'Whither are you going, oh my brother, oh fellow humble desert dweller?' he asked, valiantly fighting back a fresh attack of the giggles.

'Across the border to Morasq,' Wesley said. 'Thought I'd just pop over and visit my Uncle Ibrahim. Not seen the old boy for quite some time.'

A renewed bout of hysteria swept over the nomads.

'We will escort you,' the chief said. 'For will it not bring great honour on our house that we should be the instrument which reunites you with the "Old Boy"?'

He gestured with his hand.

One of the other nomads trotted forward until he was level with us, and then swept me up onto his camel as if I weighed nothing.

A second man started to advance hopefully towards Wesley, but the chief waved him back.

'I will carry this brother myself,' he said, 'for I have much to learn from him.'

We travelled through the night – the rest of the caravan following a respectful distance from Wesley and his chortling companion. It was dawn when we reached the outskirts of Morasq City.

'We can go no further with you, for I have many enemies in Morasq,' the chief said, helping Wesley to dismount.

'No problem,' my partner told him. 'Been awfully decent of you to have brought us this far.'

'You have given me much to think about, and many things to tell my grandchildren,' the nomad said. And then, switching – grotesquely – from Arabic to English, he added. 'Three cheers for the old school. Hip-hip-hooray … hip-hip-hooray … hip-hip-hooray.'

'I taught him that,' Wesley said, with obvious pride in his voice. 'He says he's going to use it as his new battle cry.'

'May Allah grant you many wide-hipped wives that you might fill the world with little Donningtonians,' the nomad chief said, reverting to his own language. 'Goodbye, my brother.'

He wheeled his camel round, and rode reluctantly away.

'Jolly fine chap,' Wesley said, as we watched the Bedouins disappear over the nearest sand dune. 'Would have made a damn good House Captain.'

Jolly fine chap he might have been, but I'm convinced that if I'd been in any other company but Wesley's when I met him, I'd now be nothing but a set of bleached bones lying in the hot sand.

5

One of things I *didn't* tell Joyspear about was my next meeting with Les Fliques.

The meeting took place in Paris this time. It had been over three years since I'd last seen the intrepid policeman, but knowing him as I did, it came as no surprise when, stepping out of my modest eighth arrondissement hotel, I found him – croissant in hand – loitering with intent.

'How did you find me?' I asked.

'It's never difficult to keep track of a lad with an obsession,' Fliques said. 'I'd have been to see you earlier, but a lot of the time you've been in places well beyond the travel budget of a humble chief inspector.'

'You made promotion again!' I said delightedly. 'Congratulations.'

'You made it again, too, didn't you, Bobby?' Fliques said.

'Don't call me Bobby,' I told him, with a sudden anger which was so unexpected that it caught me quite off-guard. 'Aunt Sadie always called me Rob, so that's the name I go by now.'

Fliques nodded, understandingly. 'Rob it is, then.' He took a bite of his croissant. 'They're not at all bad, these foreign cakes. Shall we go for a little stroll, Rob?'

The hotel was just round the corner from the Champs-Elysées, and soon we were walking up the broad avenue towards the Arc de Triomphe.

'There's only one thing I don't really understand about your Aunt Sadie's death,' Fliques said. 'Where did you get the fake coins from?'

'You're not wired for sound, are you?' I asked.

Fliques looked offended.

'Of course I'm not. This is between you and me, Rob, and when I collar you, I don't want it to be because some bloke in a white coat has fitted me with a souped-up deaf-aid. So tell me, where did the coins come from?'

'I made them myself,' I said. 'I did it in the school's art and craft workshop.'

Fliques stopped dead in his tracks. 'You admit it? Just like that?'

'Just like that!'

'You've never admitted anything at all before,' Fliques said, clearly baffled by my new openness.

'I never had an "accident" happen to anyone I really cared about before, either,' I told him.

Fliques nodded, and we started walking again.

'I suppose you told your aunt that it was Digger Morton's buried treasure,' he said.

****

Yes, that was what I'd told her, running breathlessly into the house and waking her up at five o'clock early one June morning.

'Digger Morton's treasure,' she'd repeated excitedly, holding the coin I'd given her as though it were a holy relic. 'Where did you find it?'

'It was in that big hole on the building site.'

Her eyes narrowed, suspiciously.

'What were you doing there?' she demanded.

I was well-prepared for that question.

'I was looking for some way to sabotage the project,' I said. Sadie nodded, as if, knowing me as she did, that was just the sort of thing she'd expect me to do.

'I'll get a shovel,' she said. 'We can start digging before anyone else wakes up.'

'And with all the money we'll get from the treasure, you won't have to sell your shares in Shelton Bourne plc, will you?' I suggested.

'We'll see,' Aunt Sadie said absently, as she pulled her green wellington boots on.

We rushed to the building site, and squeezed through the gap I'd previously cut in the wire. Before us stretched the hole into which the foundations were soon to be poured.

'Where's the ladder?' Sadie said, half-mad with greed.

I showed her, and we descended into the pit.

'Show me where you found the coin,' she ordered me.

I pointed to the far edge of the pit. 'Over there.'

'Then that's where we'll start.'

I had buried ten of the fake coins in all, and it took her over two hours to find them. She worked like a demon, and wouldn't allow me to take over the digging – not even for a second. By the time there was the noise of heavy machinery starting up overhead, her hair was a mass of sweaty rat-tails and her face a mask of ugly obsession.

'This is only the start,' she gasped, not easing off her effort one iota. 'There has to be a trunk or something further down.'

More machinery snarled from beyond the lip of the shaft.

'It's not safe to be down here any longer, Aunt Sadie,' I said. 'They'll probably be working on this hole any minute.'

'It has to be here somewhere,' Sadie muttered wildly.

'We could be killed,' I told her.

'Then go and tell them to stop working,' Sadie said impatiently, slashing at the earth again.

I made one last effort.

'Come with me, Aunt Sadie,' I begged. 'We can stop them together, and then we can come back down here and have another look.'

'You go!' my aunt said, turning over a clod of earth, and gazing hopefully at the looser soil underneath. 'You bloody go! I've got to keep looking.'

According to my master-plan, I should have climbed calmly back up the ladder, strolled inconspicuously to the gap in the wire, and been well away from the site when the accident occurred.

I thought I could do it.

I really did.

After all, I'd always kept my head before. My hand hadn't shaken when I'd phoned Tom and told him about Aunt Jacqueline's plans. My voice hadn't cracked when I'd shopped Aunt Peggy to Les Fliques. My heart hadn't beaten any faster when I'd exposed Aunt Catherine for the heartless blackmailer she was …

But this time was different. This time, I wasn't dealing with one of the others, it was Aunt Sadie – and however much other people might suffer as a result of her deliverance from danger, I couldn't allow her to be hurt.

I scrambled wildly up the ladder, the roar of machinery filling my ears. My head cleared the top of the shaft, and I could see a large tipper truck, filled with hard-core, backing towards the edge under which Aunt Sadie was digging.

'Get out!' I screamed down at her.

She couldn't hear me above the noise. Truth to tell, she probably wouldn't have heard me even without it – she was deaf to everything but the all-compelling voice of her own avarice.

The truck had come to a halt on the edge of the hole, and the tipper was beginning to tilt.

'Stop!' I shouted, running towards it. 'Stop!'

More and more, the tipper tilted. One or two old house bricks rolled off the top of the pile and plummeted down the shaft. I reached the lorry and tried to open the door on the passenger side. It was locked. I pulled myself up, and hammered furiously on the window.

The driver turned his head in my direction.

'Don't tip!' I yelled.

'Can't hear you,' he mouthed back at me. 'Be with you in a minute – just as soon as I've finished this job.'

Through a film of tears, I watched as several tons of rubble slid off the back of the lorry – and into the hole.

****

'Must have squashed her as flat as a pancake,' Les Fliques said.

'Yes, it did,' I agreed, dully.

'Sorry, Rob, that was thoughtless of me,' Fliques said. 'She meant so much more to you than the others, didn't she?'

'I loved her. I really did.'

Sensitivity from either side was not part of the game, and it embarrassed both of us. For several minutes we continued walking, passing pavement artists and flower sellers, but not saying a word.

'Well, at least you achieved what you set out to do,' Fliques said finally, as if he were offering me some consolation.

I gave him a sharp look, suspecting a trick. 'Set out to do?'

Fliques chuckled. We were back on track.

'You stopped the old 'uns being evicted,' he said. 'Oh, don't look so surprised, I know all about the property company. I'm almost as good at working out *why* you bumped off your aunties as I am at figuring out *how* you did it. So who's got your Auntie Sadie's shares in Shelton Bourne plc?'

'They're in trust, but in three weeks' time, when I turn twenty-one, they'll be mine.'

'And you'd never sell them to Cypher, would you?'

'No.'

'Not that you'd have the option now. He went bankrupt.'

'I didn't know that.'

'Apparently he was in a hole – a bit like your auntie.'

'Don't talk about her like that,' I said, getting angry again.

'Sorry, Rob,' Fliques said apologetically. 'Old habits die hard. Anyway, Cypher was apparently hoping the Shelton Bourne project would bail him out, and when that fell through—'

'It broke him.'

'Exactly.'

The Arc de Triomphe lay ahead of us.

'Bloody big traffic island, that,' Fliques said.

'It's supposed to serve as both a symbol of the greatness of France and a monument to those who selflessly gave up their lives for their country,' I told him.

'Hmm,' Fliques mused. 'Bloody big traffic island! And look at the way those cars are going round it. Half those motorists should be summonsed. What do the French police think they're doing?'

'Does this mean our little talk's over?' I asked.

'For the moment,' Fliques said. 'But I'd tread carefully if I were you, Rob. Now I'm a chief inspector, I've got a lot more resources at my disposal than I used to have. And I'm prepared to use them, because although I've come to like you – and maybe even admire you – I really can't allow you to go on killing people.'

6

It was night. Wesley and I stood on one of the bridges over the Seine, looking at a moon-bathed Notre Dame.

'I saw somebody I know today,' I told him. 'It was a police chief inspector from England.'

'Jolly good. It's always nice to meet a fellow Englishman abroad – even if he is a member of the constabulary,' Wesley replied.

But his heart was not really in it, and his bounce was gone. It was almost as if he suspected what was about to come next.

Should I tell him? I wondered.

Could I tell him?

'*Never put off until tomorrow what you can do today*,' said Mother's voice, the words lapping as gently against my mind as the water below lapped against the river bank.

I took a deep breath. 'The thing is, seeing this man got me thinking. I've decided it's time to go home.'

'Yes, I suppose it is,' Wesley said noncommittally.

'I mean, I really want a future as an international bridge player, and I've already left it a little late,' I argued.

'Quite so,' Wesley agreed. 'Err ... who were you thinking of having as your partner?'

This was the moment I'd dreaded.

'It can't be you, Wesley,' I said. 'You're good – but you're nowhere near good enough.'

Wesley's jaw quivered, and for a second I thought he was about to burst into tears.

Then he remembered he was an old Donningtonian and pulled himself together.

'Not good enough?' he repeated. 'Well, for heaven's sake, old boy, I already knew that. No, I was just wondering if you'd anyone in particular in mind as your new partner.'

'I'll have to see who's available.'

'Exactly,' Wesley agreed. 'Good plan.' He sighed. 'I'll be moving on in the morning, then.'

'Moving on? Why would you want to move on?'

Wesley shrugged. 'Won't be needing me anymore, will you? Not once you've got a new partner.'

'Of course I'll need you. Look, I'm going to be starting at the bottom, but if I'm successful—'

'No "if" about it. You're the best player I've ever seen.'

'… if I'm successful, there'll be all sorts of complications – sponsorship deals, lecture tours, the whole package. I can't handle all that myself, now can I?'

'Can't you?' Wesley asked.

'Of course I can't. So I shall need a business manager.'

'Expect you will,' Wesley agreed – then his mouth dropped open in surprise. 'Are you talking about me?'

'Yes, I am.'

'A business manager,' Wesley said, savouring the words. 'Never been in business before. Should imagine I'll be quite good at it.'

****

Good at it? Wesley was to business management what Aunt Peggy had been to animal welfare.

At the beginning, when I was a nobody, he could only cause minor inconveniences, but as my fame grew, he started to have the scope to enact real disasters. It took me twice as long to untangle the messes he'd got us into as it would have done to fix the whole thing myself. And still, even with all my efforts to straighten out the arrangements, I'd find that we'd been booked on a flight to Iceland when we were due in Rio. *And still* we could arrive at a hotel to discover that Wesley had either reserved no rooms at all, or else commandeered an entire floor.

It didn't really bother me – I'd expected nothing better. And it was worth suffering the odd inconvenience to keep a friend like Wesley.

7

I was just leaving Bush House – flushed from my success on *Joyspear* – when I heard a silky voice say, 'Mr Bates?' and, turning round, saw Rosalyn for the first time.

She was a petite blonde, with an oval face and a nose which stopped just short of being a button. Her mouth – which could be hard when she chose to make it so – was at that moment soft and alluring. She was wearing a mid-length dress which showed off her figure without being too sexually aggressive. She'd chosen it especially for me – I realise that now. If I'd come across differently on television, she might have turned up in a split skirt and fishnet stockings, but she'd assessed, quite correctly, that this particular outfit would please the man she'd watched on *Joyspear*.

Looking back on it, I suppose she reminded me a little of Mother and Aunt Sadie. At the time, my only thought was that she was the most attractive woman I'd seen in months.

'You *are* Rob Bates, aren't you?' she asked.

'Do I know you?' I said.

'No, you don't.' She laughed prettily – she could always laugh prettily when she wanted to. 'My name's Rosalyn Russell and I'm a reporter.'

'A reporter?' I repeated.

'That's right. I saw you on Cadbury's show and I called a taxi straight away. I'd really like to talk to you if you could spare the time. Do you think we could go somewhere for a drink?'

The night was young and she was beautiful – so why not? We found a mock-Victorian pub not far from the studio.

'What would you like to drink?' I asked when – as Mother would have wished – I'd escorted her to a table.

'A white wine, please.'

Playing to her subject again, you see. If I'd been one of those butch men who go around putting out fires on oil rigs, she'd have ordered a straight bourbon. Had I been of the ecclesiastical inclination, she'd have stuck to fruit juice.

I bought the drinks and took them back to the table.

'What paper do you work for?' I asked, as I sat down.

'*The Globe.*'

'*The Bonker's Daily!*' I said before I could stop myself.

Rosalyn laughed, though I could tell she was not really amused.

'Yes, I suppose we do have something of a reputation,' she conceded, 'but we cover some pretty serious stuff, even if it is in a popular format. That's why I'd like to do a story on you.'

'On me?'

Rosalyn grinned. 'You sound surprised.'

'I am,' I admitted. 'I mean, I know I've appeared on national television tonight, but I wouldn't have thought I was all that interesting.'

'All that interesting! Are you kidding? You've got the looks, and, by God, you've got the patter. Those stories you told about your friend Wesley, in which you made him out to be the hero—'

'He was the hero,' I said.

'Doesn't matter,' Rosalyn said dismissively. 'The important thing is that you come across as incredibly modest. You know what you are, don't you?'

'No,' I said. 'What am I?'

'You're a personality. What Bobby Fischer did for chess a few years ago, you're doing for bridge. People will be interested in the game because they're interested in you.'

We drank some more, and she told me a little about herself.

Her father, it seemed, worked on a provincial paper.

'Thirty years of covering weddings and WI meetings,' Rosalyn said with contempt. 'And he's never had the balls to try to climb any higher up the ladder.'

'Maybe he's happy where he is?' I suggested.

'Happy!' Rosalyn snorted. 'How *can* he be happy? I was out in the sticks for less than two years before *The Globe* offered me a job. And *The Globe's* only the start – because as soon as I've got a bit more experience at the national level, I'm intending to move into some really serious heavyweight journalism.'

You might have said it, but you were fooling yourself, weren't you, my love? Yours was a temperament ideally suited to working for *The Globe*. We may all be lying in the gutter, as Oscar Wilde once said, but while some of us are looking up at the stars, you were actually peering down the grid.

****

I don't want to give the impression that all these thoughts were flitting through my mind as Rosalyn and I sat knee-to-knee in the pub near the BBC. No, my thoughts were somewhere else entirely. And – apparently – so were Rosalyn's!

'Would you like a guided tour of my flat?' she asked when the pub landlord called time.

'I'd love it,' I said.

It was not so much a flat as a bed-sit – or, as the estate agent had probably said, "a quasi-maisonette" – but the guided tour, as we both knew, had nothing to do with fittings and furnishings. The moment she'd closed the door, Rosalyn was on me – guiding my hands, tearing at my clothing – and it was not until we were after our second orgasms that she suggested we continue on the bed.

Sex with Rosalyn was fantastic. She made Mrs Cynthia Harrap seem like a repressed nun. Next to her, Glynis, the Llawesuohtihs nymphomaniac, seemed as prim as Little Bo Peep. She even …

But enough of comparisons – suffice it to say that just as a mouse will ignore the spine-breaking bar overhead and nibble at the cheese, just as the fly will find itself drawn towards the spider's web, so I, completely oblivious to the risk, took the bait which Rosalyn offered.

****

Straight after breakfast, Rosalyn produced a recorder and placed it on the table between us.

'I want to get some of your stories down on tape,' she said. 'Start with the story about the two Russians.'

'But I did that on *Joyspear*, last night,' I pointed out.

Rosalyn shrugged. 'That doesn't matter. My readers have the attention span of the average goldfish. Go on. Start talking.'

'No, I'd rather tell you one of the stories I didn't tell Joyspear,' I said. 'Wesley and I were still in the Gulf, and, as chance would have it, Wesley led us into our second revolution in as many months …'

****

We were stranded in a small town on the coast of Qabir. It was a filthy little place, made up mostly of mud-brick houses, but at least there was no one there – for the present – who seemed particularly eager to kill us. We'd been in the town for a couple of days, dividing our time between drinking strong coffee in the town's only hostel and trying to work out how – given that all the roads were closed, and many of them were mined – we were ever going to get away.

As usual, Wesley came up with what, on the face of it, appeared to be a solution to all our problems.

'Been talking to this chap down at the harbour,' he announced. 'Turns out he's the captain of a fishing boat. Says he's more than willing to take us with him the next time he sails.'

'And how much does he want paying?' I asked suspiciously.

Wesley beamed. 'Nothing at all! Says since he's sailing anyway, we might as well come along for the ride. Frightfully decent chap.'

With ever-growing misgivings, I went to the harbour to meet this "frightfully decent chap". He turned out to be six feet four-tall, with scars on both cheeks and sly eyes which kept settling on the Rolex watch Wesley had been given to settle a gambling debt in Nice. He was the fourth most sinister man I'd ever met – the first three on my list being the members of his crew.

I took Wesley into a quiet corner. 'He's a smuggler,' I whispered.

'Do you know, I hadn't thought of that,' Wesley said agreeably.

'And probably a pirate, too.'

'I suppose that's possible.'

'So once we're away from the shore, what's to stop him taking everything we own, slitting our throats and throwing us over the side?'

'Why do you always take such a pessimistic view of human nature?' Wesley asked. 'I've always believed that if you're nice to a chap, there's a very strong chance that he'll be nice back to you.'

'There's absolutely no way I'm setting foot on that boat,' I said firmly.

Wesley looked uncomfortable. 'I wasn't going to mention this,' he said, 'but the rebel army's on the way here and its commander doesn't like foreigners at all.'

'I know,' I agreed, 'but if we can get the townsfolk to hide us—'

'Ah, there's the rub,' Wesley interrupted. 'The townspeople have been talking about how to ingratiate themselves with the rebels and someone suggested that disembowelling us and hanging us over the main gate as a sort of welcoming present, just might do the trick.'

I had had a mental picture of us hanging from the arch, and gave a heavy sigh. 'I'll go and get the bags,' I said.

'Jolly good idea,' Wesley agreed.

****

We'd been out at sea for about an hour when the crew made their move. Wesley was standing at the prow of the boat at the time, looking out across the water. I was near the stern, wondering if we might not have been better, after all, to have risked the disembowelling.

The pirates worked as a team, the three crew members forming a semi-circle around me, and the captain heading towards the prow – and Wesley.

I tried to see beyond the three who blocked me in, but every time I moved, so did they. Finally, through a gap between their shoulders, I caught just one glimpse of what was happening at the other end of the boat.

Wesley still had his back to us, and the captain, knife in hand, was almost on him.

'Look out, Wesley!' I shouted, but my shout was muffled by the noise of the engine.

I flung myself at the men who were penning me in, but they were too strong to resist. And then I saw that resistance wasn't necessary, because instead of the knife being in Wesley's back, it was in his hand.

'What happened?' I asked him later.

'What happened when?'

'When the captain came at you with the knife?'

Wesley chuckled. 'You've got it all wrong,' he said. 'The captain didn't come at me with his knife. It's true that when I turned around, I saw it in his hand, but I never thought for a minute he intended to do me any harm with it.'

'Then why had he got it out?'

Wesley laughed. 'He'd come to show it to me, of course. They're like that, these chaps – simple people who take pleasure in their simple belongings.'

'So what did you do when you saw the knife?'

'Smiled pleasantly, and asked him if I could take a look at it.'

'And he just gave it to you?'

'Well, it was more like I took it, if the truth be told. Fellow seemed in a bit of daze, for some reason.'

'And what happened next?'

'I told him what a jolly fine knife it was, and asked him if he'd teach me to tie a few nautical knots.'

'What did he say to that?'

'He mumbled something about Allah protecting holy fools. Can't think who he was talking about.'

****

'You see, the captain might have been the worst cut-throat in the Gulf,' I said to Rosalyn, 'but he couldn't bring himself to kill anyone as trusting as Wesley. Is this any good? I mean, can you use it in one of your stories?'

'Oh, I can use it all right,' Rosalyn assured me. 'Only I might have to change it round a bit.'

'Why?'

'Because it's all centred on Wesley again.'

'But it is his story,' I protested.

'That doesn't matter,' Rosalyn said.

It seemed to be her motto – if it didn't matter to her, then it simply didn't matter.

'Look, Rob, I know I might come across as a bit unfair, sometimes,' she continued, 'but the simple truth is that it's you who people are interested in. Frankly, no one gives a toss about Wesley.'

8

Rosalyn and I began to see each other regularly – and partnering her opened doors for me which had previously been tightly closed. Whilst in the past I would have had to queue for film premieres, I simply walked to the front of the queue with Rosalyn on my arm, and handed over the celebrity tickets that she'd been sent. At restaurants where I'd been told there were no free tables, one was suddenly found once the maitre d' realised who I had with me.

She seemed to know nearly everyone, and was very popular with all kinds of people.

'A guid sort, Ros,' Eddie McGroom, the soccer star told me at one of the numerous cocktail parties we attended. 'Niver expects somethin' for nothin'. Give her an exclusive story and ye can sure she'll pay ye back in kind.'

By which he meant extra publicity, I assumed.

'I find Rosalyn so refreshing,' said Malcolm Toffler, the right-wing literary critic. 'In an age when most people are so restricted by liberal qualms and petit bourgeois ethics, it's such a pleasure to meet a woman who knows what she wants – and will go to any lengths to get it.'

And how did I feel about her? At first, I merely found her intelligent, amusing, and an outstanding partner in bed. But as time passed, I was surprised to discover that I was slowly – but irresistibly – falling in love with her.

****

Not everyone was as enamoured of Rosalyn as McGroom and Toffler, as I was to find out one night in my hotel room.

I was sitting at my dressing table, fastening my tie, while Wesley was slumped in the armchair with a pile of newspapers on his lap.

'Going out with Rosalyn again?' my "business manager" asked me, out of the blue.

'Yes indeedee,' I told him, centring the tie.

'I'm not sure that her stories in *The Globe* are doing us much good,' Wesley said.

'What do you mean?'

'Well, look at the way she covered your last tournament. *The Times* headline says: "British Success in European Mixed Pairs".'

I grinned. 'And what does *The Globe's* headline say?'

'"English Lad Pisses on Frogs and Wops",' Wesley answered.

'What? Does it really say that?'

'Not quite. They've put one of those little star thingees, instead of the "i" in pisses – but everyone understands that. It could be damaging, you know. Being associated with the wrong attitudes could turn your fans off.'

'You're over-reacting,' I said, reaching for my cuff links. 'The people who read *The Globe* aren't my public. Besides, Rosalyn needs the by-lines.'

In the mirror, I could see Wesley frown.

'Another thing,' he said. 'Not really happy, professionally speaking, about the number of nights you've been spending out on the tiles.'

'Really?' I said, reaching for my hairbrush.

'Really. Need a lot of stamina for international competitions – can't afford to sit down at the table feeling clapped out.'

I put my brush down.

'Wesley, are you starting to get jealous of Rosalyn?' I asked.

'Of course not,' Wesley said quickly. Then the frown in the mirror slowly changed to a shamefaced smile. 'Well, perhaps a little,' he admitted.

'Rosalyn's become a very important part of my life,' I said seriously, 'and I really would like my best friend in the whole world to get on with her. Will you give it a try?'

The shamefaced smile was now tinged with a deepening sadness I didn't quite understand.

'Yes, I'll give it a try, old chap,' Wesley said. 'You know me – I'm game for anything.'

9

Rosalyn and I had been going out together for about six months when I started to develop feelings of discontent. It was not long before Rosalyn noticed it.

'What's the matter?' she asked me, one night as we lay in bed after a vaguely unsatisfactory session of love-making. 'Gone off me?'

'Of course not,' I replied – shocked she should even think that. 'But there has to be more to it than this.'

'More to what than what?'

'Our relationship; when we're together, we're either in bed, or else at some fashionable restaurant or charity gala, where we can be seen.'

'And what's wrong with that?' Rosalyn asked. 'You've certainly acted like you've enjoyed it so far.'

'But it isn't real life. And it doesn't seem to be leading us anywhere.' I put my hand on her shoulder and kneaded it gently. 'How would you feel about us setting up house together?'

'No,' Rosalyn said immediately. 'No, I don't think that would be a very good idea.'

It was the speed of her response that hurt me.

'But I thought you loved me,' I said.

'I do,' Rosalyn replied, moving further away from me.

'Well, then?'

'With all the publicity you're getting at the moment, you're riding high. But you know what fame's like – the bubble could burst at any minute. Almost overnight, you could become a penniless nobody.'

'Why should that make any difference to us?' I asked her, my hurt increasing with every word she spoke. 'Do I have to be rich and famous for you to care about me?'

'Of course not, darling,' Rosalyn replied. 'But you don't know what it's like to suddenly have the carpet pulled from under you. It destroys people. I've seen it happen a hundred times.'

'And are you saying that if that happened to me, you'd want nothing more to do with me?'

'Darling, how could you ever even think that?' Rosalyn asked reproachfully. 'But you must see that I'd be in a much better position to help you – to give you strength – if I'd hung on to a little of my independence.'

'I suppose so,' I replied, though – to be honest – I couldn't quite follow the logic of her argument.

I might have said more, but just then, the bedside phone rang.

I picked it up.

'Who?' I said. 'What? … Oh, I see … No, I'd be delighted … Eleven o'clock tomorrow morning … that would be fine.'

I put the phone back on its cradle.

'Who was that?' Rosalyn asked.

'The BBC,' I said excitedly. 'BBC2 want me to do a series.'

Rosalyn gasped. 'A series!'

'They're going to call it "Learn Bridge with Bates." They're planning to put it out at prime time.'

Rosalyn moved closer to me. 'That's wonderful news, darling.'

'Yes, it is,' I agreed.

We kissed. It was soft and sweet and wonderful.

'Rob …?' Rosalyn said hesitantly.

'Yes, darling?'

'Would you think me terribly indecisive if I said I'd changed my mind about us moving in together?'

'Of course not, darling.'

Rosalyn snuggled happily against me. 'We make such an ideal couple, don't we?'

'All couples in love are ideal,' I told her.

'True,' she agreed, perhaps a little reluctantly. 'But they don't all look as good together as we do. And not many of them are both rising stars, like we are.'

****

Within a week, I had used my BBC2 money as a deposit on a short-term lease of a pleasant flat in Knightsbridge. Within a month, Rosalyn and I had moved in. I was very happy.

You can't beat having your own home, Mother used to say.

And Mother, as usual, was right.

10

In the early days of my relationship with Rosalyn, I was the jealous one.

'She's only doing her job,' I'd tell myself whenever I saw her cosying up to the latest alternative comedian, or to a dress designer whose new collection had caused a sensation.

But I would still feel a stab of pain.

Yet quite soon, things began to swing the other way. My book, *Learn Bridge with Bates* (based on the television series), was published simultaneously in London and New York, and I suppose that whilst that gave me more confidence, it robbed Rosalyn of a little of hers.

Then again, the change may have come about because I was becoming popular in London society, and now at least half the invitations we received were addressed to me.

Whatever the reason, Rosalyn grew more and more possessive.

'Did you have to spend so much time with Bazoom Bazooms?' she demanded angrily, after we'd just got home from attending the opening of a new disco.

'She was upset,' I said, in my own defence. 'Her pet dolphin, Moby, has just died.'

'Upset my fanny!' Rosalyn retorted contemptuously. 'She was practically undressing you with her eyes.'

'You're exaggerating,' I assured her.

'Exaggerating!' she screamed back at me. 'No, I'm bloody not. They're all after you.'

'Even if they are, I'm not interested in them,' I said soothingly.

It was true. Mother had been a one-man woman, and had she lived to see me grow up, I'm sure she'd have expected me to be a one-woman man.

****

I don't want to make too much of Rosalyn's bouts of temper. Certainly she would blow up quite regularly, often in public, but I soon learned how to handle it. I never regarded our little arguments – if, from my side, they could be called arguments at all – as serious. And only once – if you don't count the mammoth row at the end – did we come into serious conflict.

It happened one rainy afternoon in October. I'd just flown in from the States, where I'd been promoting my book, and had only been home for half an hour when Rosalyn stormed in, slamming the door behind her.

'Bloody weather!' she said, taking off her wet raincoat, and flinging it on the floor.

'How was America, Rob?' I asked, reprovingly but gentle. 'How did the book signing go?'

'Bloody editors!' my fiancée screamed. 'Four years, I've been working for that bloody paper. What do I have to do to be assigned one of the really big stories? Sleep with the *entire* editorial staff?'

'You're tired,' I said. 'You'll feel better after a G and T.'

But I knew her well enough by then to realise that she would not feel better until she'd had a go at someone or something else.

I watched as she searched her mind for a convenient target.

'Bloody Wesley!' she said finally. 'Where is the snivelling parasite, anyway?'

'He's—'

'You've got to get rid of him, you know.'

'He's my manager.'

'Your manager! He's bloody useless, and you know it. And yet he goes everywhere you go.'

'You could come too,' I pointed out.

'No, I couldn't,' she countered, 'because, unlike Wesley, I have a career – my own way to make in the world.'

'Well then, you can't blame Wesley—'

'Do you have any idea how much he costs us?' Rosalyn demanded. 'How much his flights and hotel rooms are every month? We can't afford it.'

'Yes, we can,' I said. 'Easily.'

'All right, then,' Rosalyn replied, stamping her foot on the floor, 'I don't *want* to bloody afford it. He gets on my nerves, swanning around the place with his plummy accent and his vague look. There's real life out there, and it's about time he found out about it.'

'Wesley and I have been through a lot together,' I said. 'There was that time in Qagmire—'

Rosalyn stamped her foot for a second time. 'Please, not the same old song again, for Christ's sake,' she screamed. 'I used up that story in the very first article I did on you.'

'It isn't something you can just use up,' I said hotly. 'He saved my life in Qagmire – more than once.'

'Yes – and he's been treating you as a meal ticket ever since then. Don't you see that whatever you owed him has been paid back in full, and now it's time to say goodbye?'

I can rarely find it in myself to be firm with a woman – it's my early training, I suppose – but I was firm then.

'Wesley and I are friends, not partners,' I said. 'We've never added up what we owe each other, because we know before we start that we could never even begin to pay it back.'

'And what, exactly, is that pretty little speech meant to mean?' Rosalyn demanded.

'It means I will not get rid of Wesley.'

'It's him or me,' Rosalyn said, her voice suddenly cold and clinical.

She was tearing me apart. Both she and Wesley were central to my existence – aces in my pack of life – and the thought of sacrificing either of them was totally horrendous.

True, as well as being an ace, Wesley also had a bit of the knave about him, too – his scant regard for the safe and strictly-legal having landed us in any number of scrapes – but in the end he'd always come up trumps. And whatever else his failings, there wasn't a malicious bone in his body.

'Well?' Rosalyn demanded.

'I'm sorry,' I said.

If I had actually slapped her, it would not have produced the mixture of astonishment and rage which now appeared on her face.

'Let me get this straight,' she screamed. 'You'd pick Wesley over me? Is that what you're saying?'

'If you forced me to, that's the choice I'd have to make.'

Rosalyn's anger suddenly evaporated, and where there had been a towering fury, there was now only a vulnerable little girl.

'You just don't love me anymore, do you, Rob?' she said, with a catch in her voice.

'Of course, I love you.'

Rosalyn ran across the room, buried her head in my shoulder, and started crying.

'There, there,' I said, stroking her hair.

'If you really love me, prove it,' she sobbed. 'Get rid of him.'

'Couldn't seem to get to sleep,' said a voice from the guest bedroom doorway. 'Hello, Rosalyn.'

My fiancée lifted her head from my shoulder to look at the new character who had just entered our little melodrama.

'Hello, Wesley,' she said sullenly.

'Wesley was tired from the flight,' I explained. 'He wanted a little rest before he travelled up to his parents' place in Hertfordshire.'

'Feel absolutely fine now,' Wesley said – unconvincingly. 'I'm fighting fit and raring to go.'

'What we were just talking about—' I began.

'I heard,' Wesley interrupted, flinging his hair out of his eyes. 'And I agree with what Rosalyn said. You're a couple now. It's only natural that she doesn't want me around.'

'The age of miracles has finally come to pass,' Rosalyn said, without a hint of her previous tears in her voice. 'Wesley, of all people, has finally started developing some common sense.'

'I want you to stay on as my manager,' I told him. 'I need you.'

'No, you don't,' Wesley said sadly. 'You never did – and we've both always known that.'

'Wesley …'

'I'll be off now,' my old friend told me.

He started to walk towards the door. I tried to move, but Rosalyn was clinging on to me as tightly as if her life depended on it.

'We'll talk in the morning, Wesley,' I said, 'when you've had time to get over your jet lag.'

'That's right,' he agreed – far too easily. 'We'll talk in the morning.'

He opened the door, stepped out into the hallway, took one last regretful look over his shoulder – and was gone.

'I can't let him leave like that,' I said.

'Let him go,' Rosalyn urged, gripping me even tighter. 'Let him go.'

And to my eternal shame, I did.

I rang his parents' home the next morning but, of course, he'd never arrived there. For the sake of my relationship with Rosalyn, Wesley chose to disappear, and though I've spent years – and a small fortune – trying to track him down, I've never been able to find him.

11

The knock on the door – as they used to say in Soviet circles – came as I was packing for my trip to Germany, where they were planning to show *Learn Bridge with Bates* with sub-titles. And since Rosalyn was out tracking down a transvestite golfing champion, it was me who opened the door to the big man with Neville Chamberlain's moustache and Jack the Ripper's eyes.

'Chief Inspector Gouge,' he announced, producing his warrant card then pocketing it again with the speed of a prestidigitator. 'Mind if I come in, sir?'

'Can I stop you?' I asked.

'Stop me, sir? Yes, I suppose you could. But then I'd have to go all the way back to the station and get a search warrant, wouldn't I? And by the time I returned here, I'd probably be in a very bad temper indeed.'

'Then you'd better come in now,' I said resignedly.

Gouge tramped down the hallway into the living room, looking around him with undisguised curiosity.

'Nice place you've got here, sir,' he said. 'There must be more money in this bridge business than I thought. Pay your income tax, do you? Got a licence for that television set, have you?'

'And are the lights on my bike working?' I asked.

'Beg pardon, sir?'

'You're not, by any chance, an acquaintance of Chief Inspector Fliques, are you?' I asked.

'Superintendent Fliques of the Cheshire Constabulary did ask me to look you up, yes,' Gouge admitted.

'Why would he do that?'

'Why indeed, sir? I suppose the short answer is that, living in Cheshire as he does, he can't do it himself.'

'And what's the long answer?'

'The long answer?' Gouge repeated. 'I'm not sure that I quite understand you, sir.'

'Yes, you do. What was it Les told you – and what message did he give you to pass along to me?'

Gouge frowned at my familiar use of Fliques' first name, and then took out his leather notebook.

'The Superintendent told me that the women you associate with are very prone to sudden and/or violent death,' he said. 'And he's got this Miss ...' he opened the notebook, '... this Miss Rosalyn Russell marked down as your next victim.'

'Very interesting,' I said.

'Yes, isn't it?' Gouge agreed. 'Anyway, he wants you to know that he'll be keeping an eye on you himself whenever he's down here, but when he's not, I'll be acting as his locum.'

'You're a good choice for that position, because you're almost as subtle as he is,' I told Gouge.

'Oh, I wouldn't go that far, sir,' Gouge said modestly.

'Isn't Les Fliques worried that by letting me know in advance that I'm being watched, he'll frighten me off?'

'Frighten you off what, sir?' Gouge asked, with Fliquesque ease.

'Isn't he afraid that with you looking over my shoulder, the next victim won't die at all?'

I said the words lightly – almost whimsically. After all, while Rosalyn could be difficult, I still loved her, and I certainly wouldn't let any harm come to her.

'If it does frighten you off, that's a good thing, because the first aim of law enforcement is crime prevention,' Gouge said. 'But Mr Fliques doesn't think that knowing you're being watched is going to stop you. "Nothing will stop Rob once he's put his mind to it", were his exact words.'

'So if nothing's going to stop me, why bother to come and tell me I'm under observation?'

Gouge fixed me with his wild razor-wielder's eyes.

'Because knowing you're being watched might put a bit of pressure on you, sir – and people under pressure often make mistakes.'

'You're good,' I told him.

'Thank you, sir.'

'In fact, you're very good.'

'That means a lot to me, coming, as it does, from a homicidal genius like you, Mr Bates.'

'But you're still no Les Fliques.'

'Maybe not yet,' Gouge agreed, 'but I'm getting there.'

'Will you be seeing him again soon?'

'I might be, sir – it's not beyond the bounds of possibility.'

'Well, when you do, tell him he's wasting both his time and yours,' I said. 'Tell him that if Rosalyn does die, it'll be nothing to do with me.'

And in a way, I suppose, I was at least half right.

12

My career went from strength to strength. The BBC commissioned a new series, *Bates' Better Bridge* – originally entitled *Bates' Master Bridge Class*, until some wag pointed out how open it was to word inversion.

I appeared on *Star Circles*, a quiz show which featured guests who were mainly famous for being famous.

And the makers of Chunkie-Chops decided that I was the ideal person to advertise their cat food – and at the kind of obscene fee they were offering, who was I to argue?

The one black cloud on the horizon was the absence of Wesley. It was somehow boring to always travel by the flight I'd intended to take, and to arrive at hotels where the room had invariably been booked ahead. Yes, I missed Wesley. He deserved to share in the success he'd worked so incompetently to achieve.

And how did Rosalyn feel about my ever-increasing fame? She was becoming more and more jealous.

In the early stages, she'd been able to tell herself that I was nothing more than her protégé, you see.

'I spotted you first,' she'd say. 'If it hadn't been for my articles, you'd have got nowhere.'

But now it was becoming harder and harder for her to play the role of my Svengali, since – despite my best efforts to counteract the trend – most people regarded her as nothing more than my appendage.

I can't blame her for her bitterness, I suppose. She was still stuck in the post of junior reporter, and evidence of my success was all around her. When we were out together, I was constantly being asked for my autograph. At cocktail parties, it was me her former friends homed in on. She couldn't walk past a book shop without noticing a stack of *Better Bridge with Bates* piled up in the window.

And then there were the television commercials …

****

A complacent grey cat, wearing a Lincoln green cap on which the word "Hood" is written, pads through the trees. Suddenly, it finds itself surrounded by legs clad in chain mail. It tries to run, but one of the men grabs it. It struggles, but its captor is holding it tightly.

All the soldiers laugh, wickedly.

'The Sheriff will pay us well for this outlaw cat,' one of them says.

An arrow thuds into the tree next to them. A second one follows, within a hair's-breadth of the first. The soldiers look across the clearing. And there I stand – bow in hand and, like the cat, dressed in Lincoln green.

The soldiers start to advance towards me, but when I smile and draw my sword, they lose their nerve.

'Run for it, lads,' one of them shouts.

Crashing into one another, and sometimes falling over, the soldiers make their escape. The cat comes over to where I am standing. I reach behind a tree, and produce a bowl of cat food.

'Rob 'n Hood,' says the rich mellow voice-over. 'Two champions of Chunkie-Chops.'

I look down at the fat grey cat.

'Not even venison tastes this good, does it, Hood?' I ask.

'Meow,' my co-star replies.

****

'Not even venison tastes this good,' Rosalyn mimicked when the advert came on the television. 'You've made yourself look ridiculous, Rob.'

Yet none of the hundreds of people who wrote to me every week seemed to agree with her, and the advertising campaign had been such a success there was even talk of making it into a cartoon series – a fact I was wise enough to keep my fiancée ignorant of.

****

The breaking point for Rosalyn came, I think, with the taxi ride to the National Theatre. The evening had started very well. We'd made love just an hour earlier, and we were sitting in the back of the cab, snuggled up and more relaxed with each other than we'd been in months.

Then the cabbie had to open his big mouth. 'Here,' he said, 'didn't I see you on the telly the other night?'

I felt Rosalyn stiffen.

'It wasn't me,' I said. 'I really think you must be confusing me with someone else.'

'Pull the other one!' the cabbie retorted. 'It was you, all right. You're what's-his-name.'

'Tom Cruise?' I suggested, still doing my best to defuse the situation.

'Nah, not him. You're Rob Bates. You were on that Jonathan Woss Show. Am I right?'

'Yes,' I admitted in defeat. 'You're right.'

'Cor, but you've got some stories, ain't you?' continued the clown I was actually paying to ruin my evening. 'What about the one when you and your mate Wesley was hiding from the police in that Turkish brothel? Laugh? I very nearly wet meself.'

'Stop the car!' Rosalyn screamed.

'What, here, lady?' said the cabbie, finally beginning to realise that all was not well in the back.

'Yes! Here! Now!'

'You'll not find another cab very easily, and we're miles away from the nearest tube sta—'

'I'll walk,' Rosalyn said. 'I'll bloody walk.'

The cabbie pulled into the side, and Rosalyn flung the door open.

'I'll come with you,' I said.

'You will not,' replied my fiancée, stepping onto the kerb. She was about to walk away, then changed her mind and leaned back into the cab.

'I'll tell you something, Rob Bates,' she said. '*The Globe* built you up, and *The Globe* can knock you down again. I've seen it happen a thousand times.'

I didn't take her threat seriously at the time. The whole outburst was nothing more than sour grapes, I told myself, and dismissed it from my mind. I should have guessed that Rosalyn's bitterness was closer to deadly nightshade than it was to anything which grew on the vine – and that from that bitterness, she was already beginning to concoct the poisoned cup.

13

On that fateful day when I got back from Singapore a full twelve hours earlier than I was expected, I'd been engaged to Rosalyn for nearly two years.

It was a fine May morning, I remember. Buds were bursting forth on what – when I'd left the country – had been stark, skeletal trees. Birds, shedding their winter misery, flitted from branch to branch, chirping happily. Young girls had donned bright new clothes, and even old men, leaning on their sticks, seemed to have developed something of a spring in their steps.

My fiancée was not at home, but her latest project was spread untidily all over the living room table.

I didn't intend to read it – Rosalyn's "work" was really of no interest to me – and I would have gone straight to bed had it not been for the fact that amidst the various papers and pages of notes, I caught sight of Mother's photograph.

Nor was that the only material relating to me. Though I had never seen a copy of my birth certificate before – Aunt Sadie having gone through all the formalities of getting me a passport – I saw one now.

With trembling hands, I picked it up.

"Mother: Jennifer Bates – Spinster

Father: Unknown …"

Mother – a spinster! It was a shock, I must admit. I'd always assumed my parents had been married, and that Father had died. Yet thinking about it at that moment, I couldn't find any solid basis for my assumption – Mother certainly hadn't gone so far as to say that she'd been married, or that she'd been left a widow.

The shock drained away, to be replaced by anger.

Father unknown!

That was what the cold, official form said.

As if Mother had had so many lovers that she couldn't be sure who had impregnated her!

It hadn't been like that at all. I was sure it hadn't. There'd only been one man in Mother's life and, for her own good reasons, she'd chosen to keep his name a secret from the snoops and bureaucrats down at the town hall.

I grabbed a piece of paper covered with Rosalyn's writing:

"Mother's Death

Drowning due to cramp – at the crucial moment

Father's Death

See above

Father's death? See above?"

I wished I could remember more of the last week of Mother's life, but all I had was a few vague images: the three of us in the taxi, going to the station; me, opening the door of Mother's hotel room, and hearing a man's voice, 'I thought you'd locked it, Jennie'; Mother suddenly appearing in the doorway, and blocking my view of the room …

I read on:

"Aunts

Did they do it, too?"

Do what, too?

'*We all had the same temptation,*' Aunt Jacqueline had screamed at me when I'd told her I would never cheat at bridge, '*even that self-righteous prig Catherine. But only your mother, your precious bloody mother, gave in to it.*'

My ears pricked up at the sound of a key turning the front door dead-bolt.

Rosalyn.

I stood perfectly still, and listened to her close the door, then walk along the corridor. She stopped half-way down the hall – as I'd known she would – to check her appearance in the mirror. I held myself as rigid as a statue – and waited.

The living room door swung open, and my back-stabbing fiancée walked in. She was wearing a crisp white blouse and an expensive grey skirt. It was just the sort of tasteful outfit that Sadie would have worn, and, despite my anger, I couldn't help loving her.

Rosalyn was intent on putting her keys in her handbag, and didn't see me at first – but when she finally noticed me, she froze in her tracks.

'Hello, Rosalyn,' I said, forcing a neutral tone into my voice.

'I … I wasn't expecting you back so soon,' she told me, looking first at me, then at the table, and finally back at me again.

'What's this?' I asked, pointing to the pile of papers.

'I'm … I'm writing another story about you.'

'Any particular angle?' I asked innocently.

'I'm going to talk about all the rewards that fame and fortune have brought you,' she lied.

'Then why do you need a copy of my birth certificate?' I demanded. 'Tell me the truth, Rosalyn.'

My fiancée shrugged her shoulders resignedly. 'All right, it's going to be more biographical than that,' she admitted.

'What do you mean?'

Rosalyn smiled maliciously, and I realised, for the first time, just how much she'd grown to resent me.

'I've discovered something very interesting – very, very juicy – about you and your family,' she said.

My Aunts!

Had my investigative fiancée uncovered anything on the violent deaths of my aunts?

Was it possible she could succeed where Fliques had failed?

Might I, as a result of her efforts, yet end up in gaol?

I could already see *The Globe's* headline: "Bridge Champion Killed His Entire Family!"

'I scarcely think my aunts could be of much interest to your readers,' I said unconvincingly.

'Your aunts?' Rosalyn repeated – and though she was a good actress when she wanted to be, I could see that, this time, her surprise was genuine. 'Who's talking about your aunts?'

'I thought *you* were.'

'Of course not. It's your bloody mother that I've got the dirt on, for Christ's sake!'

14

We stood facing each other across the living room. Only a few seconds had passed since Rosalyn had said she'd got some dirt on Mother, but it seemed like an eternity of mental torture.

'Mother died when I was young,' I said shakily.

'I know that,' Rosalyn told me, the amused, malicious look still in her eyes. 'But it's the *way* she died which is interesting.'

'*We shouldn't talk about it!*' Sadie had said at that congregation of aunts after Mother's funeral. '*For Rob's sake, we should come to an agreement right now that none of us will ever tell him exactly how his mother died. Will you promise? All of you?*'

'*Promise!*' Aunt Catherine had repeated. '*There's no need to promise. I would never soil my lips with such filth.*'

'*Me neither,*' Aunt Peggy had said. '*I mean, I just couldn't. I wouldn't know where to put myself.*'

'Mother was drowned,' I said. 'It was tragic – but these things happen. I can't see how there's a story in it – especially over twenty years after the event.'

'There's a beautiful story in it,' Rosalyn said with relish, 'a gorgeous, wonderful story. Because she didn't *just* drown, did she?'

'Didn't *just* drown?' I asked, becoming more confused by the second. 'Then what else did she do?'

'You don't know!' Rosalyn said with amazement in her voice. 'I thought at first you were hiding it from me – but you really don't know! None of those bloody aunts of yours ever told you.'

'They made an agreement,' I said, before I could stop myself. 'It was a sort of conspiracy.'

Rosalyn laughed nastily. 'Given what they were keeping quiet about, I can understand that,' she said.

'Why are you doing this to me, Rosalyn?' I asked.

'You know why I'm doing it. People used to notice me. I was getting to be important. But what am I now? I'm nothing but Rob Bates' girlfriend. You've destroyed every chance I ever had, because even if I left you now, I'd never be anything more than Rob Bates' *ex*-girlfriend. But after the story's published, they'll have to take me seriously.'

'I take you seriously,' I said. 'You're important to me.'

'That's not nearly enough,' Rosalyn replied. She ran her fingers through her hair. 'Do you want to hear the truth now – or would you rather wait and read about it in *The Globe*?'

'I don't want to hear about it at all,' I told her, as I'd once told Aunt Jacqueline. 'Not now, not in *The Globe* – not ever.'

'Really?' Rosalyn asked challengingly. 'Wouldn't you like to know who your father was?'

My father again!

My mysterious father, whose name did not even appear on my birth certificate – the dark shadow which had been with me all my life.

'*You look very like him,*' Aunt Sadie had said, advancing uncertainly – and perhaps a little drunkenly – into my room, the day that I went to live with her. '*Very like him. I could have had him, you know. He wanted me – badly. But I couldn't have done it to Jennifer – to your mother. She needed him more than I did. Yet sometimes, I wish ...*'

'*I ... I think there are some things we shouldn't go into, don't you?*' Aunt Peggy had stuttered. '*I mean, you might not like the truth when you hear it.*'

'Yes, I'd like to know about my father,' I told Rosalyn, 'but not the rest of it – not Mother's death.'

'*You can't separate the two,*' Aunt Peggy had said. Then she'd laughed – almost hysterically. '*Yes, that was the problem – you couldn't separate the one from the other.*'

And now – eerily – Rosalyn repeated my aunt's very words.

'You can't separate the one from the other,' she said. 'So what's it to be – the whole story, or nothing at all?'

'Tell me the whole story,' I said heavily.

'A Cornish holiday,' Rosalyn said, extracting every drop of drama she could from her tale. 'It is night, and you, little Bobby, are safely tucked up in your bed, dreaming of seagulls and sandcastles. And this is just what Mummy has been waiting for. She kisses you softly on the forehead, and tip-toes from your room.' She paused for a moment. 'And that's interesting, in its own right, isn't it?

'What's interesting?'

'Hotel rooms are expensive, yet you, a kid of nine, had one entirely to yourself. Don't you think that's just a little strange?'

Yes, looking at it that way, I supposed it was. But I definitely remembered that I did have a room of my own.

'Where was I?' Rosalyn asked. 'Oh yes. Mummy tip-toes out of your room, and goes down to the beach. Only she's not alone – she's got her lover with her.'

'This is ridiculous!' I said.

Except that it didn't actually *sound* ridiculous. In fact, it was beginning to fill in some of the gaps in my memory.

'So they're on the beach,' Rosalyn continued. 'Very romantic it is, what with the moon, and the sound of the tide coming in. It's a warm night, and there's nobody about, so one of them suggests a bit of nooky al fresco. She takes off her knickers, he pulls down his trousers – and they're away. They're going at it hammer and tongs, having a great time. Then guess what happens?'

'You've got a sick mind,' I said.

And yet I believed what she was telling me – I believed it all!

'Mummy gets cramp,' Rosalyn said with glee. 'And not in her arm or her leg. Oh no! It's in somewhere much more inconvenient than that.'

'You don't mean …' I gasped.

'I *do* mean! You've seen it when it happens to dogs, haven't you? Well, it was just like that. They must have tried to move, but it would've hurt like hell, and even then they couldn't have got far. And all the time, the tide was coming in … *whoosh … whoosh …*'

'Stop,' I pleaded.

'The currents are strong down there,' Rosalyn continued relentlessly. 'They were dragged out to sea with him still inside her, so, naturally, they drowned.'

'Can you prove *any* of this fantastic rubbish?' I demanded.

'Of course I can prove it,' Rosalyn said contemptuously. 'Jesus Christ, they were still welded together when they were washed up again. It's all in the coroner's report.' She picked up an official-looking piece of paper, and waved it at me. 'Do you want to read it for yourself?'

'No,' I said – because I was sure that it would say exactly what she claimed it did.

'And that's not even the best part of the story,' Rosalyn said. 'The real kicker is that the lover your mother died screwing was actually your father. Ask me who he was! Go on – I dare you.'

Who could he have been, this man Mother would never talk about?

Why had she refused to publicly acknowledge him, even on my birth certificate?

Had she kept their relationship secret because he was famous?

Or had there been an altogether more sordid reason for hiding the love affair in the shadows?

'He wasn't married, was he?' I asked.

Rosalyn laughed. 'Is that all you're concerned about? No, he wasn't married. Or rather, he had been – but his wife was long dead by the time he started sticking it to your precious mother.'

Thank God for that!

Forgive me, Mother, I thought. Forgive me for believing, even for a minute, that you could behave like that.

'Who were you living with just before your mother died?' Rosalyn asked, teasing me in the nastiest possible way.

'With Mother, of course.'

'Only with her? Nobody else?'

'We both lived with Grandfather.'

Rosalyn rummaged through her pile of papers and came up with an old sepia photograph, which she handed to me.

'Is this him?' she asked.

It must have been twenty years since I'd seen a picture of Grandfather – and this one was taken when he was a much younger man – but I recognised him immediately. I recognised something else, too. I recognised that he … that I …

'So you and your mother were living with your grandfather immediately before the holiday – immediately before your mother drowned,' Rosalyn said, cutting into my thoughts.

'Yes, I've already told you that.'

'Then why did you go to live with your Aunt Jacqueline? Why didn't your grandfather look after you?'

'Because … because he was dead.'

'And *how* did he die?'

'He … he was drowned.'

I looked down at the photograph again. The clothes were old-fashioned, the pose unnatural – but aside from that, I could have been looking in a mirror.

'*It would have been different if they'd been cats, wouldn't it?*' Aunt Peggy had said. '*Cats don't know any better, do they? They don't mean any harm – it's just the way they are.*'

'That's right,' said Rosalyn with a verbal flourish. 'Your grandfather was also your father. Your mother was bonking her own dad!'

15

Another lifetime had passed in a few agonising seconds.

Rosalyn still stood by the table; I was still in the centre of the living room.

'I want you to drop the story,' I said.

Now why did I ask her to do that?

For Mother, I suppose. Whatever she'd done – whatever she'd been unable to *stop* herself doing – I didn't want her memory soiled now.

But if I'm being honest, I have to admit I was also asking it for myself. Rosalyn had already robbed me of something of Mother – if I actually saw it in print, I would lose her completely.

'I want you to drop the story,' I repeated.

'You've got be joking,' Rosalyn replied. 'This is the chance of a lifetime for me. After this, the paper will give me whatever I want.'

'It will hurt me deeply if you publish it,' I told her.

'You'll survive,' Rosalyn said indifferently.

A powerful feeling was overcoming me, a sensation I'd never experienced before.

The room swayed before my eyes, then turned red – blood red.

My hands began to tingle as if they'd been punctured by a thousand tiny needles.

And there was a roaring in my head, like a huge waterfall or the pounding of a thousand horses' hooves, which hammered out one simple message: kill her … kill her … kill her.

'What's the matter, Rob?' Rosalyn gasped. 'Why are you looking at me like that?'

'Drop the story,' I said hoarsely.

'Y-yes, yes, of course I will, if that's what you really want,' Rosalyn stuttered.

She began backing away from me, but her eyes, like those of a frightened rabbit caught in bright headlights, were glued to my face.

'You don't mean it,' I told her. 'You're just saying that because you know it's what I want to hear.'

My hands were prickling unbearably – as if they'd been held too long in front of a hot fire – and I knew that there was one way – and *only* one way – to make the feeling go away.

'I'm telling the truth,' protested Rosalyn, who had now backed up all the way to the kitchen door. 'All the papers are on the table. They're yours. Do what you want with them. Burn them, shred them – I really don't care.'

Like a fool, I glanced down at the documents on the table, and Rosalyn used the few precious seconds that gave her to open the door, step inside the kitchen and close the door behind her.

It wouldn't do her any good, I thought as I crossed the living room. There was only one way out of the kitchen, so in seeking sanctuary there, she had done no more than postpone in inevitable.

The door would not open. Rosalyn, on the other side of it, was pushing as hard as she could. But I was much stronger than she was, and she knew it, so it was only a matter of time before she gave way.

As I increased my pressure, I could picture how strained and desperate she must be, protected from my murderous intent by only a few centimetres of wood.

The door suddenly flew open, and I half-stepped, half-fell, into the kitchen. Rosalyn had moved to the window, and was brandishing our largest, sharpest, kitchen knife.

'Don't come near me,' she warned hysterically. 'Come near me, and I'll use this. I mean it.'

My hands itched to be round her throat. Yet if I rushed her, there was a chance she might seriously wound me, and thus escape her rightful fate.

I had been patient before – with all four of my aunts – and I would be patient now. So though my thumbs screamed out for a chance to press down on her white neck – to crush her cartilage, to choke the life out of her – I waited for the moment when her guard was down, and I could safely jump her.

Still waving the knife in my direction, Rosalyn picked up the wall phone and dialled clumsily with her free hand.

'Police!' she said, never taking her eyes off me. 'I want the police.'

A few seconds ticked by.

'Police?' Rosalyn gasped with relief. 'Yes, my fiancé is trying to kill me. My name's Rosalyn Russell and my address is … yes, that's right.

Come quickly, please. I don't know how much longer I can hold him off.'

It was then that I heard Mother's voice. It was not as firm – or as confident – as it usually was. Rather it was like listening to a poorly tuned-in radio, which is drifting even further from the station.

But the message was clear enough.

'*Always try to put yourself in other people's shoes,*' Mother said.

Not now, Mother, I thought impatiently. I'm too busy to do what you want at the moment.

'*Always try to put yourself in other people's shoes,*' Mother repeated faintly.

And as faint as the message was, I could not refuse Mother twice.

I imagined how hard it must have been for Rosalyn to cope with my success when her own career was going nowhere. And then I understood that while what she was planning to do was wrong, she'd been driven to it by desperation.

She wasn't wicked – merely pathetic.

And it was pity, not punishment, that she needed.

The first thing to do was to calm her down. Later, when she was in a better state, I would return to the problem of her story on Mother, and I would use every means at my disposal to make her drop it. I would appeal to her better nature. I would offer her money.

If necessary, I would even pretend that I still loved her.

My fiancée – my ex-fiancée, as she already was in my mind – had dropped the phone, though not the knife.

'The police will be here in two minutes, so you'd better not try anything,' she hissed.

'Give me the knife, darling,' I said soothingly.

'Keep back!' Rosalyn shouted.

'You're as likely to hurt yourself as hurt me,' I said, taking a measured step forward. 'Come on. Be sensible.'

Screaming at the top of her voice, Rosalyn suddenly lunged at me.

I side-stepped and watched the knife slice through the empty air where, a second earlier, my stomach had been.

Rosalyn whirled round, ready to slash out at me a second time. I grabbed her wrist, and twisted. The knife clattered to the floor.

I flung my arms around her, and hugged her tightly to me.

'I won't hurt you,' I said. 'I promise I won't.'

'Can't breathe,' Rosalyn gasped. 'You're smothering me.'

I loosened my grip. 'Is that better, darling?'

She brought up her knee – hard – against my groin.

With a *whoof*, I sank to my knees.

'You've made things even better for me, you stupid bastard,' Rosalyn said, as I fought for air. 'Do you know what the headline will be now? "The story Rob Bates thought was worth killing for!"'

'Ooph!' I said.

Rosalyn lashed out with her leg, and the pointed toe of her expensive shoe caught me an agonising blow in my sternum.

I toppled over.

'I'll bring you down,' she screamed. 'Oh yes, I'll bring you down. This time next week I'll be the star, not you.'

A spasm of intense agony shot through my brain as she kicked me on the side of the head.

Another kick followed.

And another.

'I'm going outside to wait for the police, and then I'm heading straight for the office to work on my story,' she said … kick, kick … 'By the end of the week …' kick … 'the whole world will know that Rob Bates' precious mother bonked her own dad.'

I heard the sound of her footsteps as she left the kitchen, crossed the living room, and entered the hallway. It hurt to even think of moving, but I didn't have any choice.

I simply had to persuade her not to run the story – not to sully Mother's reputation.

I rose slowly, and, using the walls as support, made my way painfully to the front door.

Rosalyn was standing in the corridor, calmly waiting for the lift.

'Please, Rosalyn …' I gasped.

She hadn't been expecting this – by rights, after the beating she'd given me, I should have been out for hours – and when she turned to look at me, her eyes were wide with horror.

'Don't … want … to hurt you,' I managed to say. 'Just … want … to talk.'

Rosalyn gave the call button a frantic jab, then, abandoning the idea of escaping by the lift, ran towards the service stairs. I staggered after her, but in my condition I had no chance of catching her up, and half-way down the first flight, I abandoned the chase.

'I'm sorry, Mother,' I said. 'I did the best I could.'

Then I turned, and made my way achingly back to the flat.

16

Rosalyn's papers and documents still sat on the table – mocking me. I collected them up and fed them into the waste disposal system. But it wouldn't do any good, I told myself, even as I went through the motions. Rosalyn could easily obtain other copies of the material. There was nothing I could do to stop her story now.

The doorbell rang just as I was shredding the last of the notes.

Rosalyn – having a change of heart? No, that was too much to hope for.

Then who?

If I'd thought it through logically, I would have realised it was probably the police, come to arrest me for attempted murder – but my logic was not at its best at that moment, so it was a surprise to me, when I opened the door, to see Les Fliques standing there.

'You look like you've really been in the wars, Rob,' Fliques said. 'Mind if I come in?'

'No,' I said wearily.

Fliques stepped past me, and strode into the living room.

'Nice place, Rob,' he said appreciatively. 'Very nice indeed. Where is she, then?'

'Rosalyn?'

'Yes, that's who I mean. Miss Rosalyn Russell. Your fiancée. It was on the car radio that you were threatening her life. Quite a coincidence it should happen when I was in London for a conference, don't you think? Or maybe it's not so much coincidence as fate.'

'Rosalyn's not—' I began.

'No, don't tell me,' Fliques said. 'Let me find her for myself.' He marched into the kitchen, opened the chest freezer, and peered inside. Finding nothing but frozen meals, he turned his attention to the broom closet. When he'd drawn a blank there, too, he opened one of the small, wall-hanging cabinets.

'You surely don't imagine that you'll find Rosalyn in there, do you?' I asked him.

'Thought that would be where you'd keep them,' Fliques said, holding up a packet of chocolate biscuits with some satisfaction. 'Don't mind, do you, Rob? Only I'm feeling a little peckish. It must be all the excitement.'

'Be my guest,' I said. 'Where to next?'

'The bathroom,' replied Fliques, who had a biscuit in his right hand and had cupped his left to catch the crumbs. 'People are always hiding bodies in their bathrooms.'

I led the way.

'I must admit, I'm very disappointed with you this time, Rob,' Fliques told me. 'I mean, direct action is scarcely your style, is it? It's far too crude.'

He pulled back the shower curtain, and did not seem unduly disappointed when he didn't discover Rosalyn's mangled corpse hanging there.

'Well, at least you weren't *that* obvious,' he said.

'You're wasting your time,' I said. 'Rosalyn isn't—'

'Please, Rob,' Fliques interrupted, 'I've been waiting for this for years – don't take my bit of pleasure from me.'

I shrugged. 'All right. Where do you want to go next?'

'The master bedroom – that's another favourite place for folk to stash the recently deceased.'

We checked the master bedroom and the guest bedroom, and then, since the body of my fiancée still hadn't turned up, we went back to the living room.

'All right, Rob, I give up,' Fliques said. 'What have you done with her?'

'Nothing. She left just before you arrived.'

Fliques froze. '*Just* before I arrived, you say?' he asked – almost fearfully.

'That's right.'

'And what was she wearing?'

'A grey skirt and white blouse … Oh, and a pair of black shoes which probably have bloodstains on them. Why?'

Fliques scowled. Then the scowl became a grin, and he shook his head with what could only be called admiration.

'Brilliant!' he said. 'Your best yet.'

'I don't understand.'

'No, you never do, do you? Well, I'll explain it to you. I get this call on the radio that you're about to kill your fiancée, and naturally I want to be the one to collar you.'

'Naturally,' I agreed.

'So I tell my driver to get his clog down. Now we're doing a fair lick when we turn into this road, but we've got the old blue light flashing and the siren blaring away, so anybody who's not blind and stone deaf can tell that we're coming from a mile away. You following me so far, Rob?'

'I'm following you.'

'As I said, anybody could hear us coming from a mile away. But this young woman seems to have something very important on her mind, and doesn't even notice us. She dashes straight out into the road, as if she's running for her life. Well, we have no chance, do we? We slam straight into her. Flying into the air, she goes. Must have travelled twenty feet before she came crashing down again.' Fliques took another nibble of his biscuit. 'Well, there wasn't much I could do for her personally, and since my main aim was to either save your fiancée or to arrest you for murder, I left it to the local lads, and came straight here.' He paused again. 'Only now you tell me that Rosalyn was wearing a white blouse and a grey skirt—'

'Is she … is she dead?' I asked.

'She wasn't when I left the scene, but I'd be surprised if she makes it through the day.'

'I'm sorry,' I said.

And I was – although I wouldn't have been human if I hadn't felt a small prick of satisfaction that now Mother's tragic story would never be told.

'Getting her knocked down by my driver,' Fliques said. 'Absolutely brilliant! How the hell did you manage it?'

'It had nothing to do with me. It was an accident.'

'An accident,' Fliques scoffed. 'When people around *you* die, it's never an accident.'

'It was,' I protested. 'This time it really was.'

'Oh, I believe you. It was definitely an accident.' Fliques looked longingly at the packet on the coffee table. 'Is there any chance of another of them biscuits, Rob?' he asked.

'Of course. Feel free.'

He picked up the packet and took out a biscuit.

'If there were Oscars for the perfect crime, you'd win them all,' he said. 'Best Forward Planning: Rob Bates – for somehow persuading the victim to call the police herself. Most Imaginative Murder Weapon: Rob Bates – for using a police Rover as his blunt instrument. Best Alibi: Rob Bates – who can actually produce a police superintendent to swear he was nowhere near the scene of the crime. Best Appearance of Innocence after the Event: Rob Bates. Oh, you'd sweep the bloody board.'

A sudden look of sadness came to his face. 'It's all over, isn't it?' he said.

'What's all over?'

'Our ... err ... encounters ... me popping up unexpectedly, and explaining how you killed your Auntie Peggy or your Auntie Catherine. We've been doing it for fourteen years or more, and now we've finally reached the end of the road.'

'Why should you think that?' I asked.

'Because you're an artist, Rob, and you know when you've painted your masterpiece. Anything after this would only be an anti-climax for you.' He took another half-hearted bite out of his biscuit. 'I shall miss you, Rob.'

'Perhaps we could meet for a drink now and again,' I suggested.

Fliques shook his head. 'Without the possibility of my feeling your collar, it wouldn't be the same for either of us.'

'There's still a chance you can catch me,' I said. 'Who knows, in a few years I might feel like making a come-back.'

Fliques shook his head again. 'You're being very kind, but I'm a long way yet from wanting charity.'

He took another chocolate biscuit, wrapped it neatly in his handkerchief, and walked towards the door.

I waited patiently for him to do his famous turning around trick.

He did not disappoint me.

Just on the threshold, he whirled so he was facing me again.

There was a reproachful expression on his face.

'I can't even nick you for riding with no lights, can I?' he asked. 'Now you're so rich and famous, you don't even have a bike anymore.'

17

Rosalyn died soon after that. I had expected that, with my fiancée's demise, Mother would return to me stronger than ever … yet somehow she never did.

And strange as it may seem, I didn't find her absence as frightening as I'd thought I would. In fact, for the first time in my life, I felt really free.

30263316R00137

Printed in Great Britain
by Amazon